MEN OF BRETTON

BAEN BOOKS by
RICHARD FOX

A DREAM OF HOME
Men of Bretton

ASCENT TO EMPIRE (with David Weber)
Governor
Rebel

SHATTERED STAR LEGACY
Light of the Veil

MEN OF BRETTON

A DREAM OF HOME: BOOK 1

RICHARD FOX

A Baen Books Original

Baen Publishing Enterprises
P.O. Box 1403
Riverdale, NY 10471
www.baen.com

ISBN: 978-1-9821-9374-4

Cover art by Pierluigi Abbondanza

First printing, November 2024

Distributed by Simon & Schuster
1230 Avenue of the Americas
New York, NY 10020

Library of Congress Cataloging-in-Publication Data

Names: Fox, Richard, 1978- author.
Title: Men of Bretton / Richard Fox.
Description: Riverdale, NY : Baen Publishing Enterprises, 2024. | Series: A dream of home ; 1
Identifiers: LCCN 2024027927 (print) | LCCN 2024027928 (ebook) | ISBN 9781982193744 (hardcover) | ISBN 9781625799883 (ebook)
Subjects: BISAC: FICTION / Science Fiction / Military | FICTION / Science Fiction / Space Opera | LCGFT: Science fiction. | Military fiction. | Novels.
Classification: LCC PS3606.O95628 M46 2024 (print) | LCC PS3606.O95628 (ebook) | DDC 813/.6—dc23/eng/20240621
LC record available at https://lccn.loc.gov/2024027927
LC ebook record available at https://lccn.loc.gov/2024027928

Printed in the United States of America

10 9 8 7 6 5 4 3 2 1

MEN OF BRETTON

"From a distance, it's easy to see how the
Hegemony's collapse mirrored so many other failed states:
It rotted away slowly then fell apart all at once."
—Francesco Muston, Umbrian Coalition Scholar, 2689 A.D.

CHAPTER 1

The rebels would kill him, Felix Ibensen was sure of it. Bullets ripped through the wide fronds of a *jerjama* bush and thudded into a tree whose top vanished into the canopy. Felix ducked behind the just-pockmarked tree and fought for breath.

"Gunnar? Gunnar, where are you?" Felix said into the mic built into his visor. The faceplate over his helmet did a decent job of cycling fresh air to his mouth and nose, but the exertion of running and fighting made every breath stuffy. This wasn't the time for "helm terror," as the Flankers called it: when a soldier couldn't get enough oxygen in his helmet and threw the damn thing off before it could kill him.

Things were bad enough. The highway ambush had killed most of the company in the first minutes. The Dahrien insurgents usually preferred to hit and run, but this time they'd swarmed over the convoy with no intent of taking prisoners.

Single shots cracked a few yards from him, answered by a squeal of pain from the jungle.

"Sarge, peel back!" Gunnar yelled from somewhere close by. "Who's that out there? You got frags?"

Felix tapped his chest rig; the exo-frame built around his arms and hands and extending down his back, waist and legs worked well enough to haul his weight, and the flack plates over his interception bivy suit. But when it came time for the fine motor control needed to activate a grenade, his Flanker panoply became difficult. Especially when his hands were shaking.

"Got one frag!" Felix tried several times to flick the pin onto a small hook on his chest rig.

"Then use it, by *faen*!" Gunnar yelled back.

Felix yanked the grenade off his chest rig, saw the pin tumble into the underbrush, then swung around and barely cleared the side of the tree. The grenade flew away, and Felix wasn't exactly sure where it would go, but grenades had always been more of a "to whom it may concern" weapon.

The brief movement of his hand was enough to highlight his position to the insurgents and they opened up on him before the grenade could even hit the ground. The thud of impacts shook the tree against his back. Lumps of bark were sheared off as heavy caliber rounds tore past him, missing him by inches.

Felix shrank into himself like a child afraid of thunder as the fire continued.

The thermobaric grenade exploded into a wall of overpressure that enveloped Felix with a brief, yet awful, embrace. The interception bivy and helmet automatically stiffened to offset the effects. The insurgents trying to kill him were having a much worse time than he was. Ruptured ear drums, collapsed lungs, and concussions might be enough to give him and his company's survivors the chance they needed to escape.

Felix glimpsed Gunnar and another Flanker moving down a hillside. He took off into the jungle, more scared of losing sight of them than the rebels following him. *Jerjama* fronds bent and slapped at him as he went along with the snap of bullets from an insurgent who was far too motivated for Felix's liking.

"Was that 'nade not enough to convince you I don't want to play? Fuckers," he muttered to himself. He stepped over the edge of the hill and followed the obvious path left by the other two Flankers. His stride increased with the slope. Green and brown undergrowth slapped at him as he moved faster and faster down the hill, until he lost his footing and tumbled forward.

His bivy absorbed most of the impact as he rolled down. Felix hit flat on a small patch of grass, forcing air out of his chest in a horrible sounding *hurf*. Momentum carried him over and flopped him into a shallow pool.

Felix flailed about, unsure if he was sinking or swimming as water washed over his helm. A hand grabbed his carry handle and dragged him out of the pool and into an abandoned farmhouse. The roof was rotted out and rays of sunlight lit up dust and mold particles over him.

"What the hell, Felix?" Gunnar checked Felix's biometrics panel on his chest, then gave him a playful slap on the side of the helmet. "You trying to break a leg and make this day even worse?"

Felix unlocked his visor and lifted it up. He took a deep breath of thick, earthy air and rolled to his side. He coughed for several seconds, clutching his carbine to his chest. Water oozed out of the suit. He touched the inflation lining around his breastplate, surprised it hadn't gone off.

"Trips when you're vertical, not when you're playing in the kiddie pool, dumbass," Gunnar said.

"I just...gimme a minute," Felix said.

The other Flanker knelt in the corner, a holo map projected off of his forearm screen.

"Sergeant Hamar...that you? From Second Platoon?" Felix asked.

"One each," Hamar said. "Central walked us straight into that ambush."

"Why would Central do that?" Gunnar asked. "Patrol Base Equity was begging for support before we left the wire."

"Equity went dark within an hour of the convoy rolling out," Hamar said. "SOP is for us to return to base until a vacuum breather or some other collection platform can figure out what's going on, but Commodore Malthus had other ideas. Fucker."

Felix looked over the holo map. Several cities and towns had red borders, indicating significant rebel presence.

"We need to get back to base, tell Central what happened," Gunnar said. "Organize a rescue mission for the others. Did either of you see what happened to Captain Olin?"

"I saw the Flags scalping him," Hamar said.

"He said he'd always keep us alive." Felix slapped his visor back down and crouched just high enough to look over a windowsill. The house had once been a farm, ramshackle at best. A pile of rusted-out tools lay against a small shed made of slightly off-sized bricks, the mortar laid down sloppily. Patches of gardens and a single large field were overgrown with weeds. The jungle was retaking the place inch by inch and day by day.

"Wasn't his decision to make," Hamar sighed. "Something tells me we're not going to find anyone else from the company."

"Can we even get back to base?" Gunnar asked. "Flags are all over that hill. Bet they're on the highway too."

"The way we came is a no go." Hamar nodded. "We need to get to ... Rabak? Rabak should still be ours. Got a whole battalion of Skien tanks there."

"Where?" Felix made a quick squint of his left eye. The sensors in his helm read the gesture and activated his onboard map pack. The onboard navigation plotted out a course to the city.

"We might get there by morning," Gunnar said. "Maybe."

"Master Sergeant Kerr ran a tight ship in 1st Platoon. You two have full batteries?" Hamar asked.

"Oh shit, he was in the truck right behind me," Felix said. "Did it get hit too?"

"Burned out from a rocket hit," Gunnar said. "I think we're all that's left."

"W-we can't be." Felix's shoulders tightened up. "The whole company was in the relief force and—"

"Captain's own drones counted almost a thousand Flags during the couple minutes we fought back. We never stood a chance," Hamar said. "Sitting here feeling sorry for ourselves does nothing. I've got the stripes. I've got command. Staggered line march through the valley to the bridge over the Baror River. We'll follow the road to Shendi, there's still a garrison there. Let's go."

Felix took a swig of water from a tube inside his helmet. Hamar was a good sergeant and Felix had a glimmer of hope that he might live to the end of the day. Maybe.

Hamar bumped a fist against his chest, the Hegemony salute, and jogged out of the house in a crouch.

The sniper's bullet arrived with a crack against Hamar's shoulder. The round pierced through his torso and burst out of his thigh, leaving a crater of blood and shattered bone in his leg big enough to stick a fist into. Hamar collapsed forward, dead before he hit the ground. The report of the high-powered rifle echoed through the farm.

"Run. Run!" Gunnar snatched Felix by the arm and pulled him through a side door. They sprinted through weed-choked rows of abandoned rice and potatoes. Gunnar made a random jump to one side. Felix did a double take as Gunnar was now a few steps behind him.

Felix's boot caught on a potato leaf and he pitched forward. A bullet snapped over his head and annihilated a potato plant. Insect-eaten, yellowed leaves rained down around him.

"Keep going!" Gunnar yelled as he stumbled past him, zigging and zagging to throw off the sniper's aim. "Get to the tree line!"

Felix rolled to his left. The sniper's next round punched the ground where he'd fallen. The impact reverberated through the ground and into Felix's body. He let out a pitiful cry and ran towards the jungle that Gunnar vanished into. Felix pushed his frame's leg braces harder than they were rated to run, ignoring the warning icons on his visor.

His right leg frame seized up and he slowed to a limp, still short of the green hell that might provide him a bit of protection from the sniper. Felix could feel the crosshairs on his back as he slowed to what felt like a leisurely stroll.

A burst of fire rattled leaves in the jungle as Gunnar laid down cover. A tree trunk ahead of Felix cracked open into ivory colored wood and shattered bark. Felix leapt into the jungle and landed in a shallow puddle. He crawled forward through slick mud, not caring where he was going, just trying to get out of the sniper's line of fire.

His breathing grew labored. His arms and shoulder burned and mud caked his visor. Felix bumped into something and gave up. The phantom sound of sniper rounds cracking overhead still rang in his ears.

Then something moved.

"Aah!" Felix scrambled back onto his haunches and snapped his visor up.

Gunnar was there, shadows from the thick overhead canopy nearly swallowing him.

"You done acting like an idiot?" Gunnar asked. "Because I don't think we want to stay here. Flags are *pissed* about something. I don't want to be here if they've got ripper drones to spare."

"Th-they killed Sergeant Hamar." Felix waved behind him as he got to his feet. He cycled the function on his right leg brace and a double *ding* sounded in his ear. The stiffness along the limb abated.

"Yeah, pretty sure that was a .60 cal anti-armor rifle." Gunnar flipped up his visor and wiped sweat from his face. The stress of months of combat were written across his twenty-something-year-old face. "Waste to use that on us squishies. Like I said, Flags are *pissed* right now. How many do you think you got with that grenade?"

"I dunno...didn't look. Too busy pussying out from the fight," Felix said, following Gunnar through the woods, walking a few steps to one side of the stream.

"Nothing wrong with runnin' from a fight you've already lost. We did stop getting shot by the lot of them, so maybe they'll be happy with taking out the whole convoy and let us slide. Except for that sniper—who was very much a 'fuck you in particular' sort of asshole," Gunnar said.

"Flags haven't ambushed an entire company for...months?" Felix patted the mag pouches on his chest rig. "Not since they scalped that division from Nazare over in that province that got X'd. I'm green on ammo. One smoker 'nade left."

"Yeah...how'd intel miss the buildup? I'm amber on mags. Zero 'nades. Didn't even grab my frickin' go bag. That had all my *lefse* in it..."

Felix handed over a pair of ammo magazines.

"I've got some *tong* if you're hungry." Felix tapped a pouch hanging from the back of his utility belt. The locally produced beef jerky was far too spicy for his taste but it held up in Dahrien's heat and humidity.

"That was *lefse* from home, Felix." Gunnar shook his head. "My sister made it for me. It came in the last batch of care packages. When was the last time you even heard about a ship coming here from Syddan? Only reason that one even came was to take casualties back home. Did you get anything—oh, that's right. You're Syddan by descent."

"I've been to the home world a couple of times. Did basic there," Felix said.

"We don't call it the 'home world,' you weird-ass spacer, it's the *arinheim*...listen to us. No NCO to bust our balls and we're yammering like territorials. Watch our left flank and our six. We cross the bridge and it'll cut almost thirty klicks off the walk to Tabuk City," Gunnar said.

"What's the chance the Flags are—"

"Shh! Don't jinx us," Gunnar snapped.

The canopy shook with the occasional bird or small simian species as the pair worked through the jungle. Felix kept a close eye on his Flanker suit's power readings, cutting back the onboard cooling to save the battery and cracking his visor to breathe untreated air. The humidity clung to his face, pulling out a constant stream of sweat.

The suit was rated for full power operations for up to thirty-six hours, but just how long it would be before they could find a friendly unit or a battery resupply was an unknown. While the visor could run off his body heat and muscle power captured by the frame, trying to fight with zero effective power to the rest of the system would be like going into battle with one arm tied behind his back and a leg hobbled.

"Not optimal for survival or victory," as the officers liked to say.

They reached a steep embankment high over a river, the surface white with rapids. The sun was high and blazed through the occasional break in the tree cover.

"Down." Gunnar went to one knee and tossed pics from his optics to Felix. A double lane bridge stretched over the river, burnt out cars jamming any possible traffic. The electric vehicles were of local manufacture, all scorched on the sides and bottoms from the batteries melting down.

The road leading away from the bridge on their side of the river led to a small village. Thin columns of cooking smoke mingled through rooftop solar panels.

A zoomed-in pic of a manned guard post on the near side of the bridge sent a chill through Felix's chest. A pair of armed men lounged in a small guard shack made of jungle leaves and branches near the bridge.

"Ah . . . shit," Felix said. "Something tells me those aren't the only two out there."

"Bridge's been out for months. Probably just lookouts for the village. You see the *Fedayeen* red on them?" Gunnar asked.

"Huh, sure don't. So, they're just local militia and not proper Flag insurgents?" Felix asked.

"Prolly. The ones that swear they're going to kill every Hegemony citizen and soldier they can are pretty proud of those red bandanas they like. But just because they're locals doesn't mean their bullets can't kill us," Gunnar said. "There's no sneaking by them. We wait for dark and word'll get here that there were survivors from the ambush. We've just got to get across the bridge, then it's nothing but old tea plantation roads and backcountry to Tabuk."

"How do you know we're not going deeper into Fedayeen territory? There are civvies in that town over there." Felix ducked a little lower.

"Everything over the river was X'd by Central almost a year ago. Dagger drones detect anyone without the right IFF transponder and their life ends in a high-pitched squeal and a *splat* when the warhead goes off. I bet that's why they've got a guard post over there. Keeps idiot kids from scrounging through the no-go zone," Gunnar said. "We're this close to being home free."

The warble of Gunnar's stomach sounded through his suit.

Felix took out a lump of shrink-wrapped dry meat and gave it to Gunnar. His squadmate tore it open and bit off a chunk before giving it back.

"Damn, Felix." Gunnar dry coughed. "Why'd you get the super spicy *tong*?"

Felix took a bite and his lips immediately burned.

"Do they make any other kind? Hangar I got it from said they have to use the strong stuff or it'll go moldy." He mashed his eyes shut as they began to water.

"Friend of mine on squadron staff said he's had it mild. Locals just sell us the painful shit because they fucking hate us," Gunnar said. "Guarantee this'll give us the wet shits later . . . still better than being hungry. Thanks, brother."

"Who needs caffeine supps when we can eat dried out fire?" Felix slipped the *tong* back into his pouch.

"Set for suppression," Gunnar said.

Felix twisted the flash suppressor on the end of his carbine barrel, opening up a honeycomb of holes down the length. He dialed back the power setting on the carbine, slowing the velocity of the bullets the next time he fired. The setup was ineffectual against any armored targets or anything behind substantial cover, but it would cut down the distance the sound of their shots carried.

"You get left, I'll get right. Let's go." Gunnar reached back and slapped Felix on the leg. Felix smacked Gunnar on the shoulder and the two crept through the jungle side by side. They moved through a muddy depression, the sound of their boots sloshing through water masked by the churning river. Tall light-green fronds swayed in the breeze and blocked most of their view of the guard post.

Sweat dribbled through Felix's mustache and into his goatee. It tasted of salt and grime, but he didn't want to huff it away for fear of fouling up his visor's display. They crept closer to the guard shack until he could hear the a capella music the locals preferred playing from the simple structure.

A man stood up, rifle slung across his chest, and came around the back of the hut. His arms and shoulders were bare, and he wore an older pattern of camouflage pants, the cuffs folded neatly over a pair of sneakers.

Felix and Gunnar froze. Gunnar raised his carbine slowly.

The guard stretched his arms overhead, then fiddled with his pants in preparation for a piss.

"Mine," Gunnar said through their suit-to-suit connection.

A sudden gust of wind depressed the foliage around them, exposing Gunnar's weapon for a brief moment. The guard froze, then leaned his head forward, eyes squinting. He said something to one side and clutched his weapon.

Gunnar fired off a three-round burst that stitched up the guard's chest and neck. The man crumpled to the road, then rolled into the basin with the two Flankers.

A much younger voice cried out in terror, then repeated a phrase over and over again.

"Felix!" Gunnar trudged forward.

Felix aimed where he thought the other guard was in the shack and opened fire. The lower-velocity bullets broke through the sticks and leaves. Bits of green and splinters flew into the air with every squeeze of the trigger.

The screaming got even higher pitched.

Felix switched to full auto in frustration and brought the shack down through a long *tat-tat-tat* of fire. There was a rustle as leaves and branches fell away from the collapse.

"Move it!" Gunnar shouted through their channel. Felix struggled to move from where he'd sunk into the mud, then finally jumped into Gunnar's tracks through the muck. He tried to ignore the dead man that lay at the bottom of the embankment. The man's arms and legs were lopped at painful angles that sent a shiver down Felix's spine.

He scrambled up the embankment and looked down the road to the village. There wasn't any immediate activity and Felix had a spark of hope . . . until he saw the collapsed hut. An arm and head stuck out from the sticks and leaves, and a cell slate lay in a growing puddle of blood. The head of the man he killed was turned away from him, a small favor from the All Father.

There was an open call on the cell and the only word Felix could make out was "crab," the Dahrien locals' preferred term for Hegemony soldiers. Felix stomped on the cell and ran after Gunnar.

The cars on the bridge were mashed together, parked haphazardly across lanes to make it even more difficult to get across.

Gunnar shuffled from side to side next to a rusted car, looking for an easy way through, but it was bumper to bumper from one side to the other and from side to side.

"Just go over?" Felix asked.

"We'll highlight ourselves, but I don't think they're—" Gunnar craned his neck up to look back at the village. He ducked down fast as bullets cracked overhead. Felix raised his carbine up and fired back toward the village. Dozens of men were streaming out of the homes towards the bridge.

"Smoke!" Felix pulled his last grenade off his chest rig and rolled it away. Purple smoke billowed out. Felix went prone as bullets cut through the smoke, leaving curling trails behind them.

"Stop waiting for the perfect time and move your ass." Gunnar hopped onto a car trunk and started jumping from vehicle to vehicle.

Felix ignored the snap of rounds overhead and that thumped into the dead cars. He went through the worst game of hopscotch to get to the other side of the bridge and the overgrown road leading the hell away from this awful place.

Gunnar cried out and grabbed his left thigh. He fell onto a hood, groaning in pain.

Felix got to the car and tried to snatch a quick-clot patch from Gunnar's chest rig.

"Get out of here!" Gunnar pushed him away. "I'm not going to make it."

"You know I can't." Felix got Gunnar's arm over his shoulder and slid him onto his back. He pulled two belts built into Gunnar's suit and connected the powerful magnets together across his own waist. He used the built-in buddy sling to carry Gunnar. Moving across the cars was hard before; hauling around a bleeding man while being shot at made it even worse.

Neither saw the rocket-propelled grenade that came screaming in from the riverside where the smoke screen hadn't spread. The warhead struck one of the mashed-together cars several yards from the two soldiers.

Felix felt a sharp pain in his back as the blast wave carried them both over the side of the bridge and into nothing but air. The buckle lost its hold and Gunnar fell away from him. Felix hit the river hard. The air was knocked out of him, and his visor filled with water.

The current pushed him along and Felix completely lost his bearings. His boots struck a rock, spinning him around. His visor was supposed to be sealed, but there absolutely was water filling it. Felix gulped down the last bubble of air and a mouthful of the river. He jammed his thumbs under the edge of his helm and tripped the emergency relief. The helmet was carried away but now the rapids were in his ears and rushing all around him.

He kicked hard and finally broke the surface. He thrashed about, unsure why his suit was trying to drown him after all his training led him to believe it was supposed to do otherwise. He slapped his chest rig and felt a pair of inflated air bladders built into his armor. The other four flapped in the current, torn and useless.

Gunnar bobbed up and down as they were carried away, face down.

Felix attempted to call out Gunnar's name and swam toward him. He got a grip on Gunnar's foot and pulled him over as whitecaps washed over them. Gunnar's back was a mess of torn up ballistic fabric and hunks of ceramic plates. Felix rolled Gunnar over and clung to him like he was a life preserver.

"Gunnar? Gunnar?" Felix tapped the man's helmet. Bubbles and air popped out of Gunnar's life vest as shrapnel damage slowly deflated them. Gunnar moved along with the current, his head lolling against Felix.

"Damn it, hang on, brother." Felix kicked hard and slowly swam them toward the shore. The current carried them towards a boulder in the river. Felix gripped Gunnar tight and turned his back to the rock, striking it hard. Felix cursed in pain and frustration. The muscles in his back tightened as the adrenaline dull wore off.

One foot scraped against the bottom of the river and he giggled in nonsensical joy. He got another foothold and swung Gunnar around onto the pebbled bank. He dragged Gunnar's limp form into a patch of grass and fell to the ground next to him.

"Gunnar?" Felix snapped out of his momentary rest and pressed a button on the side of his helmet. The visor popped up. Water poured out the sides. Gunnar stared at the sky, his eyes still. A red stain spread from a tear through his abdomen.

"No . . . no, buddy, don't leave me." Felix shook Gunnar gently. "*We are supposed to get out of here together.* Please . . . I'm no good on my own!"

Felix winced as a sharp pain knifed up his back. He reached around and pulled out a hunk of serrated metal that had buried itself into his suit. Felix looked at the wound through Gunnar's body and where he found the shrapnel. Gunnar had taken the hit and shielded Felix with his own body.

And not by accident.

"All Father, I'm sorry." Felix touched Gunnar's still chest, then snatched his hand back. "I was trying to help him. I didn't mean to . . . I didn't . . ."

Felix's shoulders fell and tears joined the river water on his face. He glanced at the bullet wound on Gunnar's thigh. The exit wound was too large to survive without actual treatment from a field hospital or a medic with a trauma kit.

"What am I doing? Where the hell even am I?" Felix pulled his knees to his chest and rocked for a moment, listening to the river and the wind rustling through the jungle. He looked to the sky and the pale blue overhead.

A moment later he reached under Gunnar's breastplate and fished out a small double-sided hammer on a plastic chain; the silver was painted over with black paint but the hard edges still shone through. He wrapped Gunnar's hands around the talisman, then kept his own hands wrapped around Gunnar's. He mouthed words, then closed his eyes. Then he said out loud:

"All Father, your brave son lies here. I feel his soul next to me. His body still claims his spirit, but he cannot remain here. His life has run. Take him to your hall where the honored dead may feast at your table and carry your banner to the final battle . . . Your brave son died for another. He died for me. There is only so much room in your hall, if you must ever choose between Gunnar and my wretched soul, let him keep his place. The scraps from your table and the warmth of your walls is enough for me, so long as he remains by your side. Send your Valkyrie to carry him away. His time in the pain of this world is over. Let him rest ... please."

Felix closed Gunnar's eyes.

He sat beside the dead man for several minutes, then slipped the carbine off of Gunnar's chest rig. His own weapon was somewhere in the river. Felix took Gunnar's magazines and the battery packs on his belt, then stood and carried Gunnar's helmet in the crook of his arm.

"I have to take what you no longer need," Felix said. "Forgive me. I'll get to Tabuk and make sure word gets back to your family—oh, wait."

He felt around the edge of Gunnar's breastplate and pulled out a cord with dozens of identity chips. Names of dead men flashed on each one.

"You were the platoon ferryman the whole time? I thought it was Svenson. Falls to me, I guess." He slipped the cord beneath his own breastplate and hooked it into his own identity chip. He ran a finger through Gunnar's helmet and cleaned out a bit of mud.

He slid the helmet on, plotted a route to Tabuk, and walked into the jungle.

CHAPTER 2

Noah Tallec clutched the restraint harness over his chest as the *Izmir's* landing gear set down, jostling the entire ship. Noah pressed his head back into the cradle, one finger tapping against the thin metal handle on the harness. Coughs and grumbles filled the troop compartment. Noah rattled the harness as the overhead lights flickered.

The harness had high, padded sides to reduce the risk of injury during a rough landing. While he'd appreciated the cushion during the descent from orbit, the only thing he could see was directly overhead and an empty seat across from him.

The landing wasn't like the net vids or the recruitment blocks everyone had to watch during their final year of mandatory education. No bombastic music or the thrill of landing in the midst of battle. The *Izmir* was a civilian cargo ship, not a proper Hegemony naval vessel. The rust bucket barely had any guns on it.

"Why're we still locked in? There something wrong?" Noah asked. His multi-tool was on his belt and it would take him a minute or two to trip the emergency release if needed. He'd been taught that skill away from the eyes of sergeants as breaking anything aboard the *Izmir* would mean a dock in pay and extra duty for—

"Crew's doing their thing. Just be quiet for a minute," Mason Tallec said from the next seat over. "Everything's 'hurry up and wait' in the Army. You should've figured that out by now."

Noah's brother, Mason, seemed far more serene about landing on a new planet. Mason had the same fresh, high and tight haircut required for all the soldiers of the Bretton Eleventh, but none of the nervous excitement of greener troops. During the final days of the journey, Mason had taken on the same long-distance stare and short temper Noah remembered from years ago. He thought Mason's difficult nature then had to do with the awful news Mason had returned to, but the longer Noah was in and around the military, the less that idea held up.

"Right. Sure." Noah rattled the harness again. "But we've rehearsed emergency evac procedures so many times—they said we'd be up and about thirty seconds after landing, didn't they?"

"Hey." A boot thumped against the deck to Noah's left. "Real gravity! We're finally here." A baby-faced soldier with big brown eyes gave him a goofy smile.

"There's no difference between ship gravity plating and a gravity well, Donan," Noah said. "We've been over—"

The harness *clicked* and the pressure against Noah's chest relented. He pushed the harness up and locked it into the housing built into the bulkhead. He could finally see his squad's full compartment again. The other nine soldiers weren't as eager to get up and about as he was; most sat there with a look somewhere between dull annoyance and exhaustion. They'd adapted to shipboard time during the transit from Bretton and their landing just so happened to take place in the middle of the sleep cycle, 3 AM ship time.

Donan drummed his feet against the deck, then raised his arms and let them fall to his side, still testing gravity. The top of his fatigues was rumpled from the harness. Noah checked his own uniform and tugged at the bottom, brushing away creases. Standard Hegemony fatigues for work and training were drab gray; soldiers' bore their name over their right chest, patch for their unit on their right shoulder and the Hegemony armed forces crest on their left arm. Rank was embossed into the collar that extended halfway up their necks.

Mason peeled a short black strip from a wound-up puck of the same material and pressed it against his gums. He leaned to one side and rested a shoulder against a pile of duffel bags secured to the deck by rubber netting. Noah reached over and poked his brother in the arm; a slight raise of his chin was enough for Mason to know Noah was worried about him.

"Shipboard inspection uniform!" Sergeant Corre read off from a small screen on the underside of his wrist. He stood up from his seat next to the bay door, his face darkening as he continued to read. "Inspection uniform *plus* rain slicks. Battalion formation in ten minutes in the cargo bay."

Corre, the oldest man in the squad bay, had a lean, angular face. His hairline had lost the battle against middle age and he'd opted for a bald shave, else the horseshoe around his bald pate would garner attention and jokes no one would make to his face. He had a perpetual air of seething annoyance to him, which Noah wasn't sure was part of his nature or a consequence of being the squad leader for a bunch of mostly raw recruits.

Noah touched his belt over his left hip where the rain slick was supposed to be attached. It wasn't there, of course; the plastic could melt in the event of a crash and wasn't supposed to be worn during landings.

"Are the zeros serious?" Corporal Boyle said from across the compartment. The man was larger than the rest of the squad, and his thick arms and torso bulged against his fatigues. "It doesn't rain in this bucket."

"It rains on Dahrien." Sergeant Corre unfastened the webbing over their duffel bags and rolled it towards the bulkhead. "LT's orders didn't come with an option for our feedback. Get your slicks and get to the cargo bay."

Noah slid his duffel bag out of the pile and dragged it away from the others. He unlocked the top and jammed an arm deep into the bag. Now, where had he put the slick?

Mason worked his jaw from side to side as the nicotine strip on his gums activated. His rain slick was at the very top of his gear in his duffel bag.

"Mason," Noah whispered just loudly enough for his brother to hear, "isn't this bad luck?"

"What? Bad enough that we're in the Saint-damned infantry on some backwater shithole for the next 364 standard days." Mason gave him a sideways glance.

"No. Where is that damn slicker?" Noah pulled out a rolled-up set of fatigues and dropped them on the deck, then did the same with a pair of pristine boots. "It's raining. Isn't it bad luck to step off a ship when it's raining?"

"Oh, yeah." Mason nodded slowly. "I remember Grandpa saying

something 'bout that during the Union War. Don't matter. We made it dirtside without any screaming or fire, so this ain't so bad."

Mason reached into one of Noah's spare boots and pulled out a rain slicker perfectly folded into a square and shoved it into his brother's chest.

"There it is." Noah rolled his eyes and repacked his duffel. "Why are you so calm? Dahrien's got an insurgency on it, right? Isn't that why we're here?"

"Because we didn't get here in a drop pod," Mason said. "There's three ways the Hegemony infantry ever go boots-down on a world: in a coffin bolted onto the outside of a pod built by the lowest bidder that lands in the middle of a firefight, a smooth descent in a pressurized and temp-controlled ship like this . . . or as a cloud of flaming chunks when either of those options fails or gets blown to shit during descent. I did two combat drops on my last hitch. This is a friggin' pleasure cruise."

"I'm just going to leave my duffel out here," Donan said. "We've landed. No need to keep everything secure, right?"

He snapped a hook into a ring, closing his bag.

"You want to donate all your gear, private?" a short man asked as he slapped a patrol cap against his thigh. "Because anyone sticks their head in here and sees a loose bag it's free game. You think everyone's got every single bit of kit they're supposed to?"

"I kinda do, Sarge." Donan shrugged. "We've had layouts since before we even left Bretton and—"

"Rhetorical question, dipshit." The sergeant—Rochelle by his name tape—swiped his cap at Donan. "Don't let your discipline slip just because we're out of hyperspace. Lock it down."

"Yes, sergeant." Donan lugged his bag back onto the pile. Noah was right behind him.

"Uniform is rain slicker, *donned.*" Sergeant Corre leaned over the threshold to the troop compartment. "Hard time in four minutes!"

"His hard time is in four minutes." Mason shook his slicker out and squeezed his head through the hole in the center. "Platoon sergeant's hard time is five minutes after that. Then the LT's hard time is ten minutes later which is thirty minutes before the captain's—"

"Do you want to be late for any of those?" Sergeant Rochelle asked. "No? Didn't think so. Everyone move your asses. We're representing all of Bretton on this shithole and we're not going to embarrass our home. Move it!"

Major Easton Perrin rocked back and forth on his heels as soldiers filed into the cargo bay. No one ever called the *Izmir* a tramp freighter within earshot of the crew, but the general state of near dysfunction everywhere he looked was not going to ingratiate the crew in his memoirs.

The water leaking from a pipe running across the ceiling still wasn't fixed, despite his numerous work order requests. The drip landed in the middle of the formation and was so dependable that the spot where a soldier should've fallen in was left habitually empty as the soldiers complained the gray water had a certain smell to it.

The hydraulics for the main cargo door functioned, but they hadn't been polished to any sort of inspection standard in years—if ever—and no proper sailor in the Hegemony Navy would ever have tolerated such a sight.

But this was a civilian ship and Colonel Jematé seemed to have some sort of agreement with the captain to keep the ship and the cargo in separate spheres during transit. Jematé was with Captain Mehmet several yards away from where Perrin stood with the rest of the officers to one side of the battalion formation.

Perrin looked over his uniform again. His rather meager rows of medals were for training completion, one exemplary performance during field and command post exercises . . . nothing for combat. Not yet.

Just setting foot on a world eligible for combat pay meant a combat pin he could wear for the rest of his days. He was already ahead of the game for all the officers that opted to stay back home on Bretton.

Their loss.

He brushed a fingertip against his pencil-thin moustache. Few officers ever bothered with the only allowed bit of facial hair in army regulations. The precision required to keep it within standards was almost comical, but Perrin bore his with a bit of pride. He considered it a display of discipline and attention to detail.

Lieutenant Colonel Timmons, the battalion XO, touched her earpiece, then walked purposefully toward Jematé and Mehmet.

The tap of a cane sounded from behind Perrin.

"Ah, made it," a rail-thin man a few years shy of elderly said. He wore fatigues in a different pattern than the rest of the battalion; a single golden arch of rank adorned one lapel, a globe of Bretton on the other. He dabbed sweat from his brow with a white handkerchief. The man's right leg had an unpowered brace on it; the limb within was atrophied and the foot was several sizes smaller than the other.

"Mr. Lambert, didn't think you'd be here for this," Perrin said. "Logistics all taken care of?"

Lambert raised an eyebrow at him, then glanced at Perrin's rank. He opened his mouth to speak, then drew in a short breath and nodded.

"Ah ha . . . once we landed here your commission automatically transfers to the Hegemony Army," Lambert said. "My territorial rank is voided. Thanks for the reminder."

"I don't make the rules," Perrin said. "Captain Mehmet looks happy to see you."

"'Course he is. He thinks he's about to be paid," Lambert said.

"Isn't he?" Perrin sneered at the dirty hydraulics and then at the leak in the overhead pipe.

"Soon as we've completely disembarked and I finish my inventories," Lambert said. "Until then, I've got release authority for all his fees. And whoever has the gold, has the power."

"Is that the Territorial Support Corps motto?" Perrin chuckled at his own joke.

"It should be." Lambert scratched his chin, which was in need of a morning shave.

"*Habibi!*" Captain Mehmet approached, his arms wide. The civilian shipmaster's head bore a knitted namaz cap; big pearly teeth were visible through his thick beard as he smiled at Lambert. "Our time together ends too soon!"

Mehmet hugged both arms around Lambert. The taller captain mashed Lambert's face against his shoulder. Lambert rolled his eyes at the unwanted physical affection. Men of Bretton were more reserved in their contact with each other.

"Yes, I'm as heartbroken as you are," Lambert said, disengaging, "I'm afraid Central hasn't cleared my access to the port's networks. Our disembarkation might be delayed a number of hours until I can organize longshoreman support."

Mehmet held up a finger.

"I'll contact the port authority immediately," he said. "They did authorize our landing, after all."

"Much appreciated," Lambert said. Mehmet ducked down a passageway, a comms device in his hand as he shouted orders in his native language to someone.

"Okay . . . that was clever." Perrin nodded slowly. "You got him to jump through his ass and saved me and my staff the trouble of getting the local quartermaster into gear."

"It's amazing how helpful people are when they want to get paid," Lambert said. "Colonel's moving." He lifted the tip of his cane to point to the officer as he strode toward the front of the formation.

Lambert took a step forward but was blocked when Lieutenant Colonel Timmons poked two fingers in his chest.

"Sorry, Lambert, regular officers only," she said. "Colonel wants you off to one side. Far to one side as possible."

"Of—of course." Lambert cleared his throat and shuffled away.

Perrin raised his chin slightly and followed Timmons to the front of the formation where Jematé was waiting. Perrin moved to the second rank behind the company commanders and their lieutenants to stand with the rest of the staff officers.

Jematé locked eyes with the battalion command sergeant major and gave him a brief nod.

"Battalion!" echoed through the cargo hold. "Atten-shun!"

Three hundred and eighty-two sets of heels slammed together.

Jematé pointed a knife hand at an *Izmir* crewman, who had the same ridiculous beard as Mehmet and had the top of his coveralls tied around his waist and a white sleeveless shirt covering his chest. The sailor opened a panel and hit three buttons in a quick sequence.

Warning klaxons sounded and the hydraulics controlling the large cargo doors squealed. The top of the ramp came away from the hull with a creak of breaking rust. Wind whistled through the opening, carrying tiny raindrops that swirled about the vortex at the top like spittle. The wind grew louder as the ramp lowered.

Perrin had dreamed of a true sky during the months-long journey. At no time during his imaginings had he envisioned the soulless gray overhead. Rain came down in lashes, gusts carried it over the formation, and Perrin hardened his face as moisture spattered against his uniform.

Colonel Jematé and the officers held their bearing as more of the storm blew in.

Best impression we can make, given the circumstances, Perrin thought.

The ramp slammed onto the landing pad, sending reverberations through the deck. Most of the void port was lost to rain and fog. Wind sent ripples across standing puddles as the heavy rain continued. Ground crew in bright raincoats kept their distance from the ship.

"God damnit," one of the officers muttered.

Colonel Jematé turned his head ever so slightly to one side and Timmons hissed at someone.

Perrin rolled his eyes. Silly superstitions about stepping onto a new world while it rained were for the common soldiers, not the officers who were trained—and expected—to know better. Just because the first colony ship to land on Bretton's eastern continent ended up crashing in a rainstorm, and the survivors nearly died from a hurricane that hit the next day, didn't mean rain on this planet was an omen of anything.

Three hulking figures appeared out of the storm. Each wore Cataphract armor, the heavy infantry suits that the Hegemony preferred for most ground engagements. The frames added a foot of height to anyone wearing them. The more experience a soldier had in the system, the more natural their gait, and each of these soldiers carried themselves like they were on a casual stroll, not the stiff trudge most of the battalion's Cataphracts still had. Thick armor plates on the shoulders and arms covered the reinforced frame and servos that carried the M-97 rotary cannons. The T-shaped slits on the soldier's helms glowed from within as they marched up the ramp.

Perrin noted kill tallies etched into the thick breastplates. Each bore dents, dings and repair patches from firefights, and his heart swelled at the thought of his own suit returning home with the same hard-earned badges of courage.

The Cataphracts on the flanks stopped a few steps short of the top of the ramp. The soldier in the middle crossed the threshold, showing no concern for the thin waterfall coming off the hull. He towered over Colonel Jematé in silence.

Jematé raised his hand in salute, and almost forgot to turn his palm out in the proper Hegemony parade ground customs and courtesies, which differed slightly from Bretton's.

The Cataphract clanged a hand against his chest twice and his helmet opened into three sections. The colonel within had hard, cold blue eyes. Streaks of scars crossed his face, pale hair on his beard and eyebrows marking where the scar tissue was unseen, but still there.

"Colonel Henry Jematé, Bretton 2nd Battalion, 89th Infantry, reporting as ordered." The colonel lowered his salute and extended his left hand to Timmons, who handed over a data slate. Jematé presented the slate to the Cataphract with a flick of his wrist.

The Cataphract held out a massive hand and a data port on his knuckle blinked twice. One third of the open face plate bent back towards his face.

"Brigadier General Zimri. Central chief operations officer. Marshal Van Wyck is expecting you but couldn't be here in person. . . . Bretton was tasked with providing a brigade to Dahrien," the general said.

"My apologies." Jematé bent his head forward slightly. "Bretton is far removed from most of the Hegemony's trade lanes. Our Governor was able to secure the *Izmir* immediately to answer the Hegemony's tasking. The other battalions and the brigade command team will arrive shortly."

The corner of Zimri's mouth twitched.

"Bretton's in the Gallia sector . . . no, not much traffic that far out on the frontier. Regardless, we're glad you're here," Zimri said. "Marshal Van Wyck will see you and every captain and above now. Your soldiers will cycle through indoc and medical ASAP. Stations are on standby for them."

"That . . . is nonstandard procedure, I believe, sir," Jematé said.

"Welcome to Dahrien. We'll take a tunnel to HQ at Fort Equity. I've got a cattle car on standby. I assume your lieutenants can handle moving your men through indoc," Zimri said, and took a half step back.

"N-naturally." Jematé cleared his throat and looked over to the sergeant major.

There was a brief discussion, then Jematé scooped a hand over his shoulder at head height, the "follow me" patrolling command. The lieutenants fell out of formation and Perrin followed the line of officers behind Jematé.

The tropical rain hit Perrin and he couldn't help but smile.

⊕ ⊕ ⊕

Noah closed one eye and glanced up at the sky. It was nothing but deep gray, the cloud ceiling barely a few hundred yards overhead. The rain slicker he wore failed to keep him dry, but did manage to make him feel exceptionally cold as the slightest breeze cut through the fabric. He'd never gone through weather like this before. Granted, this was the only planet other than Bretton he'd ever been to.

"This is bullshit." Mason Tallec's teeth chattered as he and his platoon marched through the storm.

"You think they were going to turn the rain off for the infantry?" Boyle asked from the column to his right. "This ain't your first deployment, Mason."

"Them sending us to indoc on the opposite side of the void port is what's bullshit," Mason said. "We've passed at least a dozen warehouses where they could've done all this."

"You mean the Army's nothing but a bunch of 'hurry up and wait' compounded with incompetence at every opportunity?" Donan asked. "Why didn't any of that get into the recruiting videos?"

"Absolutely nothing we're doing requires jaw-jacking from anyone," Sergeant Corre said. "Next man I hear bitchin' volunteers for every shit detail that comes our way until his attitude changes."

Mason shut his mouth and kept his eyes forward. The platoon sergeant halted the formation outside a warehouse with a moldy, faded-out sign over a set of double doors.

A small man with dark skin came out and waved them through.

"Wet no good. Come dry. Dry!" His accent was completely foreign to Noah.

Lieutenant Govrien and Sergeant First Class Malo were the first inside. The doors stayed open as the rain got worse. Noah felt moisture run down his back and into the last dry part of his clothing.

"Fall in by squads." Malo waved the first squad in. "Scan your implants, or your training won't be recorded and you'll have to do this shit again."

Noah finally made it out of the rain and swiped his right wrist over a small podium and felt a slight buzz up his arm. The briefing room was several rows of old seats facing a holo stick mounted on the wall. The whole place smelled of mold and fumes from insulation made by the lowest bidder.

"Fill in from the front. Make your buddy smile!" Malo shouted as soldiers abandoned their attempts to sit in the back. Noah ended up in the middle of the room, rubbing shoulders with other members of his squad. He stripped off his rain slicker and let it drip dry between his knees.

"Hello!" The small man walked across the front of the room. "I am Amir Jok. Welcome to Dahrien. You have already met *samar*. That's our word for weather. Also our word for 'summer.' We only have one season here. I hope you like it." He laughed heartily at his own joke and Noah suspected it wasn't the first time he'd told it.

"Fuck me sideways," Mason muttered.

"Enjoy your first indoctrination video. Coffee will be ready in ten minutes." Jok waved at the platoon and moved to the back of the room.

"Coffee? There is a god," Boyle said.

"You think they make it right out here?" Sergeant Rochelle twisted around to watch Jok at a coffee station in the back of the room.

"I don't care if it's old grounds I have to rub against my gums, just give me anything caffeinated." Boyle rubbed a sleepy eye. Mason tapped the side of Boyle's shoulder, the small tin in one hand.

Boyle's eyes brightened and he mouthed "I love you" to Mason and took a strip out. Mason shifted the tin over to his brother.

"You told Mom you quit," Noah said.

"You told Mom you were drafted." Mason drew the tin back.

"Who volunteered for this?" someone two rows ahead asked.

"They were going to draft me anyway," Noah muttered.

The lights darkened and the holo bar on the wall flickered to life. A flag with a deep star field in a silver ring surrounded by a blue field appeared and the first bars of "Hegemony, My Heart" began.

Every soldier snapped to their feet and saluted as the anthem played. Noah's shoulder burned with exhaustion by the time it finished. The anthem had always struck him as being overly long, but hearing it after thirty-six hours without sleep almost got him a write up from the platoon leader for disrespect to the flag.

The holo blinked and a man and woman seated at a newscaster desk appeared.

"Hello, I'm Chad Storm." The man had perfect hair and a smile that only money could buy.

"And I'm Vanessa Blanco." The blonde woman's green eyes glittered and Noah found a new reason to pay attention. "Welcome to Front Line Heroes and welcome to Dahrien."

Noah squinted. He could've sworn her lips didn't match that last word.

"Damn, she looks the same as when I saw her as a kid," someone said. "Still damn good."

"Stow it," Malo growled.

"Dahrien is a category II world and vital to the Hegemony," Chad Storm said as a spinning green and blue globe appeared next to him. "As you're aware, anti-democratic forces have committed innumerable terrorist acts in the name of an outlawed religion. Thanks to the fine fighting spirit and noble sacrifice from soldiers—just like you!—Dahrien's civilian population remains safe and protected."

A series of graphs replaced the globe.

"Only two percent of the population have been brainwashed by the so called 'red banner' movement," Vanessa continued. "Vestigial cultural ties between family members obligate another five percent of civilians to actively support the insurgency, but the death of the Red Banner polluting the clan will allow tribal elders to openly support the Hegemony."

"Anyone catch what that meant?" Boyle asked.

"You." Sergeant Malo pointed a knife hand at Boyle. "Front leaning rest until the end of the presentation. Next one of you that doesn't want to pay attention can do burpees until I get tired."

The chatter fell to zero as Malo got up and went to the aisle where he assumed the push-up position.

"Most insurgent support is in the deep hinterlands." Chad Storm's smile grew wider. "You'll likely be called upon to support civil military affairs missions to extend Hegemony infrastructure to underserved areas. While the insurgents are capable of launching limited raids on poorly defended targets, you'll be well protected in our field outposts."

Mason shook his head.

Noah furrowed his brows. Everything he was hearing sounded like an easy deployment.

"We'll pause a moment for your local cultural attaché to explain how best to interact with local civilians who may not act in accordance with Hegemony norms," Vanessa said. "Once again, welcome to Da-ree-en." The tone and inflection of the planet's name sounded like it was said by someone else.

The holo froze.

Jok reappeared, a steaming cup in one hand.

"I haven't finished my coffee yet," he said. "Let's watch another mandatory video before we get to my part. You all have to watch the STD video anyway."

The platoon let out a collective groan.

"We watched it yesterday," one of the squad leaders in the front row said. "Part of our pre-deployment training."

"That's nice." Jok took a sip. "But you haven't watched it in this certified facility after you swiped in. You only get credit for it if you watch it as part of indoc. Did you all see the finance, sexual harassment, operational security, and food safety videos too?"

An uneven chorus told him yes.

"That sucks," Jok said. "Anyway. Coffee in the back."

He held up a remote control and clicked a button. A new video from the Hegemony Medical Authority began playing.

"I told the LT this would happen." Mason leaned back and nestled into his seat. "Could've been asleep yesterday when he had us doing 'pre-training.'"

"Eww!" Donan held a hand up to cover his eyes and Noah sighed. The first image of any STD briefing was meant to be an attention getter. Noah got up and went to the line forming at the coffee station.

CHAPTER 3

Perrin kept his back to the wall of the elevator as it continued higher. The company commanders and colonels Jematé and Timmons were closest to the doors. Jematé seemed more tense than usual. One of the captains yawned and mumbled an apology.

The elevator stopped and the doors opened with a *ding*. The Hegemony military's nerve center on Dahrien reeked of sweat and old coffee. Holo boards ringed a central dais with a tactical ring where an officer could command battles anywhere on the planet.

Perrin licked his lips, jealous of the top-tier equipment Central command had at its disposal. His attention flitted from holo to holo, trying to grasp the strategic situation. Many of the provinces far from Malakal, the capital, were dark except for a bright red X through the center of the regions.

"Bretton Eleventh?" A female colonel with her hair pulled into a messy bun stepped between the workstations. "The marshal's expecting you."

"Can my operations officer pull data while we speak with him?" Jematé lifted a hand towards Perrin.

"No . . . I don't think there's time for that." She gave them a plastic smile, then her voice fell to a whisper. "You won't be here that long."

"Certainly." Jematé followed her to a set of double doors guarded by a pair of soldiers in Flanker gear. The colonel cracked the door open and peeked inside, then held it open.

Jematé marched in and stopped two steps from a wooden desk. He stood ramrod straight and saluted. The man behind the disk didn't rise. He was bald, at least Perrin thought he was bald at first glance. A wide patch of scar tissue and synth-skin grafts that didn't match the tone of his skin stretched from the middle of his forehead to the back of his right ear. One eye was milky white; the other swam in the throes of some manner of narcotic.

A pile of empty field ration wrappers overloaded a trash can on one side of the desk. Two stacked crates of water bottles were on the other side. There was a distinct scent of urine in the office.

"Colonel Jematé, Bretton Eleventh Infantry reports as—"

"Yes yes, Marshal Jaworski." The man returned a flippant salute. "There . . . were supposed to be more of you. General McDaniels says your governor could only find *one* transport?"

"Correct, sir." Jematé remained at attention. "The rest of the brigade will arrive as soon as possible."

"I have been begging the *Highest* for reinforcements for two years." Jaworski leaned forward slightly. "The first thing the Most High Council told me to do was fall back on the Local Force Generation plan. I did that. Trained tens of thousands of Flags to fight properly and armed them with fresh gear from the printers out of the Navy's picket force. Do you know what happened next?"

Jematé's lower lip quivered.

"I sent them all to clear out the five provinces in active rebellion against the Hegemony and they were all dead in a month." Jaworski smiled, revealing several missing teeth. "At least, that's what was reported to me. Then the Flags launched a brand-new offensive that cut this city off from the thermal sinks and now the civilians are running off whatever solar panels and generators they can find. Guess how happy they are?"

"Sir, I don't—"

"Then I have to pay off the families of all my not-so-dead Flag militia and that sucks out my operation budget. Then we pull DNA off dead insurgents and it turns out I was paying stipends to the enemy. I cancel the stipends to the 'widows,'" he emphasized the word with air quotations, "and then the locals get even angrier with me. The nerve. Sheer." He banged a fist against the deck with each word. "Fucking. Hubris."

"Tea, sir!" The blonde colonel appeared with a paper cup. She held it to his lips and ran a hand down the back of his head as he drank. The marshal stared off into space for a moment, then suddenly noticed the Bretton officers again.

"Huh . . . where was I?" Jaworski's eyes darted from side to side. "I reported all this to the Hegemony and asked for more soldiers. Proper soldiers. Not a Skien detachment, those freaks make everything worse, and the locals hate them more than anything. There was a delay as the *Highest* relocated to Deseret sector and my reports went to Tirana. Of course the *Highest* doesn't announce when she moves. She doesn't answer to anyone, certainly not me. Beg beg beg. Flags start getting Alliance weapons smuggled in and then I lose the Junglei and Rumbek provinces. Then I finally get word from the Most High council and guess what they told me to do?"

There was a long pause.

"Guess!" Jaworski snapped to his feet and slammed his palms against the desk. It was at this moment that Perrin realized the marshal was not wearing pants.

"A-a switch to law and order enforcement and public services?" Jematé asked.

"Ha!" Jaworski flopped back into his chair and a waft of stale farts tickled Perrin's nose. "Listen to you, all full of practical ideas. That won't last long. No . . . the Most High, paragons of the Hegemony and the best of us—Hegemony, my heart my ass—ordered the orbital reduction of areas actively beyond my effective control. I laminated the order. Signed by all of the Most High council. Want to see it?"

"I . . . I accept your word, Marshal," Jematé said.

"You can't! I've got it locked in a vault somewhere. You think I'm going to risk losing my 'get out of war crime' ticket with actual ink signatures on it?" Jaworski laughed nervously. "So I did as ordered and donated several multi-ton tungsten rods from orbit onto a number of cities. This . . . did not defeat the insurgency. Rather emboldened it, I must admit. I did see that coming. Just so we're all aware."

One of the holo maps behind him beeped with priority traffic. The marshal spun his chair around, let out a string of expletives, then turned back to the Bretton officers.

"I can't hold the surrounding provinces anymore. As such, I've made the strategic decision to collapse my forces around the capitol administrative area and hold out until additional reinforcements arrive from Bretton . . . or from the *Highest*. I'm expecting their next rejection to arrive via courier in the next hundred hours or so." Jaworski smiled from ear to ear.

"Sir . . . I don't understand. When my governor received the force generation orders from the Most High, the situation here was described as stable," Jematé said.

"Are you . . . suggesting the Most High misled a member world?" One of Jaworski's brows ticked up.

"Never, sir," Jematé said.

"I didn't think so. But you're here now and it seems I've got a city that's about to fall to the insurgents." Jaworski rubbed his hands together. "Tabuk, about a day's convoy from here, attacks permitting. Your battalion will escort a logistics run and join the 31st Macadan Infantry that's holding the city."

An elbow to Perrin's stomach from Timmons prompted him to pull out a small pad and jot down the orders.

"That perimeter fails and the Red Banner will have a straight shot to the capital," Jaworski said. "The city's full of loyal Hegemony citizens, some even from Dahrien, and I am not interested in reporting another massacre to the *Highest*. The convoy leaves in . . . four hours and forty-nine minutes. Chop chop."

"But, sir . . . Hegemony standard operating procedure has at least two weeks of acclimatization. We haven't been able to offload—"

"That's amazing." Jaworski set his chin on his palm. "Did you catch the part where this entire planet is about to fall into anarchy?"

"Roger, sir," Jematé said.

"Don't worry." Jaworski shook a finger. "Word from the *Highest* is nigh. Nigh, I tell you. They'll finally send the reinforcements I've been asking for. An entire army of Skien troopers led by Supreme Marshal Telemachus himself. It'll be fine. Orders!"

The blonde hurried back into the office and handed over several packets of papers to each officer. Perrin received a handful of data sticks as well.

"You're still here." Jaworski opened a drawer and removed an empty plastic water bottle and unscrewed the top. "I need my privacy."

"We— Orders received and understood," Jematé said. "Thank you, sir."

Jaworski shooed them away with waggle of his fingers.

The Bretton officers left the office and made straight for the lift.

Once inside, Jematé turned to face them as he rifled through the paper orders. Perrin did the same.

"Everything appears to be in order . . . sir," Perrin said. "Looks like they generated these as soon as we landed."

"This is all highly irregular," Timmons said. "The Marshal obviously isn't well. How can he have lost effective control of so much of the planet and how were we not told—"

"Everything is in order." Jematé looked up from the papers. "This isn't ideal, but we expected to be deployed to a combat zone."

"Sir, we're still pissing ship water," Captain Dalois, a company commander, said. "None of our own logistics support elements can even be offloaded by the time we're supposed to leave with this convoy to Tabuk."

"We are infantry on orders to hold the line," Jematé said. "So long as we've got bullets, batteries and food we can do that. There should be at least a level-III-rated foundry in the city—"

"There is, sir." Perrin pointed to a paragraph. "The logistics point there has been supporting a division-sized garrison for . . ."

"Good to know," Jematé said. "Gentlemen, this is the time where leadership is needed more than ever. Our soldiers aren't going to take this well. I'm certainly *thrilled* with this situation but my opinion is irrelevant. None of our feelings matter. We have lawful orders and we are going to carry them out as the Hegemony expects of us. Questions?"

"Governor Engelier didn't know any of this," Timmons said. "The situation's been deteriorating on this planet for *years*, sir. Why didn't the Most High tell us the truth?"

Jematé gave him a dirty look.

"Forgive me, sir, I misspoke. Why didn't the Most High give us the complete situation when the troop tasking came to Bretton?"

"That is a question for later. Right now we need to figure out how we're going to get the entire battalion onto this logistics convoy. I don't even have a friggin' local line to call the convoy master. Not even a secure radio." Jematé shook his head.

"Do we at least have an operational picture of the city we're supposed to defend?" one of the other company commanders asked.

"Map on page eighty-four." Perrin pulled out a sheet that had a picture of the city taken from orbit. "No graphics. Must be an oversight from the planning cell. Colonel, can I run back up to—"

"No," Jematé said as the elevator doors opened to an underground station. "The only thing we have time for is to jump through our own ass. I need to talk to Lambert. He's suddenly become a lot more critical than I want him to be."

"The shuttle that brought us here had secure comms," Timmons said. "I think."

"I'll take a messenger pigeon at this point." Jematé whistled at a shuttle bus.

Noah closed his eyes as yet another video he'd already seen droned on. He drifted off to a quick nap, his chin against his chest. He thought of a face framed by curly blond hair and a smile that was always ready when he was around.

A rough hand shook his shoulder.

"I wasn't sleeping, sergeant." Noah's head snapped up as he looked around.

"You were nodding." Mason pressed a hot paper cup into his brother's hand. The smell of the lousy coffee didn't excite Noah into more wakefulness.

"What is this, turpentine with a drop of sludge dissolved in it?" Noah took a quick sip. "It's barely dark but plenty bitter. Even the sugar tastes fake."

"Be thankful. We get out in the field and you'll step over a naked and ready hottie for anything warm and edible," Mason said.

"Okay, listen up!" Lieutenant Govrien walked to the front of the theater with a printout in his hand. "We've got the General Order Nine video—which has been in effect the entire time and will remain in effect—so no intoxicants, unprofessional relationships with the populace or any actions that will reflect poorly on the Hegemony."

"What're they going to do if we get drunk or get laid?" Boyle asked quietly from their row towards the back. "Send us to war on some shithole light years from home?"

"You think it can't get worse?" Mason asked him as the lieutenant continued talking. "Wait, weren't you a judicial referral when the levy order came down?"

"Not … officially." Boyle sank back into his seat. He rubbed thick knuckles against his face. A semi-permanent five o'clock shadow had seemed to grow in during the few hours since planetfall.

"They going to feed us?" Noah asked as the LT walked from the front and another video from Hegemony Financial services played. "I think it's breakfast time aboard the *Izmir*."

"Just drink your coffee," Mason said.

"Ha ha, I'm in," Donan tittered from a few seats over. "Who wants to check their bank account?"

"Commo, you always come through." Boyle slid over to Donan and leaned over to read the small slate in Donan's lap. "How'd you get in?"

"There's a zero-day exploit that must not have been blasted out to the techs here." Donan frowned at the screen. "Just gets you into Hegemony's unclassified network, none of the spicier feeds...What the hell? This can't be right. 'Special tax assessment'? Eighty percent?"

"Stow it!" Sergeant Corre shouted.

"Give me that." Mason took the slate and accessed his pay stub. "Son of a bitch, they got me too."

Sergeant Corre moved up the aisle, focused like a laser on the soldiers.

The doors burst open with a gust of wind and rain. Captain Dalois, his uniform soaked through and his patrol cap a wet rag, moved to the front of the auditorium and pointed at the video of an earnest-looking financial advisor who was emphatically explaining how Hegemony war bonds had a terrific rate of return.

"Turn that shit off," Dalois ordered. The video paused a moment later, then blinked out of existence as the lights rose.

"The fuck did you do?" Mason jumped to one seat away from Donan, who slid his data slate between the seam of his seat and seat back.

Dalois huddled with his lieutenants and the First Sergeant for a moment, then stepped forward. The lieutenants had all gone pale. The First Sergeant somehow looked more angry than usual.

"Baker Company, we've received an immediate combat tasking," Dalois said. "We will move immediately back to the *Izmir* and draw gear. Full kit and as many power packs as you can reliably carry from stores. We will receive ammunition at the convoy corral. This is not how we're trained to plan for operations, but these orders came from Marshal Van Wyck himself. This is a critical mission, and he believes we're the only ones capable of succeeding."

"Holy shit, we just got here," Noah said.

"When I say time is of the essence, I am not fucking kidding."

Dalois pointed to the doors. "Form up and then we are double-timing it back to the ship. If we aren't on the ready line in . . . three hours and nineteen minutes, our ass is grass and the Hegemony will compost the lot of us. Move out."

"Fucking move!" the First Sergeant shouted.

Noah knocked over a lukewarm cup of coffee and rushed towards the exit. He made it out into the rain and saw another company already running through the storm.

"Four columns, start running!" The First Sergeant pushed soldiers into a general formation. "Squad leaders, kick asses until the last straggler figures out how serious the captain is!"

Noah dodged a boot from Sergeant Corre and fell into the scrum. His brother huffed and puffed next to him as the formation turned into a long-tailed comet of confused and disoriented soldiers.

"Mason, was your last deployment like this?" he asked.

"Uh, equally messed up but for different reasons. Just about anything the Army does is a goat rope. At least no one's shooting at us. Yet." Mason pulled his nic-strip out of his mouth and tossed it aside. "Don't write home to Mom about any of this yet. She'll just freak out."

"How can I write home when I don't know what's even happening?" Noah asked.

The *Izmir* appeared through the gloom as they ran closer.

"Just wait. I've got a feeling this'll get worse." Mason punched his younger brother on the shoulder.

Chaos reigned through the *Izmir*'s cargo bay. A riot of soldiers raced from open cargo pods. Most grabbed armfuls of gear and dropped it in piles near their company areas. The equipment was scooped up and distributed as fast as it could be pulled from stores.

Colonel Lambert stood in the center of the madness, leaning heavily on his cane.

"Your platoon grenade-launcher attachments are in cargo pod ninety-three." Colonel Lambert tapped on a screen held by a lost-looking lieutenant. "They've been there since we left Bretton. You've done at least six serial number inspections since then. They haven't moved."

The lieutenant turned and jogged away, the strap on his Flanker helm flopping.

"By the Saint this is going to be a disaster." Lambert shifted his weight off his good leg for a moment. "Property books conflated—Don't even come over here!" he yelled at a pair of sheepish lieutenants inching towards him. "I didn't move anything since we landed. It's exactly where you had it!"

"Lambert." Major Perrin had transitioned into Flanker gear, though the frame over his right arm seemed to be locked at the elbow. "The colonel wants you to have a copy of the operations order. Here."

Lambert held out a hand and a data drive landed in his palm.

"He doesn't care how, but we need our organic support assets delivered to Tabuk City immediately if not sooner," Perrin said, then looked over his shoulder to the chaos. "You're to report to Central once that's done as our rear detachment officer. Expect a fair number of loss investigations, but he'll sign combat liability waivers for every completed packet."

"How generous of him," Lambert deadpanned. "Easton, this void port isn't even connected to the main logistics hub at—"

"That's Major Perrin, if you please," Perrin said, annoyed. "I'm aware you have concerns, but there is a fire out there and Bretton's best are about to go piss on it and put it out. Your problems are your problems until I can set up an operations center in Tabuk. Anything else? Doesn't matter, I have to—"

He spun around but stopped when Lambert hooked him by the arm with his cane. The older man pulled a bright red plug from the Flanker's frame just behind the shoulder and Perrin was able to bend his arm again.

"Ah, thank you." Perrin unhooked himself and jogged back to the scrum of officers around Colonel Jematé.

"Anytime." Lambert stuffed the safety pin into his pocket.

Sergeant Boyle turned his head to the left as far as possible. Targeting systems within his Cataphract's helm locked onto black and white hash marks in the oversized closet that served as his platoon arming bay.

"Green across the board," Sergeant Corre read from a holo plate on his helmet. The squad leader was already in full Cataphract gear, with a rotary cannon locked onto a mount on his back. "Look right. Look up. Clear. Step forward for actuator check."

Boyle lifted his left leg and haptic sensors woven into his body glove transmitted the movement to the mechanized suit. Unlike Flankers, soldiers in Cataphract armor didn't rely on muscle power with frame assistance to move about. The Cataphract suits were piloted, not worn. Granted, most of the hard work of moving the two hundred pounds of armor plating, hydraulics and weaponry were handled by the onboard systems, but it still took a fair amount of skill to move about without falling over or creaking around like an old maintenance bot.

He hopped out of the arming bay and raised his arms up to his sides and over his head. The thick plating on the crablike arms moved easily enough, though the left pauldron was a bit too close to his chin for his liking.

"Wait for my command," Corre said. "Go/No Go system's sluggish right now."

"Pretty sure it wasn't meant for every single Cataphract suit in the battalion to need the diagnostics routines all at the same time," Boyle said. "This for real, sergeant, or is the old man just trying to get us riled up for nothing?"

"Forward shoulder rotation . . . rear . . . draw main weapon," Corre read off the checklist and Boyle did as instructed. He slid one foot forward over the *Izmir*'s cargo deck and locked his right arm back. The rotary cannon locked into the cradle and he swung the barrel out in front of him, left hand catching the forward handle.

"System's slow again." Corre looked back to a cargo pod locked to ceiling. "You ever known Colonel Jematé or Timmons to cry wolf?"

"Negative." Boyle revved the barrels of his weapon. "Maybe this is some sort of new guy hazing Central does? I wouldn't put it past some commander stuck on a backwater looking to have a little fun."

"What if this is one hundred percent real and we could be in combat as soon as we step outside of the wire? How about that for a possibility?" Corre chided. "We act like this is a big joke and the Patties will slaughter us the first chance we get."

"'Patties'? I don't think any Alliance are here, Sarge. That war ended a while back . . . what do they call the bad guys out here?" Boyle asked.

"Doesn't matter. Engage secondary weapon system," Corre said.

Boyle lifted his right hand, then mashed it down against a control rig and twisted a knob to the right. A long empty frame on the back of his suit popped out of a slit in the plating and it arced up . . . then froze in place.

"Damn it." Boyle shimmied inside his suit. "I told you this unit needs a factory reset."

"You're combat viable. Pull a mortar secondary when you get to the ammo depot," Corre said.

"But, Sarge, I suck at mortars. Let me reset and then I can—"

"Did I stutter? Pull a mortar and get out there and into the cattle cars. I've got to get Donan and Laeland certified in the next fifteen minutes or we'll miss movement," Corre said.

"I just . . . appreciate you keeping your head straight, sergeant," Boyle said. "Newer guys would panic if you didn't have that stick up your ass. Wait. I mean—"

"This is why I get paid the big bucks. Move out and draw fire." Corre canted his head to a transport truck loaded down with ammo and handing out shrink-wrapped packets of bullets and grenades from servo arms mounted on the back bumper.

Noah climbed into the back of a wide-bed cargo truck. The middle was full of plastic-wrapped cargo pallets locked into rails built into the floor. A row of seats braced the cargo, arrayed so those sitting could look out over the side rails. A turret over the cab bore a belt-fed machine gun.

The rain had stopped minutes after Noah was fully kitted out for the mission.

Noah sat close to the cab and set a backpack stuffed to almost bursting between his knees. More Flankers loaded up, and Mason took the seat next to Noah.

"Saint preserve us, what a cluster." Mason popped the seal on his helmet and slid the visor up. "You got a full load out?"

"Huh?" Noah slapped magazine pouches and counted grenades by touch, then checked that his carbine wasn't loaded. "Full battle rattle."

"Whew!" A soldier climbed into the turret ring from the cab. He had a simple ballistic helmet on, with thick goggles over his eyes. He was shirtless but had thick gloves missing the fingertips. Tattoos with a variety of languages ran up and down his arms. He sat on a strap hung from one side of the ring to the other and spun around, mimicking shooting at something in the air.

"Uh . . . hi?" Noah lifted his visor. "We-we-we're new here."

The gunner raised one side of his goggles and looked at the Flanker.

"No shit, slick shoulder, it hot enough for you?" the gunner asked. "What pasture did fresh meat like y'all come from?"

"Bretton," Noah said. "It's a star system on the outer edge of the Gallia Sector that—"

"Cool story, I don't care." The gunner tapped his palm against the left ear of his headset. "Hey you." He raised his chin to Mason. "You've got a combat patch. You get it here?"

"Tolmen Campaign," Mason said. "Vac fight most of the time."

"Sounds like it sucked. Watch your sector, call out anything with two legs you see off the road. If we're past Yambio, any human you see is hostile. Armed or not, got it?" the gunner asked.

"That's not our rules of engagement," Noah said. "We're supposed to positively ID a threat before—"

"Oye." The gunner lifted his goggles onto his helmet. His other eye was an ugly knot of scar tissue. "There's no such thing as a friendly Flag once Yambio's in the rearview, you get me? They all hate us. They all want to kill us. You see something, you shoot something. You don't and they'll holler back to the Red Banner and then we get ambushed."

"Don't you have Dagger drones for security?" Mason asked.

"Flags have enough IFF transponders off our dead to mask themselves from the drones. Sometimes they'll work as advertised when we cycle new IFF, but they've cracked the 'sponders and then things don't work as advertised within a few hours." The gunner shrugged.

"What's your name? Where you from?" Noah asked. "I've never met someone from off world. Except for the *Izmir*'s crew, but they're all Union so that doesn't count—"

"I'm Amos. Don't matter where you're from when you're in hell." The gunner pulled his goggles on their strap and snapped them back onto his face. He danced in the turret, bouncing to a beat only he could hear.

"You short yet?" Mason asked.

"Short? Short means somebody can leave." Amos laced his fingers behind his helmet and kept dancing. "No one gets off this shithole, not without a toe tag and a form letter and some copy-pasted signature from the Most High. Uh oh, getting low."

He reached into a pocket and pulled out a small box, glanced around, then stuck a nozzle up his nose and sniffed hard.

"Whew. That's laced with all sorts of shit. Don't trust any Buzz you get off the Flags." He shook the box at Noah. Noah reached for it until Mason stomped on his boot.

"You have any idea what that is?" Mason growled at him.

"No..."

"Then get by with caffeine tabs and shitty coffee," Mason said. "Don't get hooked on the first shit that comes your way. What'll happen when you're in the field and get whatever the hell bathtub uppers he's on?"

"Like that time you couldn't get your nic-strips during the plague years and you threatened to stab dad when he switched your coffee to decaf?" Noah asked.

"It wasn't a threat. I was going to stab him," Mason grumbled.

"Hey, sergeant." Donan nudged him with his elbow. "Is it always like this? Getting jerked around and sent to the front line within hours of making landfall?"

"Ugh... the Army is usually a soup sandwich, but getting thrown out there this fast is a first for me. Never heard of anything like this happening to anyone else, but it's a big Hegemony. There've been wars going since the Alliance War," Mason said.

Donan nodded along, his eyes growing wider.

"But don't worry. Enemy doesn't know we're here. We show up and it'll throw them off trying to figure out how the good guys suddenly got so many brand-new badasses on their side. We're going to reinforce the lines, not attack anything. It'll be fine," Mason said.

Amos swung his open-topped turret around and leaned across the top of the mounted machine gun. He leaned over the weapon, his jaw working on a lump of gum. His head canted from side to side, like he was considering what to say.

"Gunner, what weapons do the locals use?" Mason asked, stymieing whatever the veteran was about to say.

"Our gear." Amos spat off the side of the turret. "Cataphract rifles and carbines mostly, but they'll have some tubes with captured rockets. The Red Flaggers mostly get around on scrap trucks, but they've got higher-end gear that's been smuggled in over the years. Plenty bodies on their side, lots of bodies and they don't seem to care if they die. They just want to kill us. You get captured and they'll scalp you before they hang you from a bridge with your guts dangling between your knees."

He stuck out a thumb and mimed running a blade over his head.

"That wasn't in the videos," Noah said quietly.

"That's your sector." Mason pointed from side to side in front of Noah and then for Donan. "Same drill we did back home. Just with live ammo and live targets this time."

"Hey, it's quiet out 'til Buri Buri. Get some shut-eye. Wake up if I start shooting." Amos gave them a thumbs up.

"Where are all the Cataphracts?" Noah asked.

"They'll be in cattle cars." Mason tilted his head to the truck behind them with a cargo container behind it. "Keeps them charged up and ready to deploy. Their ride looks just like the usual loggy truck. Enemy has to guess which targets are the easy ones and which ones bite back."

Amos slapped the top of the cab twice.

"Rollin' out!" the gunner shouted. Holo emitters built into the side rails of the flatbed truck sputtered to life. They formed a semi-opaque screen as seen through the cargo area. Vehicles in the convoy blinked on and off in a map, their route to Tabuk highlighted.

"Wow . . . never seen that before." Donan leaned forward and poked his fingertip through the holo.

"Hey hey hey!" Amos shouted. "Do you know how hard it is to find replacement emitters? You futz with that and it'll de-synch from the rest and you've given the Flags something to aim at. Stop it!"

"Sorry." Donan sat back, then looked over at Noah. "What's on the other side?"

"Holo of an olive drab tarp that doesn't draw any attention to itself," Amos said. "How is it you chuckleheads have never seen vehicle-masking 'jections before?"

"We're from Bretton," Donan said.

"Saint's balls, if you're going to jaw-jack the entire time, switch seats with me." Mason got up so Donan could slide over and be next to Noah. The sergeant sat back, stretched his legs out and rested his chin on his chest.

The electrical motors in the truck's wheels came to life with a hum and it rolled forward slowly.

"Bretton? Never heard of it," Amos said. "That one of those weirdo religious colonies like they've got out in the Sudetas sector?"

"Gallia sector, actually," Noah said. "Most everyone on Bretton belongs to the Church of the Adherents of God. Saint Robin led survivors of the failed colonies in the Moniker system—"

"You guys know how to use your guns, right?" Amos asked.

"We're all Hegemony level-two tech certified, but we don't use computation devices or anything like that in our daily life. Saint Robin taught that life should never be too easy, or the soul will rot."

"Cool story, not interested in your cult." Amos swung the turret around to point forward.

"We're big fans of electricity and air conditioning." Donan raised a hand.

Amos raised a single finger.

"We're not a cult," Donan said to Noah. "Why do people keep calling us that?"

"Because we send out missionaries. Though most people keep moving to Bretton because they want to . . . I'd rather not think about home right now. If that's okay with you," Noah said.

"Fall Festival's about to start." Donan's shoulders fell. "Ma and Pa always have their cider stand in the corner of Brigham Square. I know they make some decent coin, but they never spent any of it until Noel on me and my brothers . . . this is the first year I won't be with them. I told them to finally get themselves something for once. Ma said they'll keep saving, give it to me to start a business when I get home."

"They do make the best cider," Noah said. "Could go for some now too, but sleep seems a lot . . . Donan?"

His squadmate had his head in his hands, fighting back tears.

The truck rumbled into a slight depression and through a concrete tunnel. It drove out onto a paved road outside the void port. Sloped steel walls extended around the entire port, topped with weapon emplacements and surrounded by razor wire and cleared fields marked with posts warning of minefields.

Drones circled overhead. Noah zoomed in on one of the Daggers, noting that one of the grenade cradles was empty and the built-in machine gun had several notches scratched into the barrel.

Humidity rose as the convoy rolled into a decaying jungle.

"Had to clear out a ten-klick buffer zone to keep the damn Flags from shelling the base," Amos yelled over his shoulder. "Here's a hint: You ever have to walk back to base, stay on the road and hope the dronies are in a good mood."

"Look, there's a city," Donan pointed into the distance. Bland and identical skyscrapers faded into the mists in the distance. "Maybe we'll get shore leave or a pass eventually."

"You don't want that." Amos racked the charging handle back on his machine gun as they drove past two large orange posts. "Rebels sabotaged the replimats about a year ago. Everyone in the city's been eating re-cyc meal supplements. Can't even get rice in from the countryside without it being poisoned or turned to sludge from grain-rot. Rumor's that the loyal Heg citizens are spicing up their dead just for something to break the monotony of turd bars. But those are just rumors. Hey, weapons free from here on out."

Noah pulled the charging handle on his carbine, activating the electromagnetic coils around the breech. He touched the safety switch, feeling that it was pointed towards the butt stock, then glanced at it.

"Noah, I just... I just got real scared all of a sudden," Donan said. "I haven't slept in two days and now there's insurgents all over the place that want to scalp me and eat me?"

"They just want to kill us, not eat us," Noah said. "Okay, saying that doesn't make me feel any better. But we've got combat vets with us. My brother, Sergeants Corre, Malo and the company commander have all deployed before. It'll be fine."

"You didn't say the lieutenant," Donan said. "I swear he can't even shave yet. Did he get a commission from the governor like that idiot Perrin?"

"Lieutenant Govrien means well. Do you think all the combat veteran NCOs around him are going to let him get us killed?"

"They sure as hell let him get us lost when we were on maneuvers in the Scrublands. They had to send hover jets to get us home. You remember that?" Donan asked.

"Lieutenants get lost all the time. I'm pretty sure the platoon sergeant let him take us down the completely wrong pass through the mountains just to teach him a lesson. Did he get us lost after that?"

"We didn't go back to the field after that," Donan deadpanned.

"Then it was a one-time thing. Relax. Saint Robin trusted the Hegemony to protect Bretton from the Union. He said that protecting the Hegemony protects Bretton and the rest of the Church, which means we're protecting home... in a roundabout way." Noah shrugged.

"You trying to convince me or you? You know the Governor almost told the Most High for the sector to pound sand when the tasking came down for him to recruit a brigade? My cousin told me about it. His girlfriend works in the Governor's mansion." Donan nodded.

"And why would the governor do something that stupid? Refusing a military call up is no different than treason, according to the incorporation treaty." Noah leaned forward and squinted. In a distant ravine, brown sludge poured from a pipe big enough for their cargo truck to drive into. The waste pooled in one corner of a lake with an oily sheen across the top. The smell of chemicals and rot wafted over them with the breeze.

"My cousin's girlfriend's supervisor heard the governor arguing with the Most High rep. Turns out everyone back home is *also* getting bumped up an entire tax bracket to pay for . . . everything. More theft," Donan said.

"Damn, my parents are barely getting by on their stipend. Good thing we've got a decent garden. At least the Church isn't taxed." Noah activated the seals on his helmet and switched to scrubbed air as the smell from the lake grew worse.

"Yet." Donan buttoned up as well.

"What 'yet'? Did your cousin's uncle's mechanic's parrot repeat that too?" Noah nudged Donan with his elbow.

"Ass. No, rumor is that the Most High for the Deseret sector tried to tax the religious holdings there. It was going through the courts when the Most High seized one of those big beautiful temples they have all over the place and ten star systems went apeshit. And I heard that from my other cousin, the one that works the sky dock," Donan said.

"If that happened it would've been in the news." Noah rolled his eyes.

"You think the Most High or anyone on the *Highest* want word to get out that they're breaking the Constitution and a bunch of incorporation treaties? It's not like Bretton is on any major trade routes."

"What did Saint Robin tell us about rumors? 'Keep your eyes wide open, and when you see, feel or encounter falsehoods: become the light of truth to those around you.' This is basic priory memorization you should've gotten down when we were kids," Noah said.

"Yeah yeah, you always had more achievement jewels in your crown than me. I was interested in girls, you weirdo. So how about those wide eyes, huh? How's Dahrien looking to you?"

"Not . . . every world came to the Hegemony easily," Noah said.

"Things have been rough since the war with the Alliance ended. But the Hegemony pulled through the Union Conflict before that. Struggle makes us stronger."

"We lost the war with the Alliance. Things have been getting worse since then and that was twelve years ago. You know my dad says that the Hegemony's tax rate used to be three percent, and there were child credits. Now they're taking seventy-five percent of our pay."

"We're on active duty in a war zone. We've got insurance premiums and stuff like that to pay for. And twenty-five percent of my salary is more than the zero credits I was making on the farm. Stop complaining before someone rats you out to one of the High Guard. It won't be me, but if you do get sent off to re-education, they have a tendency to send entire squads with the offender," Noah said.

"Did you see a High Guard somewhere?" Donan shrank slightly into his seat.

"No, but they must be out there. I saw we had a briefing from one on the schedule back at the indoc center. How about we concentrate on our sector and not the doom and gloom, yeah?"

"The High Guard didn't even have to brief us to keep us in line. Got to admire that efficiency." Donan leaned forward and glanced at Mason, who was sound asleep and snoring slightly next to Noah. "How can he sleep right now?"

"Maybe they teach that at the NCO course." Noah shrugged. "Be glad we're out here. Would you rather be back at the indoc theater re-watching all the training videos we've already seen?"

"Actually . . . yeah. At least at the end of the day we'd get to eat some quality Re-cyc Bars, drink shitty coffee and sleep in a cot. Do you know what day it is here? Thursday?"

"I don't know. Things are blurry right now."

"Monday. It feels like a Monday." Donan sighed. "Does it bother you that we haven't seen a single bird yet?"

"Maybe this isn't a bird planet. Just watch your sector and I'll watch mine," Noah said.

"Boyle? Boyle, wake the hell up!" sounded in his ear. Boyle snapped back into consciousness with a kick against his Cataphract mech suit. He'd disabled the limb actuators before he'd dozed off to keep him from accidentally breaking out of the restraint harness in the cattle car.

Cataphracts learned to sleep while standing in their suits within the first few weeks of drilling in the equipment.

"Huh? What? We there yet?" Boyle checked the data feed from the truck.

"We're about ten minutes out from the village and a scheduled stop," Sergeant Corre said to him on a private comms channel. "Captain wants all Cataphracts to stay buttoned up at the stop. Keep us from being observed by the enemy."

"You woke me up to tell me to stay in bed?" Boyle chuckled. "So we're just going to let the Flankies run wild?"

"They... will be fine. They're not going to propose to the first local they see or take out a car loan at a disgusting interest rate just yet. But I want you to over-the-shoulder Sergeant Tallec and see if he can find high-magnetite tabs for Herve's power core. His suit's efficiency is amber and trending to black and those tabs—"

"We can find them in cargo truck transfer cases. I took care of it back in the motor pool when we were loading up. Herve's green if you ping his system." Boyle yawned.

"Wait, what?"

The holo on Boyle's visor flickered as Corre shared Herve's system feed. Herve's Cataphract suit appeared as a paper doll in a grid field. The power systems were green across the board.

"Why does his system still show the serial number of his bad power core tabs? He still comes up amber in the squad and platoon dashboard. This doesn't make sense," Sergeant Corre said, a suspicious tone to his voice.

"Funny thing about the dashboard; if you replace the part while the processer stack is decoupled from the onboard power supply, it'll default to the old part's serial number when it reboots. Dashboard thinks the failing part's still installed and the maintenance flag stays in the system. So we'll get a new tab replacement eventually... right around the same time someone else's tabs burn out." Boyle yawned again.

"Herve's fully mission capable but his suit is still prioritized for the replacement part..."

"Which I can trade for something if we need it. I didn't think you'd mind," Boyle said.

"Hold on, where'd you get the new tabs in the first place?" Corre asked, growing angrier.

"That was easy, boss, there was a maintenance depot at the void port and some of the guys assigned to the building were taking a break behind it. So I went over and struck up a chat with them. Decent guys. Been deployed too long, I think. Anyway, we get to talking and turns out they've got a pallet full of replacement tabs fresh from the foundry just waiting to be shipped to some place I've never heard of. So I arranged a trade. Simple as."

"We've been balls to the wall since we made landfall. When did you have the time—or even the chance to do that?"

"I snuck out the back of the auditorium during all the 'don't do this or else' videos I've already seen. Chatted up the guys at the warehouse and made the trade...they wanted a potent potable and I just so happened to have access to some. We've also got some extra armor repair kits in the squad mule." Boyle smiled.

"Alcohol? You know we're in a combat zone, and if you get caught with that you'll be scouting out minefields in a penal battalion with a stick and prayer," Corre said.

"I didn't *drink* any, Sarge. Didn't keep any either. There's a sailor on the *Izmir* that had a decent stockpile of booze, so I borrowed a couple of bottles from him while we were offloading our gear. Doubt he'll notice and if he does...good luck finding me again," Boyle said.

The line was quiet for several seconds.

"So you stole—"

"Borrowed without the intention of returning. Technical term is 'scrounging,'" Boyle said.

"So you stole one or more bottles of booze, snuck out of mandatory training and traded your illicit gains for parts the squad needed and fouled the supply system to get us another vital part in the near future..."

"It sounds much worse when you put it that way."

The hiss of an open line came on and off several times.

"I'm not saying this, but good work. I *am* saying this: don't get caught," Corre said.

"Yeah, I learned that lesson the hard way. Which is why I'm here. Tee hee," Boyle grumbled.

The line closed. Boyle leaned his head back and went back to sleep.

CHAPTER 4

"Look alive!" Amos slapped the top of the cab and swung the turret to the left. "We're almost to Buri Buri. Have to sit out in the open for a bit."

Noah clutched his carbine to his chest and scanned back and forth across his assigned sector. The jungle had greened back to life as they drove further from the void port. They'd stopped on an elevated road flanked by rice paddies and patches of farmland dotted with short, spiky plants. A wall taller than the truck he was in curved away into the jungle, covered in a dull brown coating.

"Why have we stopped?" Noah asked. "We're a giant target out—"

"Stuff it, cherry," Amos spat over the front of the cab. "We've got Daggers all over the place, ground sensors, automated turrets that pop over the walls . . . Flags know better than to fool around over here."

Noah remained tense. Donan trembled in his seat next to him.

"Noah . . . I don't like this place," Donan whispered. "What's wrong with all these trees? They're not like the ones back home."

"You're scared of the trees? Really?" Noah nudged him.

"It's what's in the trees. Do the insurgents even speak Standard here? Can we just shoot at any blah blah we hear out there?" Donan brought the stock of his carbine up to his shoulder.

"That's ridiculous, we can't just—"

"You'd better." Amos smacked his gum. "Soon as we're through this outpost, it's hostile territory all the way to the sea. Whole goddamn planet hates us, except the couple clans around Malakal, and the only reason they're on our side is because we won't kill them while the rest of the Flags will. Collaborators and stuff like that. Didn't y'all watch the threat videos?"

"We had to move out before we got to that one," Noah said.

"Did see the STD vid." Donan shuddered.

"Ha! Good news is if you get the fuzz off a local provider, the medics give you Penzodan, which'll clear it right up and will give you some wild dreams if you crush the pills up. Win-win." Amos smiled, revealing a couple missing teeth.

"Why are we sitting out here?" Noah asked Mason. "The whole convoy is one big target."

"Do you see any burnt-out trucks?" Mason asked. "Because I don't see any, nor do I see artillery craters or bullet holes anywhere. Everything is fine out here, stop pissing your pants."

"When . . . when should I piss my pants?" Noah asked quietly.

"You won't need me to tell you." Mason touched the side of his helmet. "Alright, we're moving in. Captain wants us to practice local security when we get inside."

Noah froze. His eyes darted from side to side as he tried to recall the battle drill. The truck lurched forward, pressing him against Donan's shoulder.

"Just because we're deployed doesn't mean I'm into you," Donan said.

"You just . . . shut up," Noah shoved him away.

The convoy rolled through the thick perimeter wall and into a small village. The first thing that hit Noah was the smell. A pall of rotting food and raw sewage hit him through his full-face helmet. The trucks drove to a wide gravel parking lot, Noah's stopped in the front row closest to a sewer/garbage trench between the lot and the village. Homes were built from plasti-boards used in logistics pallets with thatch roofs, laid out haphazardly to the other side of the perimeter.

"Saint's oath, what a shithole," Leroi said from the other side of the supplies at Noah's back.

"Dismount, three-sixty security, move it!" Mason grabbed the side rail with one hand and vaulted over. He landed smoothly and half brought his carbine up, but brought it down just as quickly.

Children dressed in rags and uniformly shoeless peeked around the huts. They chattered at each other in a language that sounded to Noah nothing like Standard or any of the old dialects back on Bretton.

Noah tried to keep his profile low as he jumped over the side rails. His heel caught on a post and what would've been a smooth dismount turned into a near disaster as his momentum carried his upper body over before the rest of him. Only his grip on the rail kept him from going face-first into the gravel. The frame over his fingers and up to his shoulder caught and held him in place as his legs swung down like a pendulum, kicking up rocks and dust.

"You okay?" Mason asked without looking back.

"Yup! I'm fine. Everything's fine." Noah crouched slightly into a firing stance and approached the edge of the trench.

A little girl, no more than six or seven, emerged from the hovels holding an empty water bottle. She wore an old sack tied around her waist with lengths of intertwined plastic strips. Her hair was unkempt and ragged where it fell around her neck. Noah wasn't sure if her skin was naturally tan or if she was just filthy.

"Mister mister, gimme please!" she shouted, a thick accent to her words.

"Christ the protector, she doesn't even have shoes," Mason said. "Abbie always had shoes, didn't matter how much I was making . . ."

"*Sections, cycle through water top off and bio needs,*" Sergeant Corre said through the squad channel. "*We're stopped for the command team to get a brief on the enemy situation. Should be rolling out again in twenty minutes.*"

"Donan." Mason canted his head back towards the truck. "Dump and cycle on the other side. We're not doing that where the kids can watch."

"Yeah . . . 'course not, Sarge." Donan jogged to the other side of the truck to empty his bladder into the truck's onboard recycler/ambient moisture collector.

Noah sidestepped towards the cab to cover Donan's sector.

More children appeared, but only the one little girl was brave enough to approach the edge of the stinking trench.

"Guys, show 'em your face," Amos said as he lit a cigarette. "Just crack your buckets so they can tell you're not a Skien. That's why they're afraid of you."

"There are Skiens here?" Mason asked. "I thought they were all on the Alliance frontier."

"Buddy, you've got to stop believing what you hear on the wires."

Amos shook his head. "Skiens are wherever there's fighting. The Most High love 'em, never complain and they kill everything they can. Flags ain't fans, naturally."

Mason hooked a thumb under the front of his helmet and lifted up his visor. The little girl with the empty bottle grew excited, her eyes widening. A gaggle of children crept towards the trench, some calling back into the hovels. Some adults finally emerged, mothers with babies on their hips, and a few elderly folks.

"Why don't they like Skiens?" Noah asked. "Aren't they the same as any other Hegemony soldier?"

"Because Skiens don't have souls, Cherry." Amos reached into the cab and took something from a driver. *"Challa challa, iman chi!"*

An older boy, perhaps twelve and taller than the rest of them, came up and shoved the girl aside. Amos slapped the top of the cab and let out several curt local phrases that cowed the child and forced him to look down at his bare feet.

Amos drew out a small sack, stuffed to the brim and wrapped in plastic.

"Cherry, toss this to the kid but don't let it land in the shit river. They will jump in to get it and I don't want that image on my mind again." Amos handed the bag to Noah. Inside were bright orange rectangular packs the size of his thumb.

"Refeeds?" Noah raised his visor. "Why are you giving them mineral and electrolyte gum?"

"Because they think it's candy." Amos looked at him like he was an idiot. "Bonus is that it keeps their immune systems somewhat strong and this way none of them go blind or have their limbs go permanently numb from the Blue Rot fungus that's all over this part of the jungle. You got a problem with that?"

"No, sir. Sorry, sir." Noah went to the edge of the trench and chucked the sack to the oldest child. The rest of the kids formed a line behind him. The girl tore open the top and pressed the Refeeds into grubby hands. The recipients clutched the gift to their chest and ran back to the village.

"Dumbass calling me 'sir.'" Amos took a long drag on his cigarette. "You think an officer would get this shit job?"

"There's not enough," Mason said as the bag grew lighter faster than the line shortened.

"I do what we can. Sometimes the resupply drones make their humanitarian drops from the big city. Sometimes they don't. You think it's easy to scrounge anything for them?" Amos asked.

The boy held the sack upside down and shook it. A final pack fell out and there was a quick scrum to snatch it up. The remaining children turned away, dejected. The boy flapped the sack at Amos.

The gunner reached into his pocket and tossed him a mostly empty pack of cigarettes. The boy shouted something, and Amos gave him the finger.

The girl with the empty bottle was the only one that remained. Her lips quivered and she started crying.

"Mason . . . we've got to have something for her," Noah said. "I've got no food on me at all. Everything I saved from home's in my duffel bag and that's . . . I don't know."

"You just assumed we'd be fed while we're out here?" Mason shook his head. "Empty bellies are great teachers. I've got a little something."

The sergeant reached into a side pouch and dug toward the bottom, then took out a plastic-wrapped roll that fit into his palm.

"That's mom's *buerre sale*. She said to save it for—"

"I'm aware, dipshit. Little girl's crying and I can't stand it." Mason pinched the end of a roll of caramel between his thumb and forefinger so the girl could see it, then waggled it when her gaze locked on. She nodded emphatically.

Mason tossed it to her, and she dropped her bottle into the sewer trench to catch it. She gave it a sniff, then peeled plastic off the end. She took a tentative bite, then clasped it to her chest.

"Thanks mister mister." She turned and ran away.

"What was that?" Amos asked. "Got to be careful with what you give 'em. Older kid wants it and they'll break her arm to get it. Adults will, too."

"Caramel with sea salt," Mason said. "Made by hand back home . . . it was my only one. She would've been better off with a Sustain Bar."

"Don't worry about it. It's not like there's a dentist around that can make a difference if she's— Ah shit." Amos tensed up.

In the village, a man emerged from the crowd and approached the trench. He was tall and slim, wearing a bright white tunic and khaki pants. A wide blue sash with a red tassel at the bottom ran from one shoulder to hip.

The locals gave him a wide berth. None looked directly at him.

"These assholes are here too?" Mason relaxed slightly. "Everyone's a sucker."

"You watch your mouth," Amos snapped. "They'll save your soul."

"The hell they will. Donan, what's taking you so long?" Mason went around the front of the truck just as Donan hurried out of the gap between two rows.

The man approached the edge of the trench. His head was bald, and his deep blue eyes were kind and happy. He held his arms out stiffly to his side, then slapped his hands together into a prayer position, elbows and arms level across his chest. He bowed his head and stood still. A heavy pack hung loose on his back.

"Uh . . . what's going on?" Noah asked.

"Shepherd," Amos said. "They're from the Antares Temple. Listen to me. Hey!" He slapped his palm twice against the cab. Noah and Donan turned back to him. "The Antares aren't on anyone's side, you get me? They're here looking for missing soldiers and that's all. They don't talk to anyone, don't say a thing about where any unit's at or do anything that'll help with targeting or attacks. Nothing."

"He doesn't do anything?" Donan asked. "Just stands there?"

"He's waiting for an officer or a donation," Amos said. "You can ignore 'em, but don't ever hurt 'em or get in their way. Commander's coming!"

The Antares didn't respond.

"So they can just . . . go wherever they want on the battlefield? Sounds like a great way to be a spy and collect intelligence," Donan said.

"Don't even say shit like that," Amos said, then raised his voice for the Antares to hear him. "Sorry, they're new. Trying to teach 'em."

"I bet there would've been a video about them at indoc if we were still there," Noah said. "I'm lost. So these Antares just wander about the battlefield doing what . . . exactly?"

"They're looking for the dead. Soldiers of heaven. They find anyone that's been left out on the field and either bring the body back for a proper burial or at least DNA to report the death to family. Doesn't matter what you do for them . . . they'll make sure you get last rites," Amos said.

A Hegemony officer in the same simple coveralls as Amos jogged over and jumped across the trench. He pulled a fold of plasti-sheets from a cargo pocket. To Noah's shock, the officer knelt on both knees, then repeated the arms to the side then palms together motion, the plasti-sheets pressed between his palms.

The Antares took the papers gently and slipped them into his sash. He drew out a set of dog tags, each attached to a small beige case and held them in the palm of his hand. The captain took the tags and rubbed a thumb across the face.

"He found truck 37," the captain said to Amos. Amos nodded slowly, his face darkening.

The Antares read through the plasti-sheets, then tossed them into the sewage. The papers dissolved quickly. Noah got a quick glance of maps marked with red circles denoting where combat had taken place.

"Cherry, toss this beside him. Don't ever hand anything directly to an Antares, you understand?" Amos held a ration pack over the side of the cab.

"I don't get this at all." But Noah did as requested and chucked the pack next to the Antares.

"They're pretty self-sufficient, but sometimes they need a little extra. It's bad luck to bother them, you get that? Even the Flags leave them alone, but they help find dead Flags too," Amos said. "And if you ever hurt one . . . your soul will never leave the world. You'll be a ghost for all time and all eternity. Got it?"

"Can't say I share that religious belief, but okay," Noah said.

The Antares picked up the ration pack and walked away without a word.

"Didn't they set up a Temple in Lorient? Real little place but some of the clergy were upset. Happened after your brother and the rest of the last levy were sent off world," Donan said.

"I was like ten and our province was cut off because of the plague," Noah said. "Maybe they did? I'm not . . . I really need some sleep."

"Noah, cycle." Mason came around the back of the truck.

"Great, nothing like drinking my own filtered pee for the foreseeable future." Noah hurried away.

CHAPTER 5

Felix reached up and dug his fingertips into a moss-covered cliff. The most direct way to Tabuk crossed over an extreme rise in elevation. He'd made the decision to take the shortest route to friendly troops, instead of following the lowlands, which would've taken days. The higher he climbed, the more he realized he'd made a poor decision. Getting back down the cliff would be quick, but that's as far as he'd ever go for the rest of his life.

He pulled himself up and gripped a vine. A brightly colored bird flapped out of a nest hidden in the cliff, screeching at him. It dove at his helmet, claws scraping against the metal.

"Hey. Hey!" Felix waved a hand at it. "Leave me the hell alone!"

The bird kept flapping and chirping around him as he wedged the edge of his boot into a minuscule ledge. He extended his leg and leveraged himself a bit higher, his eyes on a solid-looking outcropping close to the top of the cliff.

The green and yellow menace landed on his shoulder and pecked his helmet. The strikes rang through his ears and Felix wagged his head back and forth, trying to shoo the pest away.

"I wasn't going to feast on your children, but I'm changing my mind!" He let go with one hand and managed to brush it against the demon bird. Loose feathers floated past his visor and the bird finally flew away.

"This planet hates me," he muttered. "Everything here hates me—"

A warning icon flashed on his visor. The batteries powering the exo-suit had several minutes of power left... at rest. The system was

59

running hard to assist his climb, and the single percentages on the reader were ticking down fast. Very fast.

This cliffside was not where he wanted to be when the total weight of his Flanker gear fell solely to his muscles. He clamped onto the outcropping and strained to get higher. Roots snapped and the rock tipped over and slid out of the cliff.

Felix pressed his body against the moss and ducked his head. The rock hit his shoulder, sending one foot swinging into the air. One hand clutched hard against a vine for dear life as the other floundered about, his shoulder burning with pain from the heavy strike.

"I'll take the bird! I'll take the bird!" He thrust his hand into the hole where the betraying rock had been and found a knot of roots. They held his weight—barely—and he found another foothold. A dull buzz sounded in his ears as the battery reserves fell to three percent.

Felix looked down at the mists below him, unable to see the base of the cliff.

"Stupid. Stupid!" He swung an arm over the top of the precipice and gripped a handful of tall grass—which ripped out of the ground as he tried to pull himself up. He slammed clawed fingers into the dirt and raked away soil until he found bedrock. His upper body came over the cliff as his suit powered down.

The servos against his hips and knees locked up, and the weight of the exo-suit on his lower body dragged him back slowly towards gravity's embrace.

Felix let out a long string of expletives and grabbed the emergency release buckle on his waist. He twisted the knob hard and pulled out the fastening bolt. The exo-suit on his legs and over his boots slid off his body and crashed against the cliff. The rig cracked and banged all the way to the riverbed below.

He swung a much lighter leg onto the plateau and rolled onto his back. The crump and clatter of his suit echoed through the canyon below.

"I am an idiot. Such a friggin' idiot."

Felix tried to sit up, but the weight of his exo-suit only let him barely get his head up a few inches. He pulled the emergency release on his chest and the last of the weight fell off of him. The helmet had its own emergency batteries, but the cooling systems were offline. He popped it off and let it roll into the grass. The sky was a drab gray, promising rain and humidity.

The map on his forearm screen was still powered on. Tabuk was still a good ways away. Getting there under his own power felt very real now. He rolled to a crouch, listening to the surrounding jungle. The damned bird cackled in the distance.

"I'll fix your wagon." Felix dragged the last of his exo-suit to the edge and tossed it over the cliff. If there were any insurgents in the area, best not to let them find obvious proof that a Hegemony Flanker had been through. Let them find the battered metal and assume he was dead and eaten by whatever else was in the accursed jungle.

He put his helmet on, slid the visor to the top of his head and held his carbine low across his waist. The more advanced optics needed the suit's batteries, but the laser dot sight mounted to a top rail would still work for weeks.

Felix tapped a pouch on his waist. He had a bit of the *tong* jerky left and three magazines on his belt. The water purification tube across the small of his back felt intact, so he at least had the calories and hydration to keep going two more days. The flak plates on his front and back weighed him down, but he wasn't about to give up the protection they offered.

He made his way through the jungle, stopping every hundred steps or so to check his bearing with the compass built into his forearm screen. After an hour, he stumbled across a trail heading in his general direction. The map showed a valley ahead of him, with a few buildings.

Old satellite imagery in the data files showed nothing but clouds. There were no major roads into the area and whatever settlement had been there didn't even rate a name.

"Not much of a clearing, and who knows if there's even something there," he said to himself. "Sure as hell beats breaking my own trail."

He continued down the path, stopping every few tens of yards to listen. The buzz of insects and call of birds were his constant companions, along with the rush of wind through the canopy.

The rain began slowly. Small droplets spattered against high leaves, falling as a mist around him. The storm intensified with thunder and the flash of lightning. Rain started to sweep down in sheets, soaking through his shoulders and sleeves within minutes.

Felix appreciated the drenching as it washed away the accumulated sweat and body odor he'd built up over the last few days. He couldn't remember his last shower, but this was a decent enough wash down.

He put his back to a thick tree and dug out a hunk of *tong* jerky. The pungent smell of chili flakes, horseradish and vinegar made his nose scrunch, but the rumble in his stomach won out. He ripped a corner off with his teeth and chewed in silence as the spices set his mouth aflame.

"Why does this shit *never* taste good?" he asked the snack.

A branch snapped nearby.

Felix pressed himself into a recess in the tree trunk and moved a finger to press against the carbine's trigger.

A voice shouted from where he heard the snap, every word in the local dialect. Two men wearing dull green fatigues and red sashes from right shoulder to left hip emerged from the jungle; both had rifles slung over their shoulders.

The taller of the two pointed to the other side of a small clearing and brushed the back of his hand against the other's shoulder. The other stopped and tugged a pack of cigarettes from within the sash as the other continued into the jungle.

The shorter insurgent looked to be barely through his teens, but he bent his body forward to protect his lighter from the rain like a seasoned smoker. He puffed a cloud of gray overhead, then raised his arms and stretched from side to side.

Felix kept perfectly still. He took short breaths through his nose, his body on a hair trigger should the insurgent turn around. Shooting him in the back would only alert his battle buddy . . . and any other Flags in the area.

The teenager yelled something out and the other man laughed from where he was in the brush. He put his hands on the back of his hips and twisted his body away from Felix, then towards him. Felix saw the side of the teenager's face.

The insurgent bent back at the waist, then looked over his shoulder straight at Felix.

Felix snapped his carbine up to his shoulder and kept the teen dead in his sights. The kid had peach fuzz on his cheeks, and his mouth hung open in shock. His eyes widened with fear and the cigarette fell from his mouth and sparked against his chest.

Felix shook his head slowly.

"Makisig," the other man called out.

Felix trembled, adrenaline racing through his system.

"Makisig!"

The teenager slowly raised his hands up to shoulder height. Bushes rustled and thunder rolled overhead.

Felix turned his eyes to the disturbance at the edge of the clearing and saw the other insurgent emerge, a dead rabbit in one hand. He saw Felix and dropped the animal.

"Crab!" The insurgent went for the rifle still slung over his shoulder. Felix swung his carbine to the side and hit him in the chest with a three-round burst.

The teenager reached back and grabbed the handle on his rifle and lifted it up. Felix saw his scared, confused face through his carbine's optic. He shot him center mass and the boy fell back with a brief cry.

Felix bolted down the path. His lungs burned and the muscles in his legs felt like they had molten iron running through them instead of blood. The path took a steep downslope and Felix could not slow himself. His stride became longer and longer as the path became a small stream from the rain.

He spotted the clearing through the trees and saw the stream veer to one side at the bottom of a slope . . . into a dug-out diversion.

A topless Dahrien man with a toothbrush in his mouth stepped out in front of the end of the path, a pistol on his hip. Felix, unable to slow or stop his momentum, lowered his shoulder and smashed into him.

The insurgent went flying into a fire pit, knocking a boiling pot off a hanger. The boiling contents sloshed onto two men cutting up meat and vegetables. The sudden chaos of screams and a burning man in the midst of the camp took all the attention away from Felix as he lay in the mud, his shoulder aching.

Felix snapped his head up. There were dozens of insurgents, with more coming out of low tents to investigate the ruckus. On the other side of a fire pit was a power station, the side solar panels raised and a wind turbine mast extended high to harness the storm. Rifles were stacked together nearby beneath tarps.

Someone reached under his shoulders and tried to haul Felix up, chattering at him in Dahrien, mistaking his mud-covered form for one of their own. Felix landed an uppercut to the man's groin and he went down with a rumbling *herk*.

"Sorry," Felix muttered and shook mud from the carbine. He aimed it at the exposed batteries in the power station and switched his weapon to full auto. A half dozen men in various stages of dress stared at him in shock as he opened fire on the generator.

Pierced batteries let out streams of sparks before bursting into flames and exploding a heartbeat later.

Felix didn't wait for the camp to react. He turned to the right and ran off as fast as he could. He tore through brush and wide leaves, falling more than once. Bullets snapped through the trees and tore chunks of bark loose as he kept running for as long and as far as his body could manage.

His foot hooked on a root and he fell hard, sliding across wet undergrowth before coming to a stop between two violet ferns. He fought to catch his breath and he knew he couldn't go any further. He lay there heaving as the storm abated. Golden rays broke through thinning clouds and he took a sip from the water blister on his back. It was muddy and brackish, but it was still the best he'd ever had.

He looked at his forearm screen... which had cracked. The final residual image faded in and out then shrank to nothing.

"Figures..."

There was no sound of pursuit by the time he recovered enough to push himself up to sit against a tree. He stared off in the general direction from which he'd come, unsure if he'd run, fight or just die here if the Flags found him.

He was tired. So very tired... but he couldn't stop. Felix slid a hand beneath his front flak plate and found the dog tags of Gunnar and others from his platoon. If he died out here, no one back home would ever know what happened to them.

"Charon has to cross the river," he said, and continued on.

CHAPTER 6

Colonel Lambert limped down a long hallway. Captain Mehmet walked slowly next to him, keeping pace. The civilian shipmaster wore a leather vest over a linen shirt and baggy pants wrapped tightly around his ankles. A fez with a tassel sat tilted back on his head.

"I assure you, Mehmet, your presence here makes little difference," Lambert said.

"Ah, my dear colonel, you must not think that I am here for your sake. My sailors are rather agitated that they've been refused shore leave. I accompany you on your unusually difficult task of offloading my ship and they assume I'm trying to help. No matter what happens with the Hegemony bureaucracy, I return to better favor," Mehmet said.

"Are things not this complicated back in the Union?" Lambert checked an office number to the screen of his data slate and kept walking.

"Things work ... differently. It's not hard to find the right person as they will make themselves known," Mehmet said. "Typically, they require a small donation. The Hegemony seems to have stricter standards. Or we haven't met the right person. Yet."

"Would you prefer things be like you're used to?" Lambert asked.

"While my ship and I would likely be in orbit awaiting our slot to hyperspace with a fresh cargo contract and full hold if we were back home ... the Hegemony pays better, once they finally pay up," Mehmet said.

"Indeed. Here we are." Lambert adjusted his Bretton Planetary

Guard uniform and knocked on a door. There was a buzz as magnetic locks unsnapped from each other and the door creaked open slightly. Inside, a portly Hegemony officer sat at a desk surrounded by curved holo screens. The displays were one-directional, casting flickers on the man's mostly bald head and archaic glasses.

"Help you?" He came up slightly from his seat and squinted at Lambert's uniform. "Mister . . . Lambert, is it?"

Lambert hobbled forward. He'd become used to never being referred to by his Guard rank from anyone in the Hegemony military. Getting around the planetary headquarters seemed a bit easier when he was in some manner of a uniform, a theory he tested and confirmed by having Mehmet accompany him.

"Hello, I'm looking for the . . ." Lambert glanced at a small data slate, "Logistics Requirements Review Officer for Void Port Operations."

"Do you need the principal officer or someone with signature authority?" The Hegemony officer took a sip of coffee.

"I was told either can approve my disembarkation request." Lambert set a different slate on the man's desk. He read "Torgersen" from the man's name tape next to his Chief Warrant Officer rank insignia.

"Depends which budget pool funds have been allocated from. I happen to be both the principal and a signature designee but which authorization I might have to use is relevant." He picked up the slate and adjusted his glasses. "The . . . *Izmir*? Sounds foreign."

"It is her first journey this deep into Hegemony space." Mehmet bowed slightly. "I am her captain, and my crew and I have—"

"Doesn't matter." Torgersen tapped the corner of the slate against a reader and the screens switched. "Bretton? Where's that? So you were granted landing authorization almost twenty-four hours ago. Average cargo disembarkation authorization and longshoreman budget allocation takes five to seven days. But there's a holiday weekend starting tomorrow. Why are you even here?"

Lambert smiled. "I'm aware of the usual time frames, but my battalion's been rushed to the front lines and their logistics support foundries are stuck aboard our transport because authorization hasn't been—"

"I am losing money sitting at dock." Mehmet knocked twice on Torgersen's desk. Lambert put a hand on Mehmet's knuckles and moved them back.

"Oh! Your battalion's no longer in the indoc barracks? Why didn't you say so?" Torgersen raised a hand and moved it among the holo controls only he could see. "For me to authorize an expedited bidding process for the final disembarkation and transport, your battalion's deployment orders need to be in the system ... or you'll be on the normal schedule of five to seven days. Holidays notwithstanding."

"The orders are—" Lambert raised a finger.

"Still in the pending queue." Torgersen leaned back. "Marshal Van Wyck's adjutant hasn't ratified the orders through the system yet."

"My battalion has most certainly been deployed." Lambert swiped twice on a tablet and held up the screen. "I have the orders from Marshal Van Wyck right here with his signature block and Hegemony cipher certificates."

"And?" Torgersen raised an eyebrow.

Lambert and Mehmet glanced at each other.

"I have the orders to authorize the expedited bidding—why is there bidding? There are Hegemony naval personnel at the void port who could unload the foundry units," Lambert said.

"Civilian firms can perform the work at a ten-percent budget savings, and we are all stewards of Hegemony tax dollars. I see the orders you've got there, but they're not in the system." Torgersen sighed.

"Could you ... put them in the system?" Lambert asked.

"Impossible. Has to be done from an Adjutant-rated terminal. Do I look like an Adjutant to you?" Torgersen pushed his glasses up his nose.

"Certainly not." Lambert frowned. "What would you recommend I do to get my foundry units offloaded and shipped? Captain Mehmet can't be paid until his holds are clear."

"I suggest you send your request to the Central Adjutant's office on the eighteenth floor," Torgersen said. "But, as you've been rather polite and I don't get many visitors down here, there's no one manning that office today."

Lambert blinked.

"There's no one in the office?"

"Yes, I just said that. Seems General Fausch fell from a rather high window yesterday and the entire staff have been segregated by High Guard agents for investigation and mandatory counseling. A new

Adjutant should be appointed soon. After the holiday. Then the terminals need to be recertified and then there's the backlog." Torgersen nodded slowly.

"So when will I be paid and my ship allowed to make orbit?" Mehmet asked.

"Next week...maybe," Torgersen said.

"I don't think you understand," Lambert said. "My battalion has been sent to the front. Without their foundries they won't be able to replace parts or manufacture—"

"Oh no," Torgersen said. "If you're about to suggest that I try and authorize anything without the required paperwork, I assure you that any attempt would be flagged by the system six ways from Sunday and then my terminals would be sequestered from the network until a High Guard level investigation is completed."

"I wasn't going to suggest that," Lambert said.

"Then what were you going to say?" Torgersen tapped a button and a recording icon flashed on the reflection of his glasses.

"Thank you for your time." Lambert took his slates back and walked out of the office. Mehmet followed him outside.

"What? Where are you going?" Mehmet asked once the door mag locked behind them. "I need to get paid!"

"And I am more than happy to do everything possible to get my equipment off your ship so that can happen," Lambert said. "But as you just heard, that won't be possible in the near future."

"Can't you...can't you go back there and make a donation to his favorite charity? That works in the Union," Mehmet said. "Just give them the cash and ask them to make the donation on their behalf."

"I'm afraid that's most unwise. Are you unaware of the Richter Reforms? After the war with the Alliance a number of allegations of graft and financial impropriety came to light. Several of the Most High retired or were censured and a number of reforms were made, not reforms that made anything better, but more bureaucracy that made corruption more difficult to commit without detection." Lambert jabbed a thumb against the elevator controls.

"It's impossible to grease the skids in the Hegemony?" Mehmet asked.

"No...simply difficult. I've heard there's quite an observation period of anyone with the placement and access to divert funds. I'm so new on the scene here that I squeak. Not that I'm interested in anything illegal, mind you," Lambert said.

"So you're giving up on helping me get the *Izmir* away from this madness?" Mehmet asked.

"Madness? This is the Hegemony, my friend. Is there another option that I've neglected?" Lambert stepped into the elevator with the captain.

"You could—but—hold on ..." Mehmet looked Lambert up and down and cursed in his native language.

"What?" Lambert raised an eyebrow.

"Nothing, I doubt anyone would go for it ... my crew is going to mutiny."

"There is a small silver lining to this rather delayed thunderstorm." Lambert reached into a pocket and handed a red envelope to Mehmet. "I was given an amount of Hegemony credits by the Bretton government for 'incidentals.' I'm sure you can purchase a fair amount of items to lessen your crew's suffering. I also assume I don't have to tell a sailor where to find such things."

Mehmet flipped the envelope open and ran his thumb across the bills.

"This will tame them for a while. How much more do you have?" the captain asked.

"I may have more, I may not. That's more than enough for a week, I assume," Lambert said.

"You know some things about sailors, but you're sadly mistaken on other things," Mehmet said. "Can you at least get the port master to detach the anchors from my ship?"

"I'll be sure to ask once the cargo disembarkation authorizations are approved," Lambert said.

"And perhaps waive some port fees for the delays?"

"Don't push it."

CHAPTER 7

Noah stared out at the jungle. His entire body was sweating in the humidity and his Flanker uniform was cooling him just enough to stave off heat exhaustion. Despite sweltering inside his helmet, his eyes did not want to stay open.

He lost focus and gazed out to the distant clouds. He closed his eyes and his head bobbed forward. The drone of the truck along the road filled the darkness and for a moment, a single glorious moment, there was sleep.

A sharp poke to the thinner part of his armor under his shoulder snapped him back to semi-alertness.

"Huh, wha'?" Noah looked from side to side.

"We're in hostile territory. No sleeping," Mason said next to him.

"I wasn't—I mean—sorry. I don't remember the last time I slept, and things are sort of... blurry." Noah slapped a palm against his thigh plates.

"Why didn't you sleep when the *Izmir* was stuck in orbit for hours? Like I told you to," Mason said. "Docs were handing out z-pills."

"Because I wanted to see the planet from orbit and I had to re-check my gear. Again," Noah said.

"I told you to get some sleep before we hit atmo. There a reason you didn't listen to me?" Mason asked. "Here I am, your older brother who's been deployed before and who had to swear up and down to Mom, Dad, aunts, uncles, cousins and the grans that I'd take care of you and I tell you to do something—especially when I'm your Saint-damned section leader—and you think I'm kidding or something?"

"Okay, okay!" Noah adjusted his seat. "I just don't understand why all this is happening so fast. When we were training back home, the officers kept telling us how well we'd be taken care of when fighting for the Hegemony."

"You believed the recruiter and not the veterans who told you differently. How's that working out for you?" Mason said.

"I can't believe we signed up for two years of this," Noah said.

"Two years, 'needs of the service depending,'" Mason laughed. "Which means the Hegemony can keep us all on as long as it needs to. They normally won't, as the last time they tried that half the Deseret sector almost revolted."

"Oh . . . God," Noah said.

"It's fine. You're young and have the time and health to bounce back from this stint. Just stay awake. I let you sleep and everyone'll assume I'm letting it slide because you're my brother," Mason said.

"You could. Then I'd tell Mom and everyone what good care you're taking of me."

"Home is a hundred-and-eighty-four light-years and two months in hyper away. Our chain of command is in this convoy and a lot less forgiving of any bullshit, Noah. The only easy day was yesterday."

"That's the thing, I don't know when yesterday even was. I should've bought some caffeine pills." Noah yawned.

"Want a nicotine strip? First one will put some juice in your boots." Mason tapped a pouch on his chest harness.

"No, those things will kill—"

The first explosion came from the front of the convoy. The blast hit Noah across his entire body, a gust of pain and pressure from out of a clear blue sky. Soldiers in the truck bed cried out in fright and surprise.

Noah flinched down as the blast reverberated through the trees, sending flocks of bats into the air.

"What . . . was that?" he asked. A bit of ice formed in his chest, growing into a fist of fear that coursed through his entire body with each beat of his heart.

Mason stood atop the bench, peering forward.

"G-get down!" Noah reached for his brother's belt only to have his hand swatted away. A priority transmission flashed on Noah's visor. An image of a scorched security vehicle on its side hung in front of his vision, a red border pulsing around it. KIA notifications pinged from inside the vehicle and a burning lump half in, half out, of the jungle.

"Look alive!" Amos swung the turret to the left and lifted up an olive drab baton. He slammed the bottom against the cab and a small drone ejected with a *ploomp*. The Dagger drone's repulse rings snapped out and the device flew in a loose spiral away from the truck. He pointed a knife hand at Donan. "Eyes up. There ain't never just one—"

The crack and hiss of a rocket-propelled grenade launching caught Noah's ear. He glanced through the holo screen on the side of the truck and saw a bright orange warhead screaming at him.

Noah froze, unable to even groan out a warning.

The projectile shot between his truck and the one ahead of them and careened off trees on the other side of the road.

Amos opened fire, the rapid pulse from the muzzle clapped against Noah's helmet as the rounds chopped an arc through the green where the RPG had come from.

"Dismount. Action left!" Mason grabbed Noah by the carry handle on the back of his shoulders and chucked his brother over the side rail. Noah went head over heels and landed hard on his side, the armor plates and his Flanker frame taking the brunt of the impact, but not all.

Noah fought to breathe, his diaphragm stunned and refusing to cooperate. Bullets snapped through bushes and cracked over his head as it felt like every tree in the jungle had opened fire. Noah looked back at the truck and realized it was a giant target. Mason vaulted over the side and landed on two feet, firing off half a magazine on full auto. He moved at a half crouch and seized Noah by the carry handle again.

"Take fucking cover, you idiot!" Mason dragged Noah toward the jungle. He turned back to the truck where Donan moved spastically trying to get over the side rail, like his limbs had turned to rubber and he was trying to go two places at once.

Amos tilted the barrel of his turret-mounted machine gun up and yanked the spent magazine from one side. He did a double take at the jungle and opened his mouth to scream.

Noah didn't see what hit the cab, but the driver's door shook and the bullet-resistant glass on the window went cloudy as millions of cracks suddenly appeared. Amos looked down, his jaw open.

The front of the truck exploded into fire. The armored plating became flaming shrapnel that gouged out a hunk of the road right in front of Noah's face. The overpressure slapped him against the quickcrete and his hearing became nothing but a persistent whine.

Noah laid there in shock, frozen as the dead body of the driver, his entire corpse burning, slumped out of the inferno and onto the road in pieces.

Mason kicked Noah in the side, then dragged him down the side of the road and into the low bushes flanking the road.

"Are you hit?" Mason put his face plate against Noah's. "Are. You. Hit?"

"N-no." Noah found the strap that kept his carbine attached to his chest rig and gripped his weapon.

"Then do your job!" Mason held his carbine up and let off a burst.

Noah rolled to his knees and elbows. The sound of the ambush came to him, explosions and gunfire sounded around him. He put one foot against the ground and stood up.

He didn't see the insurgent who shot him, but he saw the muzzle flash from deep in the jungle. Bullets struck his chest plate like hammer blows. He reeled back and landed half on the road. His chest burned and breathing was a struggle.

"Mom?" He touched his chest and a hot spot stung his fingers through his gloves. He tilted his head up and saw two smoking divots in his chest plate. He managed a deep breath and didn't feel any sharp pain, nor did he cough up any blood on his exhale.

"Noah?" Mason shouted as he tossed a grenade into the jungle. More Flankers milled around the tree line, some firing, others crouching behind tight-branched bushes.

"Mmm okay. I'm okay!" Noah sat up. Adrenaline replaced the fear and he scrambled into the edge of the jungle.

A drone zipped overhead and burst into hundreds of fléchettes near the enemy. Screams of pain and shouts of warning in a language Noah had never heard before reached him. He lifted his carbine to his shoulder and fired a burst at his best guess where the enemy was.

His first shots in anger knocked something loose inside of him. He noticed his HUD again, heard the orders shouted by his brother and other sergeants. A target ID flashed on his visor. Noah lined up the optics from his carbine and set his carbine to full auto. He emptied his magazine, fighting to keep the muzzle from rising as the buttstock pushed hard against his shoulder.

"Down! Everyone down!" Mason shouted. He tackled his brother and covered him with his own body.

The whine of rotary cannons came from the trucks carrying the Cataphract suits. A stream of bullets with white-hot tracer shells tore through the jungle, cutting through tree trunks and launching branches into the air. They arced downward into the fusillade and were shredded before they could hit the ground.

"Get off of me!" Noah squirmed out from under Mason, but the sergeant kept one hand tight on his shoulder.

"Mortar strike coming, stay down," Mason growled.

True to his word, the *crump* of shells and tremors through the ground came from the jungle. The barrage continued for almost a minute, the sound lessening as the line of impact walked further and further from the road.

"Drones got us clear," Mason said. "Don't trust 'em, though. Keep your head on a swivel."

"Got it." Noah shrugged his shoulder away as Mason bent his head forward, listening to orders from someone. He looked back at the truck; the vehicle had slumped forward at an angle, the tires still burning. "Where ... where's Donan?"

Noah touched a thumb to his forearm computer and a small cover popped up.

"I'm going to ping Donan," Noah said. "I don't see him anywhere."

"Don't." Mason shook his head.

"He's my battle buddy and I've lost him!" Noah began to panic. "Donan? Donan come in ..."

He sent an IR pulse that wouldn't travel more than ten meters in the high humidity and an icon appeared on his visor, pointing to tall grass a few strides from the road.

"Why is nothing else coming through? I'm going for him." Noah slipped away before Mason could stop him. Bits of dried grass smoldered around metal fragments that had sliced through the off-gray blades.

Noah slapped a thin hedge aside and found Donan. The soldier was on his back, his visor shattered. Donan's dead eyes stared at the sky, his face cut up and still oozing blood. One arm was missing at the shoulder, the jagged ends of his Flanker frame still there, ending at the elbow. His legs were charred black, the white of the bones in his feet jutting out from melted boots.

Noah was still, not even breathing, as he refused to believe his friend was dead.

"Donan...battle brother, can you hear me?" Noah inched closer to the body. The world was as silent as Donan. He choked down a sob as his friend would never answer him again.

"I've got this." Sergeant Corre set a heavy Cataphract's mitt of a hand on Noah's shoulder. Smoke wafted from the barrels of his rotary cannon. The mortar tube on his back was stained black from use and the smell of propellant stung Noah's senses. "You've taken some hits. Go see the medic, son."

"Sarge, he...he was right next to me just a few minutes ago," Noah said.

"I'm the platoon ferryman," Corre said. "He was your friend, but he was my soldier. It's my job to take care of him. Go see the medic. Now."

"But his—" Noah pointed back to the smoking truck in shock, "—all his stuff."

The truck tipped onto the left-side tires with a groan, then fell over and rolled off the road with cracks of plastic side rails and sputters of flames and sparks from the front in-wheel engines. Noah flinched back and took cover behind the cab of the nearest truck.

The three Cataphracts that had flipped the damaged truck away put their metal-shod palms against the side-turned bottom of the truck and shoved as one, sending the wreck and the bodies still in the cab off the road and clearing it.

"There's still..." He raised a hand and let it fall to his side.

"Second Squad Flankers, cross level to 1st Squad's truck. We're not staying here and waiting for the enemy to regroup," Corre said over the squad net.

"Hey, buddy." A Flanker with a red cross on his chest and arm-plate tapped Noah on the side of the head. "Looks like you took some hits. Let's get you in the back of this truck so I can give you a once over, yeah?"

"My stuff's in there," Noah said, his tone dejected.

"It's just stuff." The medic pulled Noah up into the back of a truck and sat him down. There was a hiss against his neck and Noah suddenly felt much lighter.

"Whoa..." He wobbled from side to side.

"Easy there, champ, the Float will keep your blood pressure up while I check you out. Any spike of adrenaline and the happy feelings go bye-bye. Stay calm and enjoy it." The medic snapped his fingers open and his palm glowed.

Noah floated along in the chemically induced bliss. Glimpses of the fight flashed in his mind as the truck rumbled forward. He nodded off for just a second when there was a sharp pain against his chest.

"No sleeping." The medic rubbed his knuckles up and down Noah's sternum. He wasn't sure when his body armor had been opened, but he looked down at bare skin and two bleeding welts. Star-shaped scars the size of his pinky nail dotted his skin.

"I get shot and I still can't sleep?" Noah slurred.

"I haven't checked you for a concussion yet," the medic said. "You had the pox pretty bad, eh? Lucky you survived."

"Didn't feel that way when I was stuck in bed for months." Noah tried to swipe his hand across his mouth to wipe a bit of drool away but managed to bump his knuckles against his closed helmet instead. He pawed at the release under his chin when a hand grabbed him by the wrist and pushed his arm down.

Mason was beside him, the opacity of his face plate turned off so Noah could see his face. His eyes were heavy with emotion, his brow tense and his lips thin. Two packs with char marks were between his knees.

"He gonna be okay, doc?" Mason asked.

"Contusions look worse than they really are. Vitals are fine. I'll cc you his file so you can file a Broken Star medal," the medic said. "Go ahead and button up, champ. Meds will wear off in a couple minutes, then you're on ibuprofen and water."

"Is anyone else hurt?" Noah asked.

"Sergeant Rochelle's section's fine. Cataphracts lost ammo and that's it," Mason said. "Don't know about the rest of the battalion. Don't do this to me again, Noah. Christ, I should never have fought to keep you in my section. I can't think straight when you're in trouble."

"It's Mom's fault...I get hurt and you're a dead man when you get home," Noah slurred. "Hey, this stuff ain't so bad. Maybe I'll get shot in the plates again."

"Don't." Mason rolled his eyes. "No more getting shot. You'll get a medal eventually, but getting you new armor plates before the next fight is going to be a pain."

"I wasn't trying to get shot, you understand...Donan. Where is he?" Noah winced as the medication wore off.

"Don't worry about him. He doesn't have any problems," Mason said. "Button up. Still got a way to go."

Noah slapped his vest back together. Fragments of the broken plate in the front pouch rubbed against each other and his onboard systems struggled to automatically adjust the fit against him.

He slumped back against the bench and closed his eyes. No one protested as he fell asleep and leaned against his brother's shoulder.

Mason kept his carbine in his hands, tightening and loosening his grip on the handle.

CHAPTER 8

Major Perrin followed Colonel Jematé and Lieutenant Colonel Timmons toward a checkpoint in the gap of razor wire and electrified fencing around a squat building, the bottom level surrounded by blast resistant T-walls. The way into the building was a wide path bordered by more razor wire, with small anti-personnel mines scattered around the coils.

Jematé and Timmons were in their Cataphract suits, while Perrin followed behind. Wearing Flanker gear made the most sense as he was a staff officer and not meant to be commanding on the front line like his two superiors. Still, he was rated for the heavy armor, and it was harder to command authority over someone who was better armed, armored and taller than you.

In his opinion.

A pair of Dagger drones kept watch directly overhead the three officers. The surrounding Tabuk City was a mix of decrepit buildings and Hegemony-standard hab towers. The convoy had arrived without further attacks, though the infantry units stationed on the perimeter had been rather icy with them when they arrived.

"Evening, sirs," a military policeman in Flanker gear said just outside the guard shack. "General Brooks is waiting for you. Got a matter of policy to go through before you're authorized entry."

The guard took out a pair of cylinders about the size of a thumb.

"Why do we need restraining bolts?" Timmons asked. "We're all on the same side."

"It's policy." The guard jerked one shoulder up. "Been a number of . . . incidents in the last couple of months. At other commands, not here. Boss runs a tight ship. Enhanced security measures were put in place. I don't have the authority to allow un-vetted personnel in with active weapon systems. Sorry, sirs."

"It's fine." Jematé popped a small panel open on his suit's upper chest. He didn't squat down to make the cop's job of fixing the bolt to the receiver any easier. The breech on Jematé's rotary cannon mounted on his back beeped and clamped shut, and red lights blinked on the frame holding it, as well as the frame with his mortar tube.

Timmons accepted his restraining bolt, and both continued through the razor wire-lined path with a serpentine turn in the center.

"Need your carbine and sidearm, sir," the guard said to Perrin. Perrin's face contorted in anger at the mere suggestion he could be disloyal to the Hegemony. He was about to argue, but the colonels didn't seem interested in waiting for him. He grumbled and handed over his weapons.

"I need a receipt," Perrin said.

"Oh, sure thing, sir." The guard double-tapped a small screen on the back of his hand and a completed form blinked twice on Perrin's forearm screen. "Don't meet many that do things right by the book all the time."

"Trust has to go both ways." Perrin jogged after the two Cataphracts.

"—not even a threat briefing before we rolled out," Timmons said to the colonel. "There's a serious command and control problem on this planet, sir."

"I agree with your assessment that things are . . . brittle," Jematé said. "We're not here to fix things, Paul. We're here to perform our duties for the Hegemony."

"The Command Sergeant Major will go into conniptions if we get jerked around again," Timmons said. "Not that it bothers him, it's that he has to tamp down on our soldiers. Who are justified in asking questions, if I may add."

"You may, just not in front of anyone outside the battalion," Jematé said. "Perrin, you have the support request drawn up?"

"Roger, sir." Perrin held up a data wafer. "I'll run it straight to the logistics desk when we get inside."

"No, wait until we've seen the general. Let me kiss the ring before we go asking for favors," Jematé said.

They entered the building. The inner walls were lined with sandbags and all the glass in the windows had been removed or blown out. The headquarters smelled of mildew and body odor. A folding table near where two hallways converged bore a decaying cardboard box overflowing with small soap bottles and the same plastic-wrapped toothbrushes dispensed in Hegemony prisons.

A major in simple fatigues and a gun belt waved them towards a hallway that curved around the operations center. Perrin tried to get a glimpse inside and spot where the logistics desk was but was hurried along by a forceful stomp from Timmons.

A Cataphract with a forearm-mounted double-barreled autocannon—better for close confines—stood in front a set of double doors. His helmet was painted with ash to resemble a skull. Kill tallies stretched across his chest from one shoulder to the other.

They waited for an awkward moment, the Cataphract refusing to acknowledge them. A door opened behind him and bumped against an axe mounted where the mortar tube or rocket launcher should've been.

"They're cleared, Areca," a dark-skinned man said from behind the door. The Cataphract took two steps to the side, never turning away from the Brettons.

"I'm General Brooks." The man opened the door fully and slapped his hand over his heart in lieu of shaking hands with Jematé or Timmons.

"Bretton Eleventh, reporting," Jematé said and touched his metal-shod hand to his chest.

"Come in, come in." Brooks raised a hand and lights rose in the large office. The three-quarters waist-high ring of a battle management stations switched on and holo screens flickered to life.

Perrin noticed a battered Cataphract suit against the wall next to a cot with a single duffel bag underneath it.

"Sorry, I was asleep when you pulled in." Brooks stretched his arms out, then picked up a faded yellow tennis ball from the battle station. "I understand you took some fire on your way in?"

The general held up two fingers and the holo panels switched to an overhead view of the city. Tabuk straddled a narrow river that ran along a mountain range. Open fields beyond the city were marked with dense minefields, and the closest peaks bore drone nests with nearly full complements of Daggers and Sparrow reconnaissance platforms.

"Five dead, six wounded," Jematé said.

Brooks raised an eyebrow and put his hands on his hips.

"So, you're at well over ninety percent strength? Fresh to the fight as well. Fantastic." Brooks bounced the tennis ball off the floor and caught it. "There's a lunar eclipse coming up and you're aware of what that means."

"Sir," Jematé took a breath, "with all due respect, we do *not* know what that means. My battalion and I are true to the Hegemony, but we've been thrown out here with little to no explanation, an anemic threat briefing that amounts to 'they're out there, shoot 'em' and our foundry units are still on our civilian transport."

Brooks' brow furrowed.

"When did you arrive? The only thing I'm tracking is the next courier from the *Highest* that's supposed to come with my orders off this rock."

Jematé brought the general up to speed on their arrival to Dahrien and Tabuk City.

"Oh . . . ain't that something," Brooks chuckled. "Not ideal. Not ideal at all. The marshal needed warm bodies to throw at a problem and he tossed you in my lap. Did you get—never mind. If I start talking about something you know, tell me to skip ahead."

The general picked up a stylus and stretched it out into a pointer.

"The enemy has coalesced around the Red Banner, a quasi-religious organization that the locals have glommed onto. Their *raison d'etre* is to overthrow the Hegemony's authority over the planet and they've been successful at it everywhere but the Capitol province and surrounding territories. My city's the bleeding edge between the marshal's law and the Red Banner. Forgive the pun."

The planetary map appeared in a corner; everything on land but a small patch around the capital was shaded in red.

"The Hegemony controls that little?" Jematé asked. "The marshal's map—"

"Were there piss bottles in Van Wyck's office? Because he hasn't left his room since he was ambushed and the Banner took his scalp but left him alive. Which didn't do us many favors," Brooks said. "The marshal got his stars because his cousin is one of the Most High. The

Banner didn't kill him as he would've been replaced by someone mildly competent. Which isn't what we've got now."

Perrin's eyes widened as the general's near-insubordination continued.

"But word from the *Highest* is coming." Brooks smiled. "Me and my boys are almost set to go home. Soon as word comes. You all can hold down this fort. Where was I? The enemy."

"Computer, display western pedestrian cameras."

New screens popped up. Groups of civilians walked through automated checkpoints and onto dirt roads leading East. Most carried heavy packs and dragged children along with them.

"The locals cycle back to their ancestral homes at lunar eclipses to commune with spirits or some such," Brooks said. "At least, that's what they say. They weren't doing it until the Red Banner became a planning factor. I'm convinced they use the 'pilgrimage' to conceal the Banner's movements and move the civilians out of harm's way before an attack."

"Why let them go? Keep them in place as a security measure to—" Perrin shut his mouth when Brooks shot him a dirty look.

"A commander to the north tried that. His entire command was scalped over a single night and their bodies hung to rot in the jungle. So I'd rather not fuck around and find out with my Flags, especially when I know most of them hate my guts for existing," Brooks said. "We're beyond the classic fight for hearts and minds here. We just have to hold out until the *Highest* sends a large enough relief force to kill our way to compliance."

"Sir...killing civilians is not what the Hegemony expects of us," Jematé said.

"That's why the Hegemony has Skiens, gentlemen. They aren't made with any sort of qualms." Brooks rubbed his face. "Which is a big part of the problem.

"Computer, how many hours until the next scheduled courier from the *Highest*?"

"Next transit from the Elko system scheduled to arrive in fourteen hours" came from the battle tracker.

"So close." Brooks smiled again. "None of my boys want to be the last one killed on this shithole. That's a planning factor."

Perrin made a mental note.

"Attacks aren't guaranteed, but possible during the lunar eclipse,"

Brooks continued. "You've had a brush with the Red Banner's tactics, but they've got a good number of Alliance-designed light tanks and knock-off Shrike drones. Local manufacture, the Patty licenses which those shitheels claim is pirated, but no one believes that. The Alliance won the war and then just had to keep rubbing our noses in it. Hmmph."

"That class of tank shouldn't be an issue for us," Jematé said. "Not with the plumbata missiles Cataphracts carry."

Brooks nodded.

"You are correct, but the Flags figured out what our complement of missiles is and figured if they attack with significantly more tanks than that . . . we get overmatched. There's a company of Wolverine tanks at an outpost on Highway Seven leading to Ifugao City. They can be here in less than an hour, but they're also supporting the forward operating base at Port Abra."

Perrin opened his mouth.

"And before you ask, the company's sequestered from the locals as it's a Skien unit. Locals don't care much for them. At all." Brooks tossed the ball up and caught it with his other hand. "Could've saved a lot of lives if even a platoon was stationed here, but the marshal outranks me, and I'm not interested in waking up with my hair cut down to the bone by trying to be cute and outsmart him."

He tapped the end of the stylus in the holo and the map zoomed in on a trench line on the eastern edge of the city.

"You'll relieve the Eighth Etruvia Infantry. They're actually rotating out on schedule, for once. I've got bunkers and auto-gun emplacements through the sector so it's not open trenches. Lunar eclipse is in . . . nine hours. Attacks usually happen plus or minus a couple hours from the planetary shadow completely crossing the moon," Brooks picked up a paper cup of cold coffee, swished it around, and took a sip.

"Is there any specific intelligence about an upcoming attack?" Timmons asked. "I saw friendly units on the map in towns further to the East. Anything from them?"

"Yes, them," Brooks chuckled. "Local militia units. Nominally under my command but the only convoys that ever make it to those towns are full of ammo and weapons sent by Central. Those same convoys would get hit on their way back after they delivered the supplies. I've had their regular re-supply drops held in my yard. Loggies don't mind, paperwork they send up keeps Central happy and they sure as hell aren't coming here to investigate."

"Then what about those militia units? When was the last time they were inspected?" Jematé asked.

"The last time someone wanted to, they visited the incinerators with a tag on their toe," Brooks said. "Are you going to believe what Central has on their boards or what I'm telling you?"

"Boots on the ground always have the best read," Jematé said after a moment.

"Good, because I was about to invite you to go inspect them yourself and solve a problem for me, but you're a sharp cookie. Brandon doesn't produce idiot officers, nice change of pace."

"It's Bretton . . . sir," Jematé said.

"Yes. Anyway . . ." Brooks wiped a sleeve across his mouth. "Captain Tharsis is in command of the Eighth. She'll send an escort for you. Be in position in the next six hours. Rotations last a week. Whoever replaces me when the *Highest* sends reinforcements might change it. Send your foundry requirements to my S4. Heck, I'm almost done, I'll approve anything."

The general laughed and reached under the battle tracking station and pulled out a small bottle held against it with tape. He unscrewed the top and took a long swig.

He coughed and held it out to Jematé with a slight shake.

"No, thank you, sir," Jematé said. "Is there anything else?"

"Dismissed." Brooks wagged a hand at them. "I'm drinking to good news. The Flags hearing that the Most High are finally sending reinforcements might make them behave. Might, but they don't know what's good for them. Now shoo."

The three Bretton officers left the room. Jematé and Timmons paused several steps away and just around a corner from the guard at the door.

"Perrin, take our requirements to the logistics office on duty," Jematé said. "XO and I need to speak."

"Moving, sir." Perrin tapped the pouch on his chest harness and the data drive inside. The Tactical Operations Center was unusually quiet compared to what Perrin expected. The usual central battle command station was on a raised dais, with outward holo projections of the tactical situation in and around the city. He noted the Eleventh's brief battle in a small callout box on the bottom left corner.

His presence in the TOC earned a few looks, but no one seemed particularly interested in him. Each staff section had a sign over the desk, and he went to the S4—Logistics and Supply—cluster. A single female soldier was there, her uniform blouse was hung over the back of her seat, and the sleeves of a too-big undershirt hung lower than her elbows. She was painfully thin and had sunken eyes.

"Hello, I'm Major Perrin with the Bretton Eleventh. General Brooks directed me to deliver our immediate logistics needs. Our own foundry units are still stuck back at the Malakal auxiliary void port and—"

"You just came from off world?" She rubbed an eye. "Did you come with word from the *Highest*? Are we rotating out?"

"We arrived separately from that . . . ma'am? Forgive me, I don't know your rank," Perrin said.

"Last name Nelson." She glanced at the rank on his chest. "I'm not . . . exactly sure what rank I am. The major died a few weeks ago and we haven't heard back from Control if my brevet promotion was approved. Or if it was even sent. The Adjutant went missing the same day the major was hit."

"I . . . I'm sorry to hear that," Perrin said.

"Got your reqs?" She held out a hand and track marks from needle injections were visible on her inner elbow and down her forearm.

Perrin passed the data drive to her trembling hand. She popped it into a reader and a flickering holo screen projected from it.

"Huh . . . that's all? You don't want any chem tubs?" she asked.

"What are those for?" Perrin leaned to one side and saw Jematé and Timmons engaged in an intense conversation.

"The tak tak flies. They're bad this time of the year and give soldiers the trots. Drop some insecticide cubes in the chem tubs and then you've only got the roaches to worry about." She shivered and banged open a drawer. She gulped down water from a bottle.

"Aren't there chem tubs already in place?" Perrin asked.

She leaned forward and Perrin saw an ugly jaundice in her eyes.

"Little hint about Dahrien. If you've got something, don't ever give it up. The Eighth won't leave a damn thing behind for you. See, couple years ago this levy unit from goddamn nowhere was supposed to cycle off world and go home, but Central canxed their orders while they were on the tarmac waiting to board transport. They had nothing but their bare issue and were deployed to Kurdufa Province."

"And?" Perrin asked.

"Kurdufa's a no-go zone. All Red Banner and Flags. Entire unit got wiped when they tried to hold an already looted FOB. Ran out of ammo and everything in hours."

"That's horrifying. Who was held accountable?"

The woman snorted, then broke into a guffaw.

"You're serious? Okay, new guy. I kinda like you so I'll add a couple line items to your foundry queue for stuff you'll need." She winked at him. "I'm leaving with the general anyway and if the Hegemony thinks they can recall me to fix a property booking . . ." She laughed some more.

"Thank you," Perrin said.

"And if you need anything," she rubbed her track marks, "or you *got* anything . . . swing on by. There's a market for just about everything here."

"I'll keep that in mind. What's the usual flash to bang time for this sort of a requisition?" he asked.

"You're asking for some pretty run-of-the-mill stuff. Probably by the end of tomorrow. And you should get all of it delivered to you." She leaned forward and spoke in a conspiratorial whisper. "You request anything special or valuable and I suggest you pick it up from the foundry yourself. Things tend to evaporate during transit if they're in demand."

"I'll also keep that in mind . . . ma'am?"

"Just Tonya." She winked at him. "You need anything off the books, I probably know someone who's got it." She rubbed her track marks again.

"Thank you, Captain. Or Major. Tonya."

"I've got the certs to make the Foundries purr." She tapped against an imaginary keyboard. "That's what matters. Stay safe out there."

Perrin nodded at her and hurried to catch up with Jematé and Timmons as they headed for the exit.

Noah stood in the entrance of a flash-crete bunker. The inner walls were molded over, and the distinct smell of old urine and fresh feces drifted out from the dark corners. Crude graffiti of a woman prepared for intercourse adorned the back wall. A single tap light on the ceiling flickered intermittently.

"Noah, get in there and inventor—oh my God!" Mason put the back of his hand over his mouth as he came up behind Noah. "There's a shitter dugout right over there. It works. I just used it." He pointed down the trench.

"The cam feeds are up." Noah leaned in and glanced at a bank of holo monitors showing open fields. "Why did they relieve themselves in here before they left?"

"Because they're assholes. I thought Hegemony Marines were the only ones that did shit like this," Mason said. "We're not sitting in there until it's clean. Man the gun point while I find some bleach or something."

He turned his brother around and pointed him towards a small dome built into the trench topped with a pair of autocannons. Noah opened a curved metal door so heavy that he had to use his Flanker's strength-assist ability to get it wide enough for him squeeze in. A single ratty stool, remote controls and displays were inside. Crumpled food wrappers and other garbage were smooshed against the floorboards.

The smell was noticeably better than the bunker, but still reeked of body odor and farts. Noah sat on the stool and tested out the controls. The display view shifted from side to side, and the crosshairs turned green as the aiming systems adjusted to target a low hill in the distance.

"Private Tallec." Sergeant Corre rapped his metal-shod knuckles on the steel door. His helm face was open, the thick chin piece angled down. "How you doing?"

"The ammo cans reserves aren't even." Noah tapped a display. "I don't know how that happened. I burn through the right side and the left will rattle itself out of alignment and we'll have to reset them during combat."

"No...how are you doing? Chaplains weren't on our levy assignment. We've only got each other when things get bad," Corre said. His face had a five o'clock shadow, blue eyes still sharp even though the rest of his visage spoke to exhaustion.

"Should be fine, sergeant. I had the highest score on the firing point sims back home...oh, you mean about Donan?"

"Yes, private, I mean Donan. We're Bretton, not robots. It's been go go go since we landed, but when you sit here alone and you've got time to process what's happened . . . it catches up with you. There are plenty of old hands here that know what you're going through," Corre said.

"Roger, sergeant. I don't—I don't understand what happened to him. He was in the cargo bed when the front went up. How did it even . . . ?"

"Alliance bolter-head munition," Corre said. "Designed to penetrate light armor and then explode inside the crew compartment of a vehicle. The enemy came prepped to take out the convoy; they weren't equipped for fighting Cataphracts or determined Flankers like you. The bolter popped and tossed Donan out into the jungle where you found him. It was quick, at least."

"At least," Noah said. "What'll happen to him now?"

"Hegemony policy is to cremate remains and transport them home when available. I processed his tags and the packet went back to Central. Priority traffic like that gets routed back to Bretton as soon as possible so his family will know soon. The LT and I will write letters to the family, that's our duty. Would you write one too?" Corre asked.

"Me? I'm nobody, Sarge," Noah said.

"You were his battle buddy. You've known him for a while, yeah?"

"He got drafted within a few days of the levy order from the *Highest*. I was passed over for pox exposure and didn't think I was going to get to go. Him and a couple other guys from the football team that were drafted all reported to the recruiting center at the same time. I went with them and just . . . went inside. Turns out I was eligible to enlist and didn't even need a med waiver for the scars. So I signed up to stay with him. Rest of the other guys are all over in 3rd Company." Noah kicked at a roach as it scurried along the floor.

"Do me a favor. When you've cycled off duty, write up a letter to his family. Say what he meant to you but don't mention the fight, that's the LT's job."

"Roger, sergeant, can do," Noah said.

Corre looked back at the dugout.

"Your bunker's getting bleached from top to bottom right now. Go to bunker nineteen and crash for a couple hours. Either it was unmanned or the last guys in there weren't a bunch of fucking animals because it only smells like mold and old food rations. Besco'll take your spot here. Ask the doc for a sedative if you need it."

"Thanks, sarge, but I think—"

"Did that sound like a request, private?" Corre's tone hardened just enough to straighten Noah's back.

"No, sergeant. Sorry, sergeant. Moving, sergeant." Noah shoved the door open and slipped into the trench. Thunder rumbled through overcast skies and thick raindrops spattered against his head and face. Noah looked up as rain materialized out of the misty and low cloud ceiling. The drops were warm and had a faint smell of sulphur to them. He licked a drop from his lips and spat it right out.

Thunder rolled into a sharp crack and the rain came down in sheets. Noah bent forward slightly to protect his carbine and ducked into the other bunker.

CHAPTER 9

An angular shape jutting up from behind the trees caught Felix's eye. It didn't bend with the wind of the returned storm, but remained rigid and still. He shouldered his way through the jungle and found a crashed Hegemony cargo helicopter. Repulsor technology worked well enough for lighter, more nimble craft, but the power needs to haul freight made the older technology more viable.

The skids and bottom of the helicopter were encased in soil, the fuselage had rusted out long ago, but the painted Hegemony crest on the rotor housing was still visible. Sliding doors on Felix's side were stuck fast, and the bulletproof glass was fogged out from cracks.

"Well well well, what have we here?" Felix put a palm against the door. "What were you hauling, eh? Batteries? Emergency-please-come-get-me-before-the-Flags-scalp-me beacons? Food that *doesn't* taste like the devil's shit?"

He moved around the nose. The pilot seats were empty, cockpit glass shattered. The jungle had reclaimed the seats with vines hanging from the panels and ferns sprouting from the cushions.

"Maybe the other doors are open and—" Felix let out a rather feminine-sounding shriek when he saw a woman in a white tunic sitting on the cargo floor, her legs dangling over the side. Her skin was dark as night, short hair gone to gray at the edges. She had her hands up to her sides, palms out.

The Antares priestess didn't move as Felix bumped into the helicopter and swung his carbine up. He continued the swing until the muzzle pointed straight up, flashing it across her for a brief instance.

91

"Sorry! Oh God, I'm so sorry." Felix held a hand out. "A-are you okay? I didn't mean to—p-p-please don't be mad. Are you...are you here for my soul? Oh no...am I dead?"

She lowered her arms.

"I can't be dead. Shit hurts too much for me to be dead." He rolled the shoulder that had knocked the insurgent off his feet. "So, I'm not dead. But you're here. Um...hello?"

She pressed her hands together beneath her chin and bowed ever so slightly.

"That's right...you guys—and gals!—don't talk. Don't help any side. You're out here to find..." He looked at the empty cockpit, then to the bullet holes and torn metal near the nose.

"There are some other guys." He pointed back from where he'd come. "Not happy with me. They might come from that way. Or another. I really don't *know* where I am. Trying to get to Tabuk City, don't suppose you know..."

She stared blankly at him, her eyes kind.

"No, that would be helping, wouldn't it?" He gnawed on his bottom lip for a split second. His shoulders slumped and he let out a sigh.

He gestured at the empty spot next to her. "May I?"

She didn't react as he sat on the floorboard that creaked with rust.

"It's nice to sit on something that's not mud or wet, know what I mean? Sure you do, that's why you're in here and not out there getting pissed on like me." Felix took his helmet off and set it beside him. "If the Flags show up, I'll take off running. Won't say a word about you. Seems fair."

The Antares looked him up and down, concern behind her eyes.

"Hungry?" He took out the pack of *tong* jerky from his pouch. Slimy mud had gotten in and fouled the open pack. "Ah...that sucks. Sorry, didn't know. Might taste better now, who knows." He put it back.

They sat in silence as the rain pattered against the jungle.

"Thank you," Felix finally said. "I don't think it was you, but when I was a kid a friend of mine back on a Syddan port lost his father on Ayutthaya. Missing in Action for years and years, then one day an Antares showed up at his family's house with some remains and personal effects. Didn't mean anything to me, but my friend...he started to live again after that. No more 'what if.' They had a proper burial and everything."

Felix's face lit up.

"Hold on." He reached into his flak jacket and pulled out the ring of dog tags. "Here. Can you take these? They're from my platoon. Dead in the last couple of days and I don't know if word's gone off world—"

He held the tags out to the Antares. She took in a sudden breath and covered her mouth with one hand. She sniffed hard and wiped away a tear.

"This . . . is what you do? Right? You can tell their families." Felix jangled the tags, the aluminum clinking. "Yeah, I'm their Charon right now, but I don't know what's going on. I don't know where I am. I could step on a mine or get shot and then the Flags will scalp me and leave me hanging from a tree with my guts dangling between my knees. Sorry . . . that was a bit much."

He shook the tags again.

The woman looked away.

"Is it because I'm still alive? You only work for the dead, huh?" Felix brought the ring to his lap and flipped through the tags. "I shouldn't have asked. Apologies."

He stared at Gunnar's tag, then put the ring back in his flak vest.

"Can you hear them whisper? Sometimes I do . . . a name called out in the dark, a face behind my eyes. At least they can rest." He hopped off the edge, boots rustling pebbles that had washed up against the helicopter. He put his hands on his hips and looked around the clearing. There were two paths leading into the clearing, but each went off in different directions.

"One of these should get me to Tabuk, yeah?" He shrugged. "Guess that's a rhetorical question. I won't tell anyone I saw you here. Good luck and I hope . . . I hope you find who you're looking for."

She pressed her hands together and bowed slightly again.

Felix held up a finger and bounced it from side to side like a metronome needle and went toward the path on the left. He was a few steps from the wood line when there was a small crash from the other path.

He ducked slightly and readied his weapon, but he didn't see anything moving. He looked to the Antares, but she was in the same spot.

"Rabbit? I'm hungry . . . eh, who am I kidding. Not going to catch one." He turned toward the path again.

Something stung the back of his neck. He slapped a hand against his skin and waved a hand at whatever had bitten him.

"Son of a—" He cocked an eyebrow up, looking for the culprit. The Antares was staring at him, one hand clenched in a fist.

Felix narrowed his eyes at her, then sidestepped towards the other path. He crossed the threshold into the jungle, and turned back to give her a last look. He gave her a sheepish wave and went deeper into the green.

CHAPTER 10

"Hey."

Something jostled Noah's feet. He shot partway up from the plumbing-pipe-and-plastic-strips cot he'd fallen asleep on. He blinked gunk out of his eyes and felt aches through his muscles. The dugout was surprisingly comfortable for one as exhausted as he was.

Mason smacked Noah's boot again.

"Up. We've got hot chow coming and you don't want to miss it," Mason said. The other Flanker section sat on the opposite side of the bunker. Cobwebs hung from the ceiling and clustered in the high corners. The sliding bunker door was partly open, letting in semi-fresh humid air from outside. Twilight shone through the gap.

"Huh? How long was I out?" Noah sat up.

"Longer than anyone else," Besco, another Flanker, said from the other side. Saluan, his battle buddy, leaned against a corner, snoring quietly. "Are we setting a precedent that getting shot gets you more nap time?" he asked Sergeant Rochelle, who was in the back of the bunker fiddling with the pipes of a toilet that had seen better days.

"Don't get shot," Rochelle grumbled.

"Yeah, I'd rather have pulled a guard shift." Noah pressed at the sore sports.

"Chow." Sergeant Corre slid the bunker door open and ducked under the entrance. His Cataphract armor was almost tall enough for his head to scrape against the ceiling. Behind him came the rest of the squad's Cataphracts; Boyle and Leroi carried a green plastic supply chest between them. Herve, the last Cataphract, locked eyes with Corre and posted himself on guard outside.

Herve closed the door.

"Alright, men." Corre's Cataphract armor opened with a hiss of hydraulics. The armored plates covering the front of his body hinged open and he stepped out of the suit. His bodysuit was soaked through with sweat; a cloud of salt from dried sweat ringed his collar. "Our first official meal on Dahrien. Gentlemen, please dismount."

Boyle and Leroi followed suit. Boyle started towards the toilet, his steps short.

"That thing working?" Boyle asked Rochelle.

"It'll flush but—don't you dare shit where we eat!" Rochelle moved to block Boyle.

"I'm gonna piss in the next thirty seconds and you get to choose where I'll do it." Boyle put a hand against the bunker wall.

"Doesn't your suit come with a piss tube?" Rochelle tossed his hands up and sidestepped away from Boyle.

"Damn filter's shot!" Boyle got to the toilet and unzipped the front of his bodysuit.

"This is such a magical moment," Saluan said. "I can't wait to have my grandkids at my knees asking me how I spent the Great Dahrien Action and then I describe this very moment."

The sound of fluid striking linoleum sounded through the bunker.

"I'm starting to think my uncles lied about the Alliance War," Besco said. "Because all they talked about was the 'recreation stations' and the hooch fermented in plastic tubs that they drank on Colima."

Corre put a hand on the supply crate, glaring at Boyle until he finished relieving himself.

"Why talk about rec sections?" Noah asked. "The tent back at training had board games, a broken holo and other wild excitements."

"Bit better equipped on Colima," Besco said. "Very entrepreneurial staff of local ladies, if you know what I mean."

"I don't," Noah said.

"Anyone else need to tinkle before we eat?" Corre snapped. "Hold it until we're done eating. Can't believe they built a shitter into a bunker, but it beats using empty ration packs."

"Another riveting tale for the grans." Saluan swung a fist across his chest.

Corre opened the chest and removed a shrink-wrapped bundle of cylinders.

"Cataphract batteries for two days of operations." Corre handed them off to Mason. "Combat loads for Flankers and two mortar shells, and chow." The sergeant hefted out an olive-drab can as long as his arm and twice as thick. He twisted the top off and crinkled his nose at what was inside.

"What've we got, Sarge?" Besco asked.

"Looks like some sort of local bread." Corre handed over a pack of flatbread laden with moisture to Boyle.

"They call this bread?" Boyle shook the pack. "It's not even leavened. What a waste of flour. They could've given the ingredients to me and—"

"You haven't even washed your hands." Mason snatched the flatbread away. "You think we want the runs already?"

"There's egg . . . loaf?" Corre used an aluminum ladle to scoop out a rubbery mass of off-yellow eggs. Grey bits jiggled in and around the substance.

"Not this shit again." Mason tore the plastic open and handed the bread to Noah. "I'm not that hungry. Yet."

"What is it?" Noah sniffed at the bread and noted a distinct lack of smell.

"Reconstituted faux egg powder with bits of mystery meat rubber disguised as sausage," Mason said. "That was all I ate for months on my last deployment because some loggy screwed up the req and none of the other units were willing to trade their food for our cache of egg loaf. Hey, Sarge, let me guess, white rice in there too?"

"Rice." Corre held up a smaller sealed case.

"You'd think the unit we replaced would be a bit more accommodating," Saluan said. "Instead they shat all over the place."

"Eat it now, taste it later." Corre doled out rice and egg loaf to a pressboard tray and handed it over to Noah. Noah peeled off a spork on the underside and poked it into what were labeled "eggs."

Once everyone had a tray, Corre looked around the squad.

"Prayer," the sergeant said.

"Donan usually led us," Mason said. "He was in the junior priesthood."

The room went silent.

"Saint Robin." Corre said and bowed his head. "Lord Above. We are less without Private Alexander Donan. We ask that you judge his duty well done and worthy of a soldier's rest at your side. We thank you for the courage to defend the Hegemony and thank you for protecting Noah Tallec. We thank you for this meal. I beg that your hand be upon us as we stand between the innocent and the wicked. If we are worthy of your mercy and peace, give it to our families and our honored dead. In Jesus' name we pray. Amen."

"Amen," the squad intoned.

Noah took a bite of the egg loaf and chewed quickly. The texture was like rubber, with cold gooey bits of "sausage" that had a salty crunch at their center. The rice was better, but not by much.

Saluan wolfed his egg loaf down and burped.

"How?" Rochelle looked at his soldier with disgust.

"Hunger is the best sauce." Saluan shrugged. "You want yours?"

Rochelle looked at his tray, conflicted.

"So what about the other bunker?" Mason asked. "It's our assigned sector and our responsibility, but we need to hose that shit bucket down before we can man it without getting whatever diseases those assholes left us."

"Lieutenant Govrien has the firing points half-manned." Corre took a nibble of his eggs and passed the tray to Saluan. "Which is why our point's empty for now. The enemy tends to attack at dawn with the sun at their backs so stand up will be at least an hour before then. We can stay in this bunker until the other's clean."

"Jailhouse rules for the shitter," Boyle said. "Poop a little, flush. Poop a little, flush. Don't let the smell build up. Wait." He sniffed the air. "That's a chem toilet. Okay, so we've got our water ration and—"

A siren wailed in the distance.

"Fuck!" Leroi tossed his tray aside and hopped back into his Cataphract armor.

"What? What's going on?" Noah snapped to his feet and tapped the bottom of his magazine to cycle a bullet into the chamber.

Corre touched an earpiece and a small holo screen appeared over one eye.

"Incoming drone swarm." Corre canted his head slightly as more information came through. "Trench defenses are coming online..."

A high whistle carried through the bunker. Sudden thunder shook the walls and the light flickered on and off.

"Figured they'd have screamers," Mason said. "Hate those things."

"Lieutenant wants our firing point up. Tallec, you're still on the cycle." Corre's helmet clamped down over his face. "Leroi, you're with me on shield."

"Moving, sergeant." Noah slapped a hand on his visor and slid it down and over his face. He gave Mason a fist bump on the shoulder and moved toward the door. Corre and the other Cataphract stacked at the door, Noah behind them.

A blast against the bunker sent a thin crack through the ceiling. A mechanical groan rumbled overhead.

"Herve, shield the squishies." Corre gripped the thick handle on the bunker door.

"Easy work, Sarge." Herve stepped close to Noah.

Noah felt smaller than usual with the Cataphracts towering around him. Hegemony squad tactics were designed around the Flankers spotting targets and keeping enemies from outmaneuvering the Cataphracts while the Cataphracts eliminated the threats through overwhelming and precise firepower. Both elements were designed and intended to support and protect each other in battle.

As more explosions sounded through the trench line, Noah felt less confident with the protection his Cataphract squadmates could offer.

Noah leaned to one side and looked at his brother. Mason was tense, his weapons tight in his hands as the rest of the Flankers moved to the walls.

"Trench cover's up," Corre said. "Moving in three . . . two . . . go!"

He flung the metal door open. The handle hit the frame an instant after the *crump* of a suicide drone slammed through the trench. The blast wave rocked Noah against Leroi. Leroi put his knuckles against Noah's back and pushed him out the door and into the trench.

Turrets and point defense gunfire rattled across the trench line. Tracers cut over the slice of sky Noah could see. Wire fencing had extended over the top of the trench, casting interlaced shadows across the front wall. A dark shape darted overhead. Noah froze as a drone looped high into the sky then came back, heading straight for him.

"Get in there!" Corre clamped onto Noah's shoulder and yanked him into the fire point. Noah's feet didn't touch the floor before he hit the control panel and fell hard, half on and half off the seat. Corre slammed the door behind Noah.

He had a moment to catch his breath before the attacking drone detonated into fire and shrapnel. Jagged metal sliced through the door and sparked off the concrete around them. A fragment struck the side of Noah's armored boot, sending a nasty sting up his leg. The bit of metal rattled around the bottom of the firing point, then sizzled amidst a sticky puddle of brackish water.

"Shoot something!" Corre shouted through Noah's earpiece.

"Moving." Noah kicked at his boot and noted that while it hurt, his foot was still there and not even bleeding. He banged his fist against the controls and most of the holos sprang to life. The machine gun housings overhead snapped open and the auto-targeting systems went to work. Noah tapped at circling reticules on the holos and the guns churned out quick bursts, downing most of a pack of incoming kamikaze machines.

A larger signature was detected, a glide bomb that could've been launched from dozens of miles away. The computer projected its flight path over the trenches and deep into the city. Noah prioritized it in the target queue and shared it with the rest of the firing points with a flick of his fingers.

The point defense guns went silent for a moment, then went fully automatic as the glide bomb came into range. The machine guns rattled the tiny compartment until the bomb sailed right over the trench line. None of the other firing points had concentrated their firepower on the target.

"Ah . . . Sarge? The synch software's not working. Can you de-conflict with the other—"

Wa-boom!

The ground shook as the glide bomb detonated in the distance. Noah flinched down, his shoulders high and tight as static washed across the holos.

"You worry about what you can shoot, not what everybody else *isn't* shooting. God damn it, cut the water supply before we drown in shit water!"

"Fine, I'll just save all our assess with this glitch—"

"Hot mike!"

Noah grimaced and stopped transmitting. Another wave of kamikaze drones appeared in the holos. He checked the ammo reserves and rubbed his thumbs against his hands. The magazines were nearly empty, and if he engaged the next wave of targets, he might not have rounds ready to shoot down another glide bomb. The enemy likely knew exactly how fast the firing points could fire and reload and if they timed their attacks just right...

"I'm overthinking this. Or underthinking. But if there's more coming then...damn it!"

Noah slid a thumb up a holo and the machine guns withdrew into their armored housings. His mouth went dry as the system lost track of the incoming kamikaze drones. One crashed into the dirt just beyond the trench line, its rotors clipped by a lucky shot from another firing point.

Another went into a terminal dive and exploded against the dome of his position. The overhead tap light shook off its housing as the warhead broke the reinforced concrete-and-steel shell above him. More drones fell into a cluster around his firing point, each explosion beating him lower and lower until he was crouched under the controls against the scuff marks around the bottom.

The assault ended and he glanced up at the holos.

Two glide bombs were coming right for him.

"Shit shit shit!" Noah swiped up on the arming screen and only one machine gun came back online. The other was a pulsing red in the holo, the housing damaged from a direct hit. Noah jabbed two fingers into the screen, targeting one of the glide bombs. The still-functioning machine gun burst into staccato life. Chugging out rounds that sailed toward the flying bomb.

The first target lost a wing, nose diving into the ground. The bomb blew up, sending a plume of shrapnel and dirt that enveloped the second glide bomb. The other target wobbled, then lost altitude.

It bounced off the dead zone that was No Man's Land and arced back up...then straight for Noah's firing point and the bunker with the rest of his squad.

"Brace! T-take cover! Something!" Noah ducked back under the controls and realized he was about to die like an idiot, cowering under a plywood shelf, hoping that would protect him after the concrete and steel armor of his firing point failed.

There was a dull *thud* against the firing point.

Noah peered over the desk. One of the camera's views was full of the nose cone of the glide bomb. Crude red and white rings of a target were painted on the tip along with a scrawled message in the local alphabet.

Noah carefully—very carefully—deactivated the remaining machine gun.

"Sarge...got an unexploded ordnance situation here." Noah snapped a pic with his helmet optics of the holos and sent it to Corre. "Can we call in the engineers?"

"Saint's bones, Noah...don't even fart," Corre said.

"All puckered up," Noah said. "If it's okay, I'm just going to shut off the holos. Attack seems to be over anyway...no more sky tracks."

"No, keep your sensors active and transmitting for the rest of the line. Just don't look at it," Corre said.

"Heard." Noah took a magazine from his pouch and set it over the holo lens projecting the image of the several-hundred-pound warhead resting a few yards from him. The holo was snuffed out. Only one screen remained up, casting a dull light over him.

"I haven't even been on this planet for a full day," Noah lifted his visor and rubbed his face, "and I'm ready to go home."

"Hot mike," Corre snapped.

Noah nodded slowly.

The vault door to Noah's firing point opened with a squeal of metal on metal. A Cataphract mitt wrapped around the edge and pushed it aside. The door was wrenched open just enough for Noah to squeeze through.

The buzz of insects and humid air rolled into the firing point, along with the stench of stagnant sewage.

Mason knocked on the door and looked inside.

"You okay?" he asked.

"Ugh, what happened?" Noah put the back of his hand against his nose, then closed his helmet and activated his air filters.

"Insurgents managed to blow up the sewer system." Mason waved his brother out. "Not sure if they were targeting it or if it was a shitty stroke of luck."

Some of the drone screens over the trench were mangled and blown out towards the ground. Bits of electronics and plastic casing were scattered about. Part of the trench had collapsed into mud and concrete fragments.

"Did we win?" Noah asked.

"Shh!" Mason pointed toward No Man's Land and where the glide bomb had landed. He motioned for Noah to follow and the squad followed Corre to a communication trench leading away back towards the city. Leroi took up the rear behind Noah, stalking behind the soldier. The squad turned into the other tunnel and a weight lifted from Noah's shoulders.

Leroi tapped Noah hard on the back, then pointed to the top of his helmet. A gash had been cut in the top. Leroi turned a mitt over and gave Noah a bit of jagged shrapnel the size of a pinky finger.

"I've got a new scar thanks to you," Leroi said. The report of small arms fire and the infrequent explosion rumbled in the distance.

"Sorry?" Noah held the shrapnel up and examined the edge in the low light as night settled across the city. Dried blood stained the tip.

"Somebody's got to take care of you squishies," Leroi said.

"You know where we're going?" Boyle asked over his shoulder as they walked through the next empty trench line.

"No? I figure if I just keep following everybody I won't go wrong," Noah said.

"A veteran already," Boyle chuckled. "Flags have broken through the lines on the northeast side of the city. We've been re-tasked to keep them from crossing the river and getting into the soft underbelly."

"What about back there?" Noah waved toward No Man's Land. "Isn't the brass worried about the Flags coming over the wide-open fields?"

"Temp minefield got drone-dropped after their attack fizzled," Boyle said. "They were dangling keys at us with the swarm while their infantry broke through the other part of the city. Guess the intel weenies figure the big push won't come through here."

"Are we going to catch a break at some point?" Noah asked. "We just got here."

"Yeah, we just got here," Boyle said. "And before that we were safe and happy on a ship or we had our feet up back home. You think the old hands here care that much about us?"

"How bad's the attack?" Noah asked. "Just light infantry?"

"Corre heard some snippets about tanks, which doesn't make any sense. How'd they get tanks this close to the city without anyone noticing? I swear the brass at division don't know what the hell they're doing," Boyle said.

"So what're we doing?" Noah asked.

"Left foot right foot. Maybe they'll convince the Flags to piss off before we have to do it for them. Least I've still got some of that local purchase jerky from the food drop." Boyle pulled a small pack out from inside his flak jacket and passed it to Noah.

Noah took a sniff and popped a hunk in his mouth. He chewed for a few seconds and swallowed a bit, then spat the rest out.

"Why does it hurt?" Noah squeezed his eyes shut as tears began. "It burns. It burns!"

"Yeah. Burns on the way in and the way out. Weird cuisine they've got here. We need to introduce them to cheese and proper baguettes," Boyle said. "Maybe we bring some of those murder peppers back to Bretton and start something new. Open a restaurant and challenge people to eat a pile of poutine with the spicy and give them a shirt if they can do it."

"Pretty sure they'd throw us in jail for that." Noah rinsed his mouth with water from his shoulder tube and opened his helmet to wipe his nose. "How long is my mouth going to hurt?"

"My gums still sting since chow. You'll be good in a while. Frickin' Saluan's loving this stuff. And the cops back home won't throw us in the clink for the spicy spicy. Unless we stole it. And then tried to sell it to an undercover officer. On camera . . . assholes. I am one hell of an idiot. There's the lieutenant."

He pointed to a pile of supply crates at the back of a gravel parking lot.

Lieutenant Govrien was in a Cataphract suit, speaking intently to Sergeant First Class Malo with his helm up and open. Three Flankers near them had a supply case open, blocky objects in their hands.

The platoon command post was little more than the crates and the comms specialist, the junior-most soldier in Cataphract armor with antennae and a foldable sat dish jutting up from his shoulders and back. The other three squads from the platoon converged on the lieutenant as they came in from the trench line.

"Red platoon," Govrien's voice hissed with static through Noah's earpiece. So much distortion so close to the officer could only mean the highest levels of broadcast encryption were being used. "Order of march is Second Squad, followed by First, Third and Fourth. We've been re-tasked to take up defensive positions on . . . Novachik Street."

A map of the city with a blue rectangle over a civilian neighborhood next to a highway appeared on Noah's visor.

"Soon as the battalion's in place, division's going to recall the units holding the Flags back in the slums," the lieutenant continued. "Flankies, pick up Shrike units and bolt on to your Cataphracts. Black air's in effect across the city. It flies, it dies. Do not employ Dagger drones or the point of origin'll get flagged for artillery."

"It's that bad?" Mason asked.

"Shut it," Corre growled. "Boyle, grab Shrikes and get them loaded onto our hardpoints."

"Moving." Boyle and his two Flankers trotted over to the supply point and took the blocky objects from the waiting soldiers. They returned to the squad and screwed the equipment onto the upper right shoulder of each Cataphract.

New alerts appeared on Noah's visor as the Shrikes came online, blinking on each wire diagram for the Cataphracts.

"Black air's been called," Mason said to Noah. "Shrikes are passive sensors, they pick up any airborne EM sig—or even enough air disturbance—and they'll launch counter-drones. They suck power though, gotta have them on the Cataphracts."

"Why aren't we carrying reloads?" Noah asked as the squad continued down a dark avenue towards their next position. The boom of artillery and endless beat of machine gun fire carried from distant plumes of smoke. Fires cast a dull red through the gloom, embers of hell waiting for them.

"Probably don't have enough," Mason said.

"Enemy armor reported at the breach," Govrien continued. "All Flanks, pick up Pikes. Five per soldier or as many as you can carry."

"It's worse than I thought, come on." Mason slapped Noah on the shoulder, and they ran over to another open crate and were given plastic-wrapped packs of cylinders with plastic handles. The Pikes were heavy, and Noah had to recruit his frame's strength to carry a pack under each arm.

"I've never used these live," Noah said.

"Same as the sims back home, but they will dud on you." Mason ripped the packaging open and handed the grenades over to Boyle's Flankers. "Throw it straight at the target, they can point detonate if the sensors fail. The anti-tank warhead can cut through Cataphracts so don't let the enemy get these. Which is generally good advice for anything we've got."

"How'd..." Noah fumbled with the grenades and almost dropped a pack, "how'd the enemy get tanks into the city?"

"The how and why don't matter," Mason said. "They're here. They're gunning through the slums on the outside of the city. They're comin' for us. We better stop 'em or Mom and Dad'll get a 'regret to inform you' form letter from the Hegemony because everyone'll be dead if we don't hold that position."

"Oh." Noah handed off a pack to Mason.

"Did I tell you what an idiot you are for volunteering for this mess?" Mason asked.

"Not today," Noah said.

"Noah, you're an idiot for—"

"I get it. I get it." Noah kept three Pikes for himself and attached a ring on the bottom of the handle to his chest rig.

Noah rushed up a concrete stairwell that reeked of the spicy local cooking and decaying trash. Bright graffiti marred the walls as he came up to the fourth-floor landing and put one hand on the emergency exit door. Mason flanked the other side.

"Covered," Boyle said from the stairwell, his weapon trained on the door. Two more Flankers were behind him, weapons aimed up and down the stairwell.

"Moving." Mason grabbed the door handle and flung it open. Noah caught the door and pinned it behind him as Mason entered the floor. Noah cut around the corner, scanning for targets. The hallway was unlit, the only light coming through the windows from distant fires burning through the city.

"Clear," Mason announced. "Get into the apartment and set up the observation post."

Boyle went to a wooden door and put his palm against it. Noah did a combat peek around the side of a window. A four-lane highway with a dirt median cut through the city, running close to the building. On the other side, rows of slums made of old construction material dotted with sturdier buildings extended out into the night. Fires raged uncontained, putting out enough smoke that the smell seeped through his helmet.

"Heartbeats inside," he said. "One adult and three kids at least."

"Damn it, they said the whole place had been evaced," Mason said.

"Frag it?" Besco asked from the emergency exit.

"There's kids in there," Boyle said. "Maybe they didn't get the word." He moved to the hinge side of the door and reached over to knock hard. When there wasn't a response, he knocked harder.

"Hegemony forces!" Mason yelled.

"Do they even speak Standard here?" Saluan asked.

"Bet they speak frag grenade." Besco tapped the explosive device on his chest rig.

"Shut your mouth before I—" Boyle jumped back from the door as it creaked open.

"Hashan! Hashan ui tal!" a woman squealed. A pair of hands stuck out over the door's threshold.

"Out!" Boyle snapped the light mounted to the front of his carbine on. The woman was painfully skinny, wearing a baggy shirt and pants, her hair covered by a cloth. Noah couldn't determine her age, as she looked like earned a living doing manual labor and the light in her face kept her eyes shut.

A child mewled in fear, clutching her leg.

"Go go." Boyle lowered the light slightly and pointed at the stairs.

The woman broke into rapid-fire language, waving her hands in front of her face.

"Hey!" Mason banged the stock of his carbine against the wall, then turned on his own light to illuminate the emergency exit.

The woman sobbed, then nodded quickly. She picked up two toddlers and hurried out, a third child clutched to her belt. The boy gave Noah an evil look as his mother led them downstairs.

Boyle and his fire team slipped into the apartment.

"How'd you do that?" Noah asked Mason.

"It's all in the tone. Transcends language." Mason shrugged. "Letting them go was probably a mistake."

"We can't have civilians up here. The shooting's getting closer, isn't it?" Noah asked.

"Yeah, but she definitely knows we're up here and she'll see the Cataphracts on the bottom floor and more of the rest of the battalion. Sure hope she doesn't have a phone on her and reports our positions and strength back to the Flags," Mason said. "Ain't no perfect decisions to make in combat. Just the ones that'll keep you alive until the next decision."

"Clear. Mason, take the other apartment!" Boyle called out from the doorway.

Noah and Mason ducked under the windowsills. Mason used the EM sensors in his glove to check for heartbeats and when none were found, he kicked the door open. The apartment didn't appear to be occupied. The concrete floor and walls were bare. Roaches scurried over cheap plastic dishes piled in the sink.

"Get eyes on our sector," Mason said as he cleared the only bedroom.

Noah unsnapped a small box off his carbine and pressed it against the windowsill. Tiny staples clutched the wood and held the optics in place. Video from the box flickered on his visor and another angle from the other apartment joined it.

"Don't silhouette yourself." Mason pulled Noah away from the window and opened the squad comms channel. "Corre, observation post set. We need over watch on the roof?"

"Negative, you go out there and the enemy will feed you a drone within minutes. Third squad's already expended half their Shrike munitions," Corre answered. "Squat and hold."

"Roger, squatting," Boyle said over the channel, and it closed.

"That's it?" Noah looked at a small two-person table against the wall in the kitchen. "Hurry up and wait?"

"You want to cut across that wide open space face-first and see if the enemy's close?" Mason asked. "Or do you want to sleep?"

"S-sleep?" Noah felt a glimmer of hope. "Really?"

"Yeah, wedge yourself against a corner and get some shut-eye." Mason opened his pouch full of nicotine strips. "Don't suggest using the bed. Ain't no body in there since we arrived, but it looks like someone died on it."

"Finally." Noah pressed his back to the wall and slid down. "Huh... don't feel that tired all of a sudden."

"Too much adrenaline for too long. I'm going to tranq you." Mason flipped open the cover on his forearm computer.

"Huh? Don't, Dad said those are habit forming and—ow!" Noah clutched his left forearm when something pricked his skin. "How's that even going to work when I'm so amped...up..." His head lolled to one side and he began snoring.

Mason turned a chair to face the tiny living space and sat down. He flicked a roach off the table and sighed.

The squad channel hissed in his ear.

"He good?" Corre asked.

"Yeah, boss . . . he's alright for now," Mason said. "Any word on when the shit storm's going to hit?"

"Not yet. Lieutenant's trying to get some Expedients for the ground floors, but the nets at battalion and higher are compromised. Flags are jamming everything they can. Only reason we can get anything from the colonel or other companies is because we're on the Hegemony ciphers Bretton was given."

"The enemy's in our nets? Saint's Bones, this is getting worse all the time. Why haven't we cloned our ciphers with the rest of the city?" Mason asked.

"Good question. You want to go find Jematé and ask him why?" Corre chuckled.

"Forget it. Let the zeros worry about zero problems. We'll hold down this part of the fort," Mason said. A sharp crack against the wall jolted him out of the seat. An artillery shell landed nearby, rattling the windows.

Noah stayed asleep.

"Think we took some small arms fire." Mason examined a fresh fissure in the wall.

"Stray rounds are all over the place . . . wait one." Corre switched the channel to include every member. A pic grab of a deep red moon in the sky appeared on Mason's visor. The edge of an eclipsing shadow covered a third of the surface.

"Maybe that's why they attack when there's a lunar eclipse," Boyle said. "Can't jam a shadow."

"What if it's cloudy?" Saluan asked.

"Shut your mouth," Rochelle snapped. "Anyone wants to take a dump, now's your chance. It's one of those weird squat kinds, though."

"Heads on swivels," Corre said. "Things'll get worse before they get better."

"Same as it ever was," Mason mumbled.

CHAPTER 11

Colonel Lambert made his way down the main hallway to Central HQ slowly. The staffers and other employees ignored him as usual, just another non-entity compared to everyone else this close to the flagpole.

Lambert touched his blouse and felt the certification slate that needed only two more signatures before he could submit an emergency funding request to finally unload the *Izmir* and move the battalion's heavy equipment to the front lines.

Those with access badges walked through a weapons detection field and into the Situation Room. Lambert kept to the side of the hallway, out of the way of those moving with more purpose and speed than he could manage.

Someone still bumped into him from behind. Lambert bumped hard against the wall but managed to keep himself upright. The person in such a rush had the off-yellow branch insignia of Void Comms on her epaulets. She didn't even look back at him before rushing ahead.

"Hurry hurry," Lambert said to himself. "That's the only person that's actually in a rush to get anything done in here."

Once he got to the main entrance, a hulking guard in Flanker armor that looked almost too small for him held out a beastly paw of a hand to Lambert, palm up. Lambert forced a smile and swiped his identity band around his wrist through the detection field.

"Lambert...you were here yesterday." The guard lifted his chin slightly, displaying alabaster white skin on his neck.

"Indeed, the JAG review officer wasn't on duty, but he is now."

Lambert's smile quivered as he felt the eyes of the guard looking him over. "Or so I heard. You'll see my HQ endorsement is still valid until the review officer can confirm or deny my request."

"Marshal is on the floor. In and out. Don't disturb him." The guard pointed to a small hallway. "Better hurry before Marshal Van Wyck insists on full cavity searches for the un-cleared. Again."

"Indeed. Failing that, I must wish for a doctor with small hands." Lambert made his way into the claustrophobic tunnel and felt parts of his body tingle as the heavy scanners made sure he carried nothing explosive or dangerous in him or on him.

He shivered as he came out of the scanner and made out the JAG lawyer on the far side of the operations center. There being only one way in and out for everyone but the marshal, Lambert's excitement grew as his scavenger hunt for authorizations and signatures neared its end.

In the center of the operations center, the marshal and a pair of generals and the Void Communications officer stood at the strategic holo tank. Whatever they were looking at was distorted by a semi-opaque privacy screen projected over them.

Lambert heard nothing, but the conversation seemed very intense between the three flag officers. The lieutenant inched away from the marshal, her hands set on the control ring.

A Cataphract soldier with a skull mask and crude sigils on his armor plating watched the men talk keenly.

"—it's confirmed!" a general shouted as the privacy holo fizzed out. The Comms lieutenant raised her chin slightly and drew her hands back from the controls.

"I-Impossible," Marshal Van Wyck sputtered. "This is a forgery. It is a fraud created by our enemies!"

"It came direct from the courier ship. Straight from the Elko system and the *Highest*." The other general slammed a hand against the controls. "It's real!"

The command center fell silent. The brute in Cataphract armor stomped towards the dais. A raised hand from the marshal stopped him in his tracks.

Lambert froze. He wasn't entirely sure how serious this spat between the senior officers was, but the nervous silence from the combined staff officers and sections around him filled him with a growing dread.

A general twisted a knob and a large holo sphere appeared over the dais, coalescing into the *Highest* in orbit over a verdant world. The capitol ship of the Hegemony looked as pristine as ever. It was several times larger than the *Authority*-class carriers that formed the nucleus of every Hegemony task force and fleet. The vessel bore statues of notable members of the Most High council over multi-story hangars. A grand dome rose over the dorsal hull, a shining beacon of light against the darkness.

Children across the Hegemony were given toys of the *Most High* when they entered Standard Academia at age seven. Every day of class began with singing "Hegemony, My Heart" to a holo of the ship and portraits of the Most High council. Every time Lambert saw the ship, it filled him with a bit of pride, though he'd never come within light-years of the vessel in his entire life.

The holo shifted to a naval tactical plot. Dozens of capital ships, all with Hegemony Naval insignia, converged on the *Highest*.

"This is Supreme Marshal Telemachus," came from the holo. The voice was low and even, one used to giving commands and being obeyed. "The Most High have failed the Hegemony. Their corruption has sabotaged our military on every front. My soldiers have died, their patriotism and fidelity exploited to fill the Most High's pockets. Worlds pried away from our Hegemony, campaigns lost from their graft and incompetence. What is the reward for calling out the corruption? What is the prize for integrity? Arrest and execution on the order of the Most High.

"It ends. Now. By my will."

The holo lit up with torpedoes, trailed by squadrons of fighters all converging toward the *Highest*. Cries of shock went up as the *Highest*'s escort fleet peeled away from the vessel, leaving it helpless and exposed.

Lambert's mouth fell open as the munitions closed in. Memories of his teachers telling him to imagine the *Most High* in the skies above and know the Hegemony was always watching over him lingered in the back of his mind.

Someone broke into sobs as warheads burst into brief stars against the *Highest*'s shields. More cried out in shock and dismay as the grand vessel reeled under the assault. There was no interdiction fire from the ship, the cannons and point defense turrets mute as the shields quivered. Shield emitter nodes overloaded and burst into brief pinpricks of stars.

Eleven shuttles burst from the forward bays and swept towards one of the retreating escort flotillas.

The massive vessel's shields failed under the onslaught. The next wave of missiles fired by bombers erupted against the hull, shattering the grand dome into millions of shrinking comets as the atmosphere blew away. The ship listed to port, exposing the ventral hull to the final attack that broke the ship's spine.

The *Highest* broke apart, gouts of fire bursting from the ruptured hull. The flames died quickly, leaving behind trails of smoke and still venting air. The next wave of missiles was unnecessary, but served to tear the living symbol of the Hegemony into a debris field. All she was and all that remained was destined to burn up in the skies of Elko Prime.

The eleven escape shuttles—undoubtedly bearing the members of the Highest Council—sped towards a small flotilla of ships breaking away from the escort fleet. Lambert bit his bottom lip, praying that the leaders might escape.

Fighters loyal to Telemachus closed rapidly. Lambert waited for the escort flotilla to launch their own interceptors. To turn and fire. To slow their march away from the remains of the *Highest*. To do anything to help.

They did nothing.

Rebel void fighters annihilated all the escape shuttles in less than a minute. Then the fighters circled in and around the wreckage, blasting any life pods or any chunk of debris large enough to shelter a human being.

Lambert's good leg buckled. His cane saved him from falling to the floor as a final and total truth hit him: the Hegemony was gone. The *Highest* was the eternal symbol of the government and it had just been annihilated. A coup from the most lauded military commander in decades, carried out with ruthless efficiency to ensure none survived. No member of the Most High or the many senior deputies could form a continuance of government . . . not when they were all dead.

The grand network of laws, trade and the simple belief that everyone within the Hegemony existed to make life better for everyone else in the Hegemony was gone. Lambert thought of Bretton, a minor world on the fringe of the Hegemony that could only thrive under the protection of something like the Hegemony.

What would happen to his home? To all the people he knew that would desperately need protection...protection that should be provided by the men of Bretton, by his 11th Battalion.

The worst realization that blossomed in Lambert's mind was that the galaxy had just become a much more selfish place.

The holo shifted to the head and shoulders of a pale-skinned man with deep blue eyes and short, platinum-colored hair. A vine-like scar traced from his collar on the left side of his neck up to his hairline.

A Skien soldier.

Marshal Telemachus raised his chin slightly.

"The Most High are gone. The taint festering in the deepest pits of the *Highest* will never corrupt the Hegemony again. With the Senate, Council of the Peoples and the Ordinal Bureaucracy eliminated, I am now the de facto leader of the Hegemony. Member worlds will remain member worlds while the government is reorganized on more... equitable terms. I do not desire this power—"

"Liar!" someone in the operations center shouted.

"—temporary measure. Those governors and others involved in the corrupt system have no place in the New Hegemony. I have attached a list of unacceptable individuals. Sworn officers of the Hegemony military have my permission to remove and replace them where prudent and necessary."

A scrolling list appeared by Telemachus' holo.

Lambert's head tilted back, as if the length and speed that the names appeared had struck him on the forehead.

Marshal Van Wyck's name popped out from the list and pulsed red.

"Nobody move!" Van Wyck yanked a grenade off his chest with one hand. The pin clattered against the floor. "Skiens," he pointed at the two generals on the dais with him, "take them into custody for treason."

"There can be no treason when there is no Hegemony," one of the generals said.

The brute in the Cataphract armor glanced at the holo of Telemachus, then back at Van Wyck.

"What are you doing? Arrest them!" Van Wyck pulled another grenade from his rig and held them both over his head.

Lambert decided he was not going to obey Van Wyck's orders and ducked into the scanner tunnel. He ignored warning buzzers as more shouting broke out from the command center. Shrill screams rose behind him.

Overhead pressure from double explosions slapped Lambert forward. He fell face-first through the metal detector on the other side. The two guards yelled at each other, and the conflict devolved into shoves as someone banged against the main doors, begging for help. Smoke seeped through fresh cuts in the doors.

Lambert used his cane to push himself halfway up when gunfire broke out. Bullets punched through the door and struck one of the guards in the back. Lambert stayed low, crawling towards the end of the hallway as more soldiers raced towards the command center.

Bullets stitched a line down the carpet next to Lambert's head. He kept moving, his focus on the other set of doors leading out into the less critical areas of the headquarters.

Just what was still under command of Marshal Van Wyck—or anyone else—was a question Lambert didn't have time for. The more able-bodied soldiers in proper Hegemony military uniforms ignored him as he finally crawled out of the hallway.

CHAPTER 12

Noah jolted awake. His boots swayed as Mason kept kicking them.

"I wasn't sleepin', sergeant." Noah blinked hard. "I mean I was. How long?"

"Shh!" Mason pointed two fingers at the window. "Got a vehicle scoping us out from the other side of the highway."

Noah pawed around either side of his legs looking for his carbine before he realized it was still attached to his chest rig. A picture of a ground car flanked by slums flickered on in the upper corner of his vision.

"It's just a car," Noah said.

"Check the EM filters. Don't move yet," Mason said.

Noah touched his forearm computer and pulled up a spectral analysis menu and ran the feed from the optics through the program. The car changed shape under different spectrums; most showed a turret mounted on the middle and the front angled like it was designed to deflect incoming hits.

"Hold on . . . what's going on?" Noah asked. "That some sort of camo?"

"We called them cope covers during my last deployment. Emitters mounted on the chassis can spoof orbital platforms and make them look like regular civvie cars. Up close and we can see through it. It's Alliance tech," Mason said. "Same with the APC. Cheap and dirty Sabrahs. They can get churned out by a decent foundry if they've got the right printers and electronics. Bet the Patties sold it to the Flags cheap. Bastards just love twisting the knife, don't they?"

"That's a tank out there?" Noah looked around, as if the roaches and faded paint were going to help. "W-what do we do?"

"Nothing yet," Mason said. "How'd it get so close? There's supposed to be another battalion on the other side of the highway screening against this exact sort of recon."

"SALT report." Noah flipped his forearm screen open. "Size . . . one APC. Activity . . . recon. Location . . . they use grid or latitude and longitude here? We didn't even get a map download—"

"I already sent it up. Just . . . relax," Mason said.

"I was plenty relaxed when I was asleep." Noah hopped up to a squat.

"You want to get woken up by me or when that Sabrah hits the building with a rocket?" Mason asked. "Yeah, that's what I thought. Ready an AT grenade. You should have an extended range one."

Noah found the grenade with a white stripe running down the handle. He unsnapped it from his chest harness and rehearsed how to use it. One hard yank on the handle would lengthen it and activate the sensor suite. All he had to do was paint the target with the optics and the grenade would feed him the angle to fire it.

"Don't activate it yet." Mason held up a hand. "They got cope shrouds, they probably have detection systems. You paint it and it'll put a big old target on us."

"We didn't rehearse defending against tanks in training," Noah said. "Why didn't they tell us to train for that?"

"Noah, at what point are you going to pick up that this isn't the best organized or led operation in the history of the Hegemony?" Mason shook his head. "It ain't called a SNAFU because things go smooth most of the time. Or some of the times. Or at all."

"What's a SNAFU?" Noah asked.

A thrum rose in the air. Mason froze, then moved a hand slowly to the barrel of his carbine. The buzz of drone rotors passed over the windows, moving towards the other fire team's position.

Noah opened his mouth to give a warning, but Mason lifted a hand to stop him. He touched his earpiece, then waved his fingertips across his throat. Even with their short-range IR comms, the drone was close enough to detect them if they used the radio.

The buzzing stopped outside of the bedroom . . . then doubled back slowly. Mason raised his carbine to his shoulder and aimed at the window.

Noah cracked the seal on his visor.

"Do we shoot it?" he asked.

"It sees us then we're made. Least we can keep it from seeing anything after that." Mason crouched behind the small table.

The buzzing rattled the filthy dishes, flushing out even more roaches. The barrel of the machine gun mounted to the drone dipped below the top of the window, pointed down the side of the building.

"Not. Yet." Mason's carbine trembled in his hands.

The drone dropped two feet and swung back from the building, turning the weapon at the brothers.

Noah heard a sharp whine and saw a bright flash of light. The drone crashed through the shattered window and bounced off the living room wall and landed belly up. Two of the rotors had been torn off and the chassis was on fire.

Mason stomped on the drone and kicked the compact machine gun clean off. The barrel clattered against the wall as tiny fléchette rounds spewed out of the severed ammo line on the gun and the drone body. Mason picked it up and hurled it out of the same window it came in.

"Fuck. Fuck!" Mason touched the side of his helmet.

"Shrike hit, you see it up there?" Corre asked over the radio.

"Roger, target destroyed but I'm pretty sure they know we're up here." Mason pointed a knife hand at Noah. "Hallway. Now!"

Noah went for the door and fumbled with the handle. He looked up and saw the frame had been knocked askew when they broke in and was jammed shut.

"If you've got line of sight on the vehicle, engage!" Corre shot back. "We've got friendlies coming across the highway and they need cover."

"Wait!" Mason grabbed Noah by the carry handle and turned him back toward the window. "ER grenade. Hurry!"

Noah looked down at his hands where the grenade had been, then saw it on the floor where he'd been sitting and abandoned it in the excitement.

"Sorry." Noah scooped it up and yanked hard on the handle. A targeting window appeared on his visor and he selected the APC masquerading as a ground car. He handle-pulsed as the internal launchers calibrated.

Across the highway, the APC lurched forward, putting most of its chassis behind another car. The turret slewed form-side towards Noah, then the barrel elevated slowly.

A green reticule appeared over the APC.

Noah pressed hard on the activation switch and the warhead popped out of the grenade with a *ploomph* and shot across the highway. The warhead bounded up on a quick burst from tiny onboard thrusters and sailed over the top—and thinner—armor. The warhead activated over the armored vehicle and unleased a single explosively shaped blob of tungsten that formed into a molten lance and pierced through the Sabrah.

Noah watched as smoke and dust enveloped the vehicle and thrust a fist into the air.

"Hell yeah! Nailed that son of a—"

Mason tackled him to the ground. Machine gun bullets from the Sabrah annihilated the window frame and blasted chunks out of the ceiling.

"Out!" Mason low-crawled toward the door, dragging Noah by the carry handle mounted onto the armor over his trapezius muscles.

The squad channel burst into life as Corre and others tried to shout out instructions.

"I thought I got it." Noah rolled onto his stomach and kept crawling. Mason's boots heels bumped into his visor as they made for the door. Another burst from the Sabrah tore through the bedroom.

"Maybe you got the driver," Mason said. "Gunner's still alive and he's pissed."

"Frag out!" Rochelle called through the squad channel. Noah heard the warhead activate in the distance and the incoming fire stopped. "Bad shot. Besco's relocating with his ER."

Mason punched the bottom of the door and it popped open. The two crawled into the hallway as the other apartment door burst open. Besco had an ER grenade in hand and ran for the hallway windows, the nearest one still intact by some miracle.

Besco punched the grenade through the glass, shattering it. The shards caught the light of nearby fires as they fell.

Mason reached toward the Flanker.

"Get do—"

A shell from the main gun of the Sabrah hit the outside wall opposite from where Besco stood. The concussion slapped Noah against the floor and a world-encompassing whine filled his ears. Pulverized concrete dust billowed through the hallway, dissipating after a few seconds.

Besco's arm lay a few feet from Mason, the grenade still clutched in his hand.

Mason reached out and pulled the severed limb to him, ignoring the spurt of blood across his chest. He wrenched the grenade out of the dead hand and pulled the handle to activate the targeting systems.

He reached up and held it against the bottom sill of the nearest window and pressed the firing stud a moment later. Mason fell flat, hands over his head.

A sharp *crack* shook the walls.

"Target destroyed," Corre said and a pic of a fireball where the Sabrah had been flickered on Noah's visor.

"Besco?" Noah lifted his head. The Flanker was in pieces amongst the rubble, wide pools of red spread over the detritus, turning pink in the dust.

"Position compromised," Mason said over the channel. "Relocating two floors down. Rochelle! Fucking move!"

Sergeant Rochelle and Saluan forced the door to their apartment open. Rochelle stared at the remains of his soldier, one hand on the doorknob.

"Rochelle!" Mason shouted. Saluan punched his sergeant in the back and that got the man to move again.

"I need his tags." Rochelle straddled the body and poked through the broken concrete.

"He ain't going nowhere. Come back when it's calm." Mason got to his feet and shoulder-bumped the stairwell door open.

Rochelle hesitated, then lifted a block. He let out an ugly groan between shock and horror and went for the stairs.

CHAPTER 13

Lambert jammed his cane against the sidewalk as he focused on the metal doors to the auxiliary void port where the *Izmir* was docked. His bad leg ached from the brace and blisters had risen from him moving at the fastest pace he could manage all the way from Central.

He felt like a turtle trying to outrun a wolf as the sound of sporadic fighting had grown from the headquarters building and spilled into the surrounding city. He'd shared a rather tense but silent robo-taxi ride from the nexus point. None of the other passengers had seemed aware of the tragedy that had befallen the Hegemony, and most of them had seemed quite drunk or otherwise inebriated.

The usual police bots on the stretch of road from his drop-off spot were missing, which made the sense of dread from the darkness around him even worse. Ahead, two men went to the access doors of the void port and banged their fists against the biometric readers, then turned away.

"Not a good sign," he said between pants, "not a good sign at all."

A citywide lockdown made perfect sense to him, but just who was in charge of anything to make that decision wasn't an answer he had.

"Hey. You," a gruff voice said from an alleyway as Lambert passed.

Lambert continued on, in case there was some other "you" that had been addressed.

"He thinks he can run?" another man said. "Get over here, cripple."

Lambert stopped. There was no use in exhausting himself further. He turned around.

Two large men stepped from the shadows, both in Hegemony army uniforms but with all the patches torn off.

"Who you loyal to, cripple?" one with a lit cigarette in his mouth asked. The other circled behind him.

"I'm afraid I don't follow," Lambert said. "I'm just trying to get back to my ship. Loyal to my need for a drink and a little sleep."

"This one's got jokes." The other man kicked Lamberts's cane into the gutter. "You like jokes, Chester?"

"I'm not in a jokin' mood either." Chester puffed smoke into Lambert's face. "See, things are different around here now. No more Hegemony to make us soldier slaves. So are you Hegemony or are you not?"

Lambert feared there was no answer that would satisfy the men, who seemed bent on a little retribution against anyone they could blame for their lot in life.

"I am a man of Bretton." Lambert bent his chin to the planetary crest on his lapel. "It's a bit of a better place than this."

His good leg trembled from bearing so much weight. He'd succumb to his disability in a most humiliating fashion in the next few minutes.

"Wait, Bretton." Chester plucked his cigarette from his mouth. "Ain't that the—"

There was a *snap* and Chester's head canted hard to one side. Blood spurted from a bullet hole and the large man crumpled to the ground.

"Oye, wait a loving second!" The other man raised his hands. He went down from two more snaps from the alleyway.

A chubby man with a wisp-thin comb-over and skin so pale it might not have seen natural light in years stepped out of the shadows. He wore a full Hegemony uniform, though it was far too tight across his belly.

He lowered a silenced pistol to his side.

"Colonel Lambert, I presume?" the man said. "I have a proposition for you that I think you'll want to consider."

He picked the cane up from the gutter, shook off some fluid from an unidentifiable puddle and handed it back to Lambert.

"Thank you." Lambert leaned heavily on the cane. "These two were..."

"Up to no good. Amazing how the lack of overarching authority brings out one's true nature. Shall we continue this discussion aboard the *Izmir*? I'd rather not speak out here. These two likely didn't have friends, but they might have cohorts."

"I'm fine with that," Lambert said and started towards the entrance to the void port. "But I believe the way's locked." He glanced up at the top of the high walls guarded by rolls of razor wire and automated gun turrets.

"Won't be a problem for me." The man jogged ahead, holding onto his belt to keep his pants from falling. He put his palm to a biometric reader. When it went red, he bit down on his thumb and yanked the finger hard. The fake digit pulled open. He shined a red light emanating from beneath the fingernail at the reader and it went blue.

The doors chugged open.

Lambert hurried inside and his savior locked the doors behind him. In the void port, the non-Hegemony crews of several ships lounged about hookahs or kicked a soccer ball between groups.

"They have no idea," the man said.

"Wait, who are you and how did you do that?" Lambert asked.

"I am Neville Harris, Hegemony Intelligence Agency," he said. "You are Brent Lambert, Colonel (Planetary Militia), one each, supernumerary quartermaster of the Eleventh Bretton Infantry. Date of birth—"

"I know who I am," Lambert said. "What do you want? And how did you know—"

"It's best we don't discuss things here." Harris' eyes darted from side to side.

"Captain Mehmet runs a tight ship. I can't just get you aboard, not while you've still got a pistol in your hand and I've only got your name. I do appreciate the help but as you seem to have your ear to the ground as to what's happening... help me help you with Mehmet," Lambert said.

"This isn't in your psych profile. The agent on Bretton did an incomplete workup on you. Let us walk and talk on the way to the *Izmir*. Only thirteen-point-seven percent of personnel in this sealed facility have conversational Hegemony Standard ability. They likely won't understand much from any snippets they overhear." Harris pulled the silencer from his pistol and slipped both into a holster on the small of his back, though he was almost too fat to reach it.

"The news of the Hegemony's sudden and total collapse wasn't a surprise to everyone," Harris said as they walked down a wide street between docked civilian vessels. "Members of the HIA were aware of the cracks in the system and predicted that a senior military leader would take umbrage with the growing disaffection with the Most High council. That actor being Telemachus wasn't in the top five of the most likely candidates, but we did factor him into the equation."

"You knew this was going to happen?" Lambert asked.

"We predicted it with low certainty. Not enough for the HIA to take overt action but enough for us to make contingency plans for our—for the Hegemony's survival. Yes. Indeed." Harris cleared his throat. "We estimated there were at least two more years before a dissolution occurred and we assumed there would be a period of open civil war first. Actual war. Not police actions such as Dahrien."

"The HIA saw this coming and did nothing?" Lambert hissed.

"All projections were off, but it was possible." Harris waved a hand over his head. "Imagine you were one of the Most High and the HIA came to you and said there was a reasonable chance of the Hegemony collapsing and then suggesting massive corrective action. How do you think it would've gone over with the Most High council?"

"As they're all dead, they probably should've listened," Lambert said.

"Reasonable deduction but irrelevant. The HIA Director, who likely perished aboard the *Highest*, was certain he'd be suspected of plotting a coup and executed immediately. He was one of the best Mittering aberrations in the entire Hegemony. Almost never wrong with his qualitative assessments. Almost," Harris said.

"I don't see what this has to do with me," Lambert said.

"Well, it's more to do with the *Izmir* and the amount of Tollonium Energy Units in her fuel tanks and her in-atmo flight characteristics."

"What?" Lambert stopped, only a few dozen yards from the *Izmir*'s short ramp on the port side.

"Brass tacks, is it?" Harris came close and continued in a conspiratorial whisper. "I can get you off this shithole. I can get your entire battalion off this shithole, too. And then I can get you all back to Bretton and that ship back to Union space where it wants to go . . . all I want in return is safe passage."

"To go . . . where?" Lambert asked.

"Bretton is sufficient for my plans at the moment. Me entrusting my personal safety to you, along with yours, should help convince everyone that I have a vested interest in getting you all back to your voluntarily techno-archaic backwater," Harris said quickly. "My kind are about to be an endangered species across the Hegemony and I'd rather be anywhere else. Now, can I pitch the specifics to Captain Mehmet, or do I need to fall back on my secondary choice? The *Schwanz* is back there."

"Let me introduce you to the captain," Lambert said.

Lambert limped up the *Izmir*'s crew ramp, Harris moving slowly a few steps behind him, his hands high. Captain Mehmet, the look on his face growing more and more concerned as Lambert approached, held a hand out to help the colonel. Lambert pushed the offering away with the handle of his cane.

"I've found I'm more than capable of late," Lambert said. He stepped over the threshold and put his back against the bulkhead and pointed at Harris. "He's with me and you need to hear him out. I do suggest you button this ship up, Captain Mehmet, sooner than later."

"Permission to come aboard," Harris said. "I am armed. A single pistol on my belt."

"Surrender it." Mehmet took the weapon from Harris. He ejected the magazine and attached battery pack and spun the weapon in his hand. "This isn't standard Hegemony tech."

"I've quite a bit more of that," Harris laughed nervously. "Aboard? Me? Now?"

Mehmet raised his wrist to his mouth and spoke quickly. A hatch opened further down the passageway and a broad-shouldered sailor in baggy pants and with a face that looked like it had stopped a ground car the hard way climbed out. He stomped a foot to the deck and grunted.

"This is Mr. Barnes," Mehmet said. "He's here in case there's a reason for Mr. Barnes to rip someone's face off."

Mr. Barnes cracked his knuckles and grunted again.

"Permission to come aboard granted." Mehmet bowed slightly to Harris. The stairs retracted into the ship and the door locked behind them.

"You look like you've been on the front line." Mehmet glanced at the fire-singed heels of Lambert's boots. "What happened?"

Lambert took a handkerchief from a breast pocket and dabbed at his forehead.

"You have no idea?" Lambert narrowed his eyes at Mehmet.

"No one will," Harris said. "The comms networks across the planet have been disabled. Standard practice in this sort of situation."

"Idea about what?" Mehmet glared at Harris. "The entire planetary network was shut down after a ship arrived from hyperspace. I've heard nothing since you left to get our final approval to unload the ship. And then finally pay me. Did you have to burn an office down or something?" Mehmet asked.

"Yes . . . indeed." Lambert turned his eyes to a pair of sailors behind Mehmet and canted his head slightly.

Mehmet turned to the pair and spoke to them in their native language and snapped his fingers twice. The two turned and ran off, a spring to their step.

"I said we finally have good news and to prep the ship for take-off," Mehmet said. "There is good news . . . finally. Right?"

Lambert cleared his throat. Harris grimaced.

"Yes, but no. Mostly no. In fact . . . we have a problem." Lambert took a deep breath and related recent events to Mehmet, stopping the recap before he met with Harris.

The veteran spacer took the news in, then steadied himself against the bulkhead with one hand.

"We are two hundred light-years deep into the Hegemony and the entire thing just disintegrated into anarchy? How . . . will I get paid?" Mehmet looked down the passageway where his sailors had gone and covered his mouth with a palm.

"Indeed, that poses a number of questions. But there is a solution, one Mr. Harris and I would like to discuss with you somewhere with fewer listening ears. Long walk from here to the command center, I assure you," Lambert said. "It boils down to the good faith and credit of the Bretton government and our trust in Mr. Harris here. Who has saved my bacon once today."

"I . . . beg your pardon?" Mehmet asked.

"Paying your sailors and making this voyage profitable for you and your partners is attainable, captain. You remember when you signed the consignment to transport the battalion from Bretton to here, yes? As part of the Governor's instructions from the Hegemony, I was issued a letter of credit." Lambert took out a small slate and pressed a button on the side. He mumbled into a corner and a golden certificate projected from the screen, and he held in front of Mehmet's face.

"That was in the event my ship broke down and needed repairs en route to here." Mehmet swiped his hand through the letter of credit but the holo remained.

"Ah, tut tut tut . . . read paragraph fourteen," Lambert chided. "The governor's duly appointed representative—that's me—can take on debts to safeguard and guarantee travel of the Bretton Eleventh. The debt is secured by the Bretton government, not the Hegemony."

Mehmet twisted around to peer down the passageway, then turned to look over Lambert's shoulder. He looked across the ceiling, then under his boots.

"I don't see the Bretton government or any money," Mehmet said. "Stop being clever and tell me what your brilliant plan is before I throw you down the gangplank to save your own life before I have to tell my crew there's no money. No. Fucking. Money."

"There most certainly is money . . . on Bretton." Lambert nodded once with great emphasis. "If you and the *Izmir* will transport the battalion *back* to Bretton, I can guarantee your fee for both transits . . . plus a bonus."

Mehmet stared at him for several heartbeats, then finally blinked.

"Why don't I just wait for this Telemachus to take full control of the government? New boss the same as the old boss. New boss doesn't want to pay the old boss's debts? The creditors will find a new boss who will. Same as it ever was."

"Telemachus is a Skien soldier," Lambert sighed. "They're rather problematic to begin with, and he just murdered the Most High and blew up the Highest, then sent out a death list through the entire Hegemony. He's not going to gain or maintain control of anything but the forces that are already loyal to him. Deseret? Tirana? Sudetas? All those sectors will declare independence from *him*. Especially when I saw the names of their Most High representatives on his death list. Telemachus won't be in charge of much, and especially not of the treasury."

Mehmet sucked his lips in, his eyes darting from side to side.

"Then what are you going to pay me in? Hegemony credits? I don't think I can spend them anywhere, especially not when I get my ship home to the Union and never come back to this disaster," Mehmet said.

"I can pay you in kind. Goods worth current market value of your fee. Doubled. Plus ten percent."

"Only ten percent!" Mehmet shouted. He flinched and looked back to make sure no one heard him.

"I'm authorized to go fifteen percent over contracted for extraordinary events, which this undoubtedly qualifies as," Lambert said. "The governor on Bretton, Engelier, happens to be my second cousin and I have a good amount of sway with him. I'm sure a bonus can be arranged. Once we're home. All of us."

Mehmet raised a finger, waggled it back and forth, then pressed it to his lips. His eyes closed in thought.

"Staying in the Hegemony and hauling freight might've been your original plan," Lambert said quietly, "but that's no longer tenable. I imagine you and your crew—and your creditors back home—want this ship back in Union space. Bretton is on the border. I'll see your hold filled with enough of our exports to make this whole ordeal worthwhile. You have my word."

"And you see, that is the problem." Mehmet waggled his finger again. "You seem to be the only honest and aboveboard person I've met in the Hegemony. I wish you were a dishonest scumbag I could toss out of an airlock and forget about . . . but you are the best option I have for getting paid. For paying my crew. For me to get this ship home with my ledger in the black once all is said and done."

"Then we're agreed?" Lambert held out his hand.

"This is not how I agree to terms. You're going straight to your quarters to write up a contract before I say a word to my crew about any of this." Mehmet sneered at the offered handshake.

"That is legitimate," Lambert said.

"You did see that my landing gear is still locked down by the port authority, yes?" Mehmet raised an eyebrow. "And your battalion is not aboard. These are significant problems."

"I've yet to meet a lock that can't be defeated by an appropriately sized axle grinder, have you?" Lambert asked.

"I don't have—"

"I can unlock the cleats remotely." Harris held up a hand. "It's rather simple and allows us to leave without alerting the other ships that something's amiss as we cut through the docking clamps."

"He's proven rather . . . capable," Lambert said. "He got me through the outer gates with some sort of secret squirrel magic . . . and we still have the battalion's foundries aboard that can print out an industrial-grade axle grinder in fifteen minutes."

"There's a matter of fuel," Mehmet said. "I've enough TEUs aboard to get into orbit and maybe to a hyper transfer point, but nowhere else, and your battalion isn't aboard, Lambert."

"I have contingencies in place for both those problems," Harris said. "There is an auxiliary void port close to Tabuk City where the battalion is currently located. Fort Triumph, ironic but we giggle over that later. There's enough TEUs there to get this ship back to Bretton. We simply need to secure the fuel depot and land there. I have all the overrides."

"And who's in charge of this fuel depot at the moment?" Mehmet asked.

"The Hegemony, or a commander that still thinks he's in charge of something in the Hegemony's name," Harris said. "I have the fuel transfer orders signed by Marshal Van Wyck right here." He tapped a pouch within his jacket.

"Where were you when I needed something signed?" Lambert asked.

"All of this sounds ... plausible, but the *Izmir* still needs some supplies before we make for orbit," Mehmet said. "The compressors on the forward gear are shot and—"

"Beg, borrow ... bribe." Lambert shrugged. "Do whatever you need to. I'll add in a cost-plus clause to our contract to make you whole for any expenditures. But I need receipts."

"You want a receipt for a bribe?" Mehmet raised an eyebrow.

"At least an invoice." Lambert shook his head. "Now, if you'll excuse me. I need to go to the bridge and get in touch with Jematé before word reaches the front line. I suggest you work quickly before the city collapses into chaos and you have to shoot for any items you need."

"The contract—"

"Not the best use of my time. I'm not leaving without my men, and you'll get nothing until they're delivered home. Safely." Lambert's face hardened.

Mehmet considered this for a moment, then held out his hand.

Lambert shook it.

"I still want a contract," the captain said, "and we're locking Harris into a berthing until he's needed. I'm not letting a Hegemony Intelligence Agency ghost wander about and beg questions from the crew. Mr. Barnes?"

Mr. Barnes grunted.

"Take him to the chai boy room and rip his face off if he tries to leave without permission," Mehmet said.

"Oh, there are chai boys?" Harris' mood improved. Mr. Barnes put a heavy hand on his shoulder, then tugged at Harris' fatty jowls. "Let's get going then, yes?"

"Contract will be done soon as my hair isn't on fire, Captain Mehmet." Lambert limped down the passageway. "Do get this ship prepared as soon as possible. Things will only get more impossible from here on out."

"*Şeytanın bacağını kırmak,*" Mehmet called out. "May we beat bad luck."

The captain raised the comms bead built into his wrist band and began speaking.

CHAPTER 14

Sergeant Corre rubbed his back against his Cataphract armor. Wearing the suit offered a number of advantages on the battlefield, but while he was nearly immune to most small arms fire and had decent heating and cooling (to protect the electronics, not the soldier), there wasn't a Cataphract suit anywhere in the Hegemony that let a man scratch between his shoulders.

Corre raised his Gatling cannon and pushed the optics out to peek around the corner of a bullet-ridden wall. The gap across the highway was silent, but the occasional firefight still raged on the slum side of the city. Corre inched back and sent a status update to Malo, the platoon sergeant.

"Air's clear," Boyle said next to him. The other Cataphract had his helm partially open, a nicotine stick between his lips. "How'd they get an APC that close to us?"

"Holo screens," Corre said. "Now we know they've got 'em, we know better than to let *any* vehicle get that close. You'd think the units on the other side of the highway would've sent a warning soon as they knew."

"Nothing's to standard out here," Boyle said, "and our squishies are suffering for it. Besco's a good kid."

"They're all good kids," Corre said. "We're less without him. Donan. Martin and Thomas from 3rd Squad too."

"Your first day go like this on your last tour, Sarge?" Boyle asked. "Because old timers like you never mentioned a goat screw like this during the Colima tour."

"Colima was different, but—'old timers'? Don't make me straighten you out before your combat cherry gets properly popped, punk," Corre said. "Flankies always have higher casualty rates. We've got the armor to take the punch and the firepower to return the hate. And I've got a feeling we'll get a chance to earn our pay soon."

"Is the LT going to volunteer us for something brave and bold?" Boyle asked. "Not that I mind getting some licks in . . . but they've got drones. Lots of drones."

"It's almost like they've been fighting Cataphracts for years and learned getting in a stand-up fight with us is a losing proposition. They're not stupid," Corre said.

"Corre, VIPs coming in. Head on a swivel," Lieutenant Govrien said over the radio. "Think we've got a mission."

"Damn it, Sarge." Boyle raised an arm and slid his nicotine stick into a fabric slot glued to the forearm. "Do you have to be so damn eager? Gold bars like Govrien can smell it. Gives them confidence that they know what they're doing."

"We can sit here as big shiny targets for the drones, or we can kick them in the dick until they realize not to mess with us. Which do you want?" Corre asked.

"'Kick'?" Boyle snapped the mortar tube built into the back of his armor out and locked it into its firing position. "High explosives can send a better message."

"All platoon Cataphracts prep for assault." Govrien sent a graphic to Corre. The company was to attack across the highway and seize a two-story building several hundred meters into the slums.

"Ah . . . shit, that us on the front line?" Boyle asked.

"Yup." Corre sent the orders to the rest of the squad. "Tallec, move to the upper floors and provide overwatch as we move. If it ain't a Cataphract, assume it's hostile. Herve. Leroi. Buddy team on the other side of this building. Boyle and I will bound forward first."

"Roger." Herve raised a thumb where he stood against the same wall and revved his Gatling cannon several times.

"Okay . . . bounding overwatch. My fire sector's zero to ninety degrees, friendlies behind us," Boyle mumbled. A new message beeped on their visors. "Fire mission! Fire mission. One dazzler round . . . what do I do? I'm supposed to—"

Corre whacked heavy knuckles against Boyle's breastplate.

"You authorize the mission and clamp down. It's friggin' dummy proof," Corre said.

Hydraulic spikes bit into the concrete from one of Boyle's boots. He stepped out with the other to slightly more than shoulder-width apart and the other boot locked in place. There was a whir of hydraulics as the autoloader on his back put a round into the base of his mortar tube.

"Clear!"

The mortar round blasted into the air and arced over the highway. The rumble of heavy footfalls from approaching Cataphracts sounded in the distance.

"Bull rush?" Boyle asked.

"You're damn right." Corre spun up his Gatling cannon. The dazzler shell—along with a half dozen others—burst over the slums. Blinding light saturated the muddy streets and shanties with enough intensity to ignite hanging laundry and trash piles.

"Move!" Corre sidestepped out from cover and charged down the street. The Cataphract's footfalls cracked pavement as he crossed onto the highway. The suit obeyed the haptic feedback sensors built into the inner lining, moving as fast as he could.

Small arms fire broke out from a building across the highway and was quickly overwhelmed with returned hate from the Flankers covering the assault. Corre focused on crossing the open terrain where he was most vulnerable. A pip on his visor's map showed Boyle was a few strides behind him.

Corre hopped over a low concrete wall on the highway shoulder. He spotted the objective, a three-story building with bullet pockmarks across the façade, and kept moving. His suit's sensors scanned for any movement or radio transmissions. While the smoke from small fires was clouding his vision and washing out his IR optics, the enemy would be having an even worse time trying to recover from the initial attack.

A scrap metal door swung open a block ahead of him. Three men with red cloths wrapped around their heads and faces stumbled out. All had crossed ammunition bandoliers over their torsos, and one carried a Flanker carbine. The others had beaten-up rifles that looked like they were for hunting, not war.

Corre skidded to a halt and swept his Gatling cannon up. Recoil from a quick burst rocked him back. The barrels' flash stung Corre's eyes through the visor, which belatedly darkened slightly to compensate.

The three insurgents fell to the ground in pieces, the building behind them torn apart as the rounds over-penetrated their bodies with ease.

"Daggers out! Daggers out!" Govrien ordered over the radio. Corre focused on an activation icon on his visor and a camera built into the helmet read his eye movement and the icon pulsed green.

"Loose!" Corre grunted, fully activating the drone.

A drone fell off his back and shot into the air. It streaked forward, seeking out targets on its own.

Corre continued toward the objective building. Recon from the Daggers lit up on his visor. Red icons of dismounted infantry in and around the shanties and clustered against the walls of the target building almost gave him pause.

Almost.

"Boyle, drop frag rounds on the troop concentrations." Corre marked two for the other Cataphract. He didn't wait for confirmation before spinning up his Gatling cannon and firing through a cluster of shanty huts. They collapsed under the gale of fire and the target icons flickered with superimposed skulls over them.

The crump of mortar strikes broke over the near-constant gunfire of the attacking Cataphracts and the insurgents.

"Shrike deployment. Shrike deployment," a calm female voice said from his onboard system. His shoulder trembled as the counter-drones spat from the launcher. A rocket exploded mere yards overhead. His armor rang as fragmentation careened off the plating. He brought one arm up, shielding himself with the thick shoulder plate as more rockets impacted around him.

One shell landed in a hut next to him. The blast wave knocked him off his feet and sent him face first into a muddy puddle. Corre's vision darkened as the visor was covered in what wasn't all mud. He got to his knees as the visor vibrated so rapidly it made his teeth hurt. Gunk was shaken loose and he could see again.

"Armor! Incoming armor!" Govrien called out.

"They think toy cars are going to stop us?" Boyle asked. "Coming down the main route flanking the target building."

"Got it." Corre activated the rocket mount on his back and the housing extended away from his back. The servos squealed as it lifted back and over his shoulder . . . then froze. An error code flashed on his visor.

"My launcher jammed. Leroi, shift over to cover the road—"

A shell shrieked past him and took out a cluster of shanties where four of the platoon's Cataphracts had congregated. Their icons went dark instantly as smoke and flame billowed into the night sky, washing out the sliver of the moon uncovered by the eclipse.

"It's not an APC! That's a goddamn Wolverine tank," Boyle shouted. "Is it one of ours?"

"If it's shootin' at us, it ain't friendly," Corre said.

"—effective fire on that target now!" Captain Dalois cut in on the company net. "Target the optics before it can—"

Dalois' transmission echoed the explosion from the tank's next main gun round. Another volcano of smoke and flame erupted further ahead of Corre.

Corre cycled the rocket launcher mounted on his back again and got the same error. He tried to reach back for it, but the bulk of his armor wouldn't allow him to touch it.

"Hell of a time not to have Flankies. I'm dismounting," Corre said.

"You're *what*?" Boyle was across the main road, on one knee. He raised a hand and waved frantically at Corre.

The squad leader slapped the emergency release on his armor, and the breastplate, thigh plates and helmet flew open. Straps around his shoulders, waist and knees retracted into their housings and Corre jumped out of the suit.

The air was thick with acrid smoke and stank of open sewers. He darted around to the back of the suit, his feet squishing through the bottom of the puddle and sinking slightly into the filth.

He pulled the emergency release on the rocket launcher and the weapon tipped out and into his arms. It was heavy enough to make him sink even further into the muck. He found the manual controls and glanced over the glow-in-the-dark instructions printed on the barrel.

"Down. Down!" Boyle's voice came from the speakers in the suit and Corre's earbud.

Corre fell backwards, pushing the rocket away from him to keep it from getting wet. He plopped into the filthy puddle and got a taste of it as it splashed over his mouth.

Gatling rounds snapped overhead. The hurried staccato of their passing and pressure from the faster-than-sound bullets pushed him deeper into the mud.

"Clear!" Boyle shouted.

Corre rolled hard to his left, the mud sucking against his body as he struggled to his feet. The smell oozed all over him and seeped through his bodysuit.

"Where is it?" Corre brought the relatively clean weapon onto his shoulder.

Another blast from the main gun round answered him. Corre hinged an optics package on top of the launcher down in front of his face and the onboard targeting suite flickered to life.

Corre sidestepped onto the road. A wire outline of the Wolverine tank, a massive beast taller than he was in his suit and with turret armor that angled toward the main gun, appeared on the target. He flicked a finger to select a high-angle attack and waited for the outline to go green with a solid lock.

The turret slewed toward him. An amber border flashed on the targeter.

"Friend or Foe error. Confirm target," chirped from the weapon.

Corre switched to manual and pulled the trigger. The rocket screamed out of the launcher, leaving his ears deadened like they'd just been stuffed with cotton. Corre dropped the launcher and leaped back towards his armor and landed in the same puddle.

There was a *crump* of impact and then silence.

"Hit!" Boyle shouted. "Got ammo cooking off inside that mother—"

The Wolverine burst apart. A flaming wheel rolled between Boyle and Corre along with hot scraps of metal that dug into the dirt street. Another blast and more remnants of the tank sizzled through the air.

One struck Corre's suit, knocking it into a wobble. Corre tried to hold it up, but it tipped back and fell into the deepest part of the puddle. Brackish water splashed up, raining down on Corre and into the inside of his suit.

"Mounting up!" Corre stuck one leg into the suit and felt something cold and slick against his shin. He grimaced and slid back into the

Cataphract. He punched a button on the inside of the breastplate and it closed around him, fully functional.

He hopped back onto his feet and a vile smell filled the inside of his helmet. It percolated through the entire suit and Corre choked down bile.

"Dalois down," Govrien called out through the company net. "Second Squad. First Squad, secure the objective and search for any survivors. I'll maintain security with Third and Fourth squads."

"Captain's down?" Boyle asked. "How bad?"

"Bad enough he can't give orders," Corre coughed. "Move, LT's still giving us orders."

Corre bounded forward toward the two-story building that hadn't suffered any fresh damage.

"You okay?" Boyle ran along the other side of the street, a few steps behind him.

"Yes. No. I'm not hurt but my ears are ringing like a son of a bitch," Corre said. The burning remnants of the Wolverine were close to the objective building. Dead insurgents and downed Cataphracts were close by.

Only Herve appeared on Corre's visor as they approached the building.

"Where's Leroi?" Corre asked.

"He's...down, Sarge. Got clipped by a rocket when you dismounted," Herve said, his voice distant. "Nothing I could do."

Corre's jaw clenched hard.

"Keep moving. We'll pick him up on the way out," Corre said. The three turned a corner and found the doors to the target building torn from the hinges and lying in the dirt.

A Cataphract from 3rd Squad—Clement—backed out of the building, his weapon held low across his legs.

"Saint's Mercy..." Clement said.

"What? It clear or not?" Corre swung his barrel into the building. His optics adjusted so he could see the interior clearly. There was no ceiling for the second story, only exposed rafters running from wall to wall.

Dead insurgents were strewn across the ground. Corpses hung from the rafters, their arms overhead and tied at the wrists. The hanging dead wore the remnants of Hegemony uniforms. Their stomachs were disemboweled, intestines dangled amongst their legs and pooled like loose ropes beneath their boots that swayed gently in the breeze.

"Blue six...no viable prisoners," Corre's mouth went bone dry. "I repeat, no viable prisoners."

"Heard. Company, fall back in sequence," Govrien ordered. "Get to the other side of the highway ASAP. If we can't recover suits, collect tags and drop cinder grenades."

"Herve," Corre said, backing out of the slaughterhouse, "can we get Leroi out of here?"

The cinder grenades were small, barely the size of a larger toy marble, but the thermite inside would reduce a fallen Cataphract to slag in seconds.

"His arm's one place. Rest of him another," Herve said. "Don't think we can dump him in a body bag without dismounting."

"Then get us back to him and we'll do the best we can," Corre said.

"Christ almighty." Boyle looked into the building. "That's what they do to prisoners?"

"We'll knock it down with mortars soon as we're clear," Corre said. "They won't keep it."

"Fall back," Govrien said. "Everyone fall back."

"Moving." Corre crossed himself.

CHAPTER 15

Not having a map or compass didn't make finding Tabuk City impossible, not when Felix's ears worked. The *crump* of explosions carried through the valley, growing stronger as he approached.

He stayed in the jungle, a few dozen yards away from a highway leading to the city that he intersected with a few hours after leaving the Antares priestess behind. The encroaching night drew him closer to the shoulder as light faded out.

The occasional flash from explosions and delayed booms served as a wartime lighthouse to guide him in, though what he'd find in the city—or even which side of the lines he was on—remained to be seen.

Felix stumbled through low vines, cursing the darkness. He took a sip from his water bladder and spat out grit. The whine of approaching electric trucks rose behind him. He ducked behind a tree trunk before the headlights could pass over him. A pair of open-topped trucks, both full of armed insurgents, sped toward the city.

Light glinted off chrome in a slight depression next to the shoulder. He waited until the sound of the trucks died down, then rushed at a crouch to the object. The corpse-smell hit him first, strong enough to make him gag.

A dead man lay beneath a motorcycle. He was elderly and dressed in the normal Dahrien attire of linen tunic and pants that ended at the calves. Flies buzzed around his face and hands.

Felix couldn't tell what killed him, but the motorcycle's front tire was badly bent and blown out.

141

"Sorry, buddy." Felix waved the mat of flies away and lifted a small hatch on the motorcycle body just behind the handlebars. The power rod was still in the housing. He hooked a finger into a ring and twisted.

The power rods were high-density batteries. Empty rods were deposited and exchanged at charging stations for smaller vehicles like motorcycles or bundled together for light trucks. Thanks to one of the fewer brilliant moves by the Hegemony Acquisition Corps, civilian power rods were compatible with Flanker and Cataphract armor.

Felix removed his helmet and popped the rod into a recess on the back. He thumbed a panel open and almost dropped the helmet in shock when it read nearly half charged.

"Ha ha!" He lifted the helmet and shook it over his head in triumph.

A truck came around a bend, the headlights stabbing into the jungle behind Felix. He cursed and dove into the underbrush, rolling into tall grass. He slipped the helmet on and breathed a sigh of relief as the cooling systems activated.

The approaching truck was a rusted-out ramshackle wreck of a vehicle. The cab's panels came from several different models. The passenger window was missing and the windshield had a crack across the bottom. The cargo bed was full of scrap metal and appliances. It was all piled close to the cab, but the back looked vacant.

The driver must be working on a washing machine collection, Felix thought as he readied his carbine.

The truck screeched to a halt. The bric-a-brac in the bed shifted forward. A bucket full of hand tools fell out and dumped its contents across the shoulder. A man with a lit cigarette in his mouth hopped out of the cab. He kicked the tools back toward the bucket as his head craned up to look over the crashed motorcycle and dead man.

He took tentative steps towards the wreck, then jumped back waving his hand at his nose to dispel the smell. He picked up most of the loose tools and chucked the bucket into the truck bed, then went back to the cab.

An idea came to Felix, one his sore feet endorsed. He slid out of the brush and hurried toward the back of the truck. He put one hand on the back gate and peeked over it. The view to the cab was blocked by the piles of scrap metal and there was enough room for him to lay down. He waited for the truck to roll forward and jumped in the back.

It headed down the highway and didn't immediately pull over, as Felix feared. He fought the urge to sleep as it rumbled on. Not that the hunks of wood and old wrenches between his back and the truck bed were going to make much of a cushion.

CHAPTER 16

"Then where the hell is the casualty collection point?" Perrin asked another officer in a holo. The battalion's operations center was in general disarray in the basement of an abandoned school. Soldiers set up additional holo workstations while Perrin continued his discussion.

"You tell me?" A tired-looking woman shrugged her shoulders. "The Bretton...where the hell is that? Anyway, *you're* supposed to have your own aid station and doctors just like every other infantry battalion in the Hegemony. It's not my—"

"Our support units aren't due to arrive for another week. Marshal Van Wyck sent us to the front lines within hours of planetfall. Now, I've got sixteen litter patients that need to be transferred to the next higher level of care. Where is the brigade aid station? Or even division?" Perrin put his hands on his hips.

"Central doing Central things." The woman rolled her eyes and flicked through a holo off screen. "Says here your unit's in the Beta Four trench sector."

"We are not—"

"*Obviously,*" she sighed heavily. "Fine, the hospital in Denmole sector's got the auto docs running and I've prioritized your unit's urgent cases. Get them over there soon as you can before someone who's where they're supposed to be shows up."

"Thank you." Perrin tilted his head forward and the holo went blank. "Lieutenant Rutherford! Load up the casualties and get them to..." Perrin found the hospital and forwarded the location to the medical services officer.

One disaster after another. Perrin checked his messages for the next fire he had to piss on when there was a tap on his shoulder. He turned and saw a rather pale Sergeant Roux. The communications soldier had a slate clutched in his hands, the screen held tight to his chest. The half visor attached to his backpack studded with short antennae with a thick wire was lifted up on his head, not down over his eyes where it was supposed to be while the battalion was in combat.

"Um...sir? I think you need to see this," Roux said.

"Is it more important than getting reinforcements or air support before the next enemy armored attack?" Perrin turned back to the situation holo.

"Yes. Yes, sir, it is." Roux swallowed hard. "It's a message from Lambert for Colonel Jematé, but the colonel's not answering his comms."

"The colonel's with our KIAs; he's not to be disturbed. Especially not from anything Lambert has to say. He should've had our foundries ready to ship with us when we—"

"Sir!" Roux's outburst quieted the rest of the command center. "You need to see this. Right now, sir." He tapped the corner of the slate against Perrin's shoulder.

Perrin turned around, ready to give a dressing down that Roux would never forget. The soldier looked like he was on the verge of tears, his bottom lip trembling.

"Alright." Perrin took the slate and pressed his thumb against a biometric reader. He squinted hard, his eyes exhausted from too many days awake and too little rest. The major frowned as he skimmed over the header from the message; his face darkened as he continued to the end.

"This...can't be real." Perrin raised his eyes to Roux. "Must be some sort of propaganda by the enemy."

"It came through with Bretton Territorial Guard ciphers and authorizations. I only got it to my systems because I haven't cleaned out the cache on my decryption banks." Roux nudged his backpack with an elbow.

"It must be a forgery," Perrin said. "An...exceptional one at that. AI can replicate tone and mannerisms and—"

"The prayers, sir," Roux lowered his voice. "We don't write those down. We don't speak them outside of the High Holy Days."

"I'm not the most theological of people, Roux." Perrin raised the back of his hand to cover his mouth, then tapped on the screen. "This is ridiculous. Impossible."

"Colonel Jematé is a man of the faith, sir. The message is for him, and I believe he'll find it more credible than you will with Lambert's inclusion of our bonds of faith," Roux said. "Are you going to tell the colonel or—"

"I will," Perrin snapped. "You . . . are correct to bring this to me right away. Keep this close hold, you understand?"

Roux stared at him.

"See if there's confirmation of this on any other net, will you?" Perrin asked.

"There hasn't been a transmission out of Central for the last four hours and fifty-two minutes. Lambert's message was sitting in my queue for over an hour before I noticed it," Roux said.

"Keep looking." Perrin walked out of the operations center at an even pace. If the operations officer were to run around like a chicken with its head cut off, it would only spark panic and rumors across the battalion. Though, he suspected the entire headquarters would know about the message by the time he finished speaking with Colonel Jematé.

He found the colonel on the school playground, or what remained of it. The slides and swings had been peppered with artillery shrapnel and never repaired. Faded murals of children waving up at a depiction of the *Highest* made Perrin double take at it.

The colonel was out of his Cataphract armor, on one knee before a line of body bags. The colonel leaned forward and put a hand on one bag and recited a prayer. Perrin waited until it was complete and the colonel had extended his arms out to his side and brought his palms together with a sudden slap.

Jematé stood, then stepped to the next body bag and looked to the sky.

"Colonel, sir." Perrin cleared his throat.

"We don't have a chaplain with us, Easton. It's my duty to commend their souls to our Lord and you're interrupting me . . . why?" Jematé gave Perrin a dirty look.

"There's . . . a crisis, sir. A possible crisis. All based on word from Colonel Lambert. The encryption checks out, but this could be a deception operation by the enemy." Perrin held out the data slate.

"These Flags seem more interested in killing us in a stand-up fight and butchering our corpses than trying to trick us." Jematé took the slate. His jaw hardened as he read, though a growing fear shone through his eyes.

"I am unfamiliar with the prayers Lambert included," Perrin said. "Are they correct? Perhaps the enemy has some knowledge of Bretton's faith and—"

"It's the wedding prayer when a man and woman are joined beneath the gaze of God," Jematé said. "But he inserted parts in the wrong order, and he made several changes that those who hold the correct priesthood ranks are taught to make if they're ever forced to speak the prayers to those outside of the faith . . . this is legitimate."

Jematé spoke into his wristband and handed the slate back.

"It can't be." Perrin raised a hand to the child's mural of the *Highest*. "How could Telemachus do this? He's a hero of the Hegemony."

"The reasoning and the why isn't what's important right now." Jematé crossed his arms and put one hand to his chin. "What we must do next is what matters."

Timmons came out of the school, zipping up his under suit. Jematé handed him the slate and remained silent until he finished Lambert's message.

"Then it's over," Timmons said. "It's all over. The Hegemony is . . . gone."

"Sir, we can't—there has to be a succession plan," Perrin said. "The Most High council appointed sector governors. Surely they can reconvene the council or call for a new one to be elected."

"Correct." Jematé nodded. "But by the Compact the new members of the Most High would be ratified by the legislature . . . who all died aboard the *Highest*. Telemachus' coup was perfectly timed. The marshal's made it clear that he won't abide anyone challenging him with any sort of legitimate methods. Rotten son of a bitch."

"Governor Engelier won't tolerate this," Timmons said. "He fought tooth and nail against the force generation order that drafted us into the Hegemony Army . . . he was afraid this exact thing was about to happen."

Perrin raised an eyebrow.

"We go to church with him," Jematé said. "We did invite you, Easton."

"I thought the invitation was for . . . church." Perrin frowned.

"The rest of the Gallia sector won't bend the knee to Telemachus either." Timmons shook his head. "None of the sectors will! Not to some soulless bastard that just murdered the entire government."

"Telemachus has the Skien Corps loyal to him but nothing else." Jematé tapped his bottom lip. "His strength can only extend so far. If he has to pacify any sector, then the rest will have time to build up their own military . . . it's going to be a bloodbath. Old feuds will mean new wars."

"And what about us?" Timmons asked. "Lambert got this out to us. It won't be long before everyone knows. And when the Flags learn of this . . ."

"They'll realize they've won," Jematé said.

"Perhaps we can negotiate our way off world with them," Perrin said. "Rather efficient way to get rid of an occupier. Just let us leave."

"You didn't see what was inside that old warehouse. I did," Jematé said. "We surrender and it will be a massacre. The Flags want revenge for what the Hegemony's done to this planet and they mean to have it. We swap jerseys and it won't make a difference to them."

"What . . . what are you suggesting, sir?" Perrin asked.

"I'm not 'suggesting' anything." Jematé let his arms fall to his sides, then folded them behind his back. "We swore to protect and defend the Hegemony . . . and the Hegemony is gone. Forever. The fight here isn't ours. It isn't Bretton's. I'm going to get us all home, gentlemen. I owe it to my boys out there. I owe it to the families that will want their fathers, sons and brothers *back*. Lambert's plan is feasible and doable in the small window of time we have available.

"We need to get the battalion to—"

A whine rose in the distance. A Hegemony air car with General Brooks' name stenciled over the two stars on the back passenger door hovered overhead, then set down in the schoolyard. The repulsors kicked up dirt that blew across the body bags, rustling the plastic and exposing the face of a young man in his late teens.

Jematé reached for his sidearm, but relaxed as a pair of heavily armed Skien soldiers, their alabaster arms and pale green veins visible under their Flanker armor plates, jumped out. Each had a carbine with fixed bayonet ready at their shoulder. A passenger air car meandered in the distance.

A colonel in fatigues exited from the front passenger seat and hurried over as the repulsor engines idled. The air car generated a constant breeze just above the ground that tugged at Perrin's boots and shins.

"Bretton?" The colonel glanced at a slate. "General wants company commanders and above at a briefing. Call your officers in and load them onto that meat wagon." He jerked his thumb over his shoulder to the circling van.

"We're still in contact with the enemy," Jematé said. "I can't remove my commanders now—"

"The General's set up a temporary ceasefire that'll stay good until dawn," the colonel said. "You all will be back before then. This is a no-fail order..." he peered at the battalion commander's name tape, "Jematé. Do you want to do this the easy way or the hard way?"

Perrin glanced at the screen on his forearm. None of the companies reported any combat at the moment.

"It's calm, sir," Perrin said.

"Very well, XO." Jematé turned to Timmons, "Call in Captains Saul and Rothfuss."

"Tell them to double-time it," the colonel said. "There's a hard time to get everyone to the general and if I have to send my boys after them, they won't like it."

"They're en route," Timmons said, lowering his wrist mic from his mouth.

"What's this about?" Jematé asked.

"Need to know for now," the other colonel said. "I don't need to know. Neither do you. Whatever the commander's got, he'll tell us all at the same time."

"He has no idea—" Perrin said.

"What was that, *major*?" the colonel snapped.

"Forgive him." Jematé stepped between them. "Bretton military tradition has different standards when it comes to issuing orders. We have just arrived dirtside and there's been a good deal of discovery learning."

"That's right, you're all still pissing shipboard water." The Colonel turned aside as two Cataphracts came around the side of the building. "No suits. Can't take the weight in the air cars. Let's go."

He tapped twice on his wrist band and the van descended toward the playground.

"I need a word with my operations officer." Jematé took Perrin by the arm and walked him a few steps towards the command post. Jematé looked Perrin straight in the eyes. "Prepare that new defensive plan we just spoke about. We may need to implement it as soon as we return."

Perrin understood Jematé's true intent right away: make a plan to rendezvous with Lambert and the *Izmir*. Jematé couldn't risk saying more while the colonel was listening.

"Roger, sir." Perrin nodded quickly.

Jematé raised a finger and poked it into Perrin's chest, then clenched the front of his uniform and pulled him close.

"Nothing else matters," Jematé said quietly.

He pushed Perrin away and changed his pointed finger into a chest-level knife hand.

"And if you screw this up, you'll be on shit burning detail for the rest of the deployment." Jematé turned and raised a hand from his waist over his shoulder, signaling to the rest of the officers to follow him to the van.

Perrin was left with the body bags and three sets of empty Cataphract armor. Jematé was the last to board the van. He gave Perrin a quick nod before sliding the door shut.

CHAPTER 17

Jematé and Timmons stood at the edge of a mass of officers inside a large garage. The large doors were completely open, allowing humid air that reeked of the battlefield to engulf the commissioned leaders of Tabuk City's defenses.

"This is some happy horseshit," a female lieutenant colonel said and spat on the oil-stained concrete. "I'm supposed to run a convoy of wounded out to the field hospital at Burat Titi and I get dragged in here for the boss to tongue waggle at us?"

"Hey, my HQ's not getting mortared or droned for the first time in weeks," another officer next to her said and chuckled. "I don't know how Brooks got a ceasefire together . . . but I could be sleeping right now."

Jematé nudged Timmons with an elbow, then shook his head ever so slightly.

Not once had the two heard any officer speak about the state of the Hegemony or the *Highest*. Jematé was almost impressed that the news hadn't leaked further, but the timing of Brooks' summons didn't have any other plausible explanation.

And if Brooks knew and used that to broker a ceasefire with the insurgents . . . chances were they knew as well.

"All the exits have Skiens on them," Timmons said. "I don't like this, sir."

"Neither do I . . . we have to squat and hold until we're released back to the battalion. At least Perrin's working the problem," Jematé said.

The garage went silent as Brooks walked in, flanked by a pair of Cataphracts.

The general's hair had gone slightly gray and his gait was altered, like he'd been drinking. He carried a civilian cell phone in one hand, the screen lit up with an active call.

"Ladies and gentlemen!" Brooks held up his hands, his words slightly slurred. "I have news. 'Tis good or bad, thinking won't make it so. It is what it is." He belched. The general unholstered his sidearm and tossed it to the concrete floor.

"The war's over. The Hegemony, my heart. Your heart... it's all a crock of shit now." He tapped the screen of his phone. "Yes, Comrade Basa, I've got them all here. We're ready for you."

Jematé reached for his holster, but there was no sidearm. The guards had collected every weapon as the officers had arrived. The air went cold as officers murmured to each other at the display.

"Iz *over.*" Brooks stumbled against one of the Cataphracts. "It's all over. Thank God. I'll write nice letters to Telemachus for all of you. Long live the king! Or whatever he wants to be..."

"What is that bastard talking about?" someone behind Jematé said. "This is treason."

"We need an exit," Jematé whispered to Timmons.

"The garage doors might be best if things—so much for that idea," Timmons grumbled.

A small utility truck rolled into the garage. The driver looked like a local; her hands were white-knuckle tight on the wheel and she wore a red bandanna wrapped around her head. Even from more than ten yards away, Jematé could see she was sweating profusely.

Brooks moved aside to let the truck through. The driver parked next to the general.

"Nobody panic!" Brooks waved a hand over his head. "I've worked out the terms of our surrender to the Flags. We'll be allowed to leave with all of our— Hey." He put the phone to his ear. "Comrade Basa. I thought you were gonna be in the truck to accept—hello?"

The woman at the wheel held up a detonator and squeezed her eyes shut.

"Out!" Jematé turned and got one step towards a door before the car bomb annihilated the garage and everyone in it with a flash of fire and screaming metal.

CHAPTER 18

The truck slowed to a stop. Felix propped himself up on his hands and knees, listening as it idled. When there wasn't any movement after a few seconds, he held the detached optic from his carbine over the edge of the truck bed. The video played on a small screen on his visor.

It was pitch black, but the night-vision optics and false-color filters made it look nearly like he was in daylight. The truck had stopped on the outskirts of the city. Shanties and other crude huts were separated by trash-strewn dirt roads. Flashes of mortar and artillery rounds deeper in the city marked the front lines . . . not too far away. Just how the insurgents had managed an assault so deep into Hegemony territory was a concern, but not one he had to solve.

Felix just wanted to get to some friendly faces without getting shot in the process.

He spotted skyscrapers further away and knew he'd arrived at the right city. Just how he was going to reach the Hegemony without getting shot in the back by the Flags or in the face by the Hegemony was a problem he hadn't solved yet, but he'd been making it up as he went along and was still alive.

So far.

The driver's door opened. Felix lowered the optic and waited, his entire body taut. The driver let out a puff of smoke that billowed around his face as he reached into the truck bed. Felix snatched him by the wrist.

The cigarette fell from his mouth.

"Hey, how ya doing?"

Felix yanked the driver to one side and hooked a punch into his chin that knocked the man out cold. He kept his grip on him as he went limp and pulled him into the truck bed. Felix gave him a pat on the cheek and patted him down. He plucked a mostly empty pack of cigarettes from a breast pocket and shoved them into his pouch.

The Flanker hopped out and ran towards the sound of gunfire.

Another shot from a high-caliber rifle rang out through the city. Felix slid his back against a tin-walled shack and inched the optics on his carbine around the edge. He hadn't encountered many civilians as he snuck through the outskirts. He suspected most had opted to go on a very convenient lunar eclipse "pilgrimage" to avoid the fighting.

There'd been more feral dogs on the muddy streets than people, and with his night vision and thermal optics powered up, avoiding them had been easy in the dark.

A flash burst from the top of a two-story high tower connected to a brick building. He wasn't sure if the building was some sort of place of worship, but it had avoided any obvious signs of taking damage in the battle raging through the city and it didn't have trash piled against it.

"Hey . . . there's a vantage point," Felix said to himself. "If he's shooting at something, bet I can see what it is and figure out how to get there."

A door near the tower was open, typical for buildings without air conditioning in places with high humidity. A shadow moved across a heat source near the door.

Felix unsnapped the safety catch on his bayonet and drew the matte-black blade. He reversed the grip and beat his fist against his chest twice.

"All Father . . . be with me." Felix whirled, then rushed the open door. A man squatted next to a hot plate, a pot of boiling water on it. He had his back to the opening and twisted around just in time to see Felix's knife plunge at him.

The blade buried to the hilt where the shoulder met his neck. Felix pushed him onto the floor and tugged the knife out. Arterial spray splattered against the wall, black in his faux-color vision.

The dying man kicked out and knocked the boiling pot over. It clattered over worn carpet and down a hallway.

"*Oi, si pau?*" There was a rustle from a darkened doorway. Felix hopped over twitching legs and put his back as close to the wall next to the doorway as he could. An insurgent with a red handkerchief around his neck stepped into the small foyer and froze when he saw his dead comrade.

Felix swung the still-bloody knife into the man's chest just below the sternum. The tip pierced his diaphragm and stuck there, keeping the insurgent from crying out for help or breathing at all. Felix felt the man's body quiver for a moment before he collapsed to the floor. Felix kept a solid hold on the handle and the dying man's weight pulled it free from the body.

The Flanker waited, listening for anyone else that might be nearby.

The sniper rifle atop the tower boomed again.

He turned a corner and found a curved stairwell leading up. He took the steps two at a time, hoping that the constant beating the sniper's ears had taken from firing his weapon, and that he had a security element downstairs, would keep him from noticing Felix's approach.

The rifle fired, and dust shook from the old brick and mortar of the tower. Felix saw a pair of sandals sticking out over the top of the stairwell. He raised his bayonet and found the sniper, a woman, kneeling against the rifle, the muzzle jutting over a low wall of the minaret.

She had long dark hair in a braid over one shoulder and did a double take as Felix charged into the space. Felix crashed into her, pinning her against the wall, and stabbed at her. She brought her arms up and deflected the strike. The edge sliced across her cheek and she shrieked in pain.

The blade bounced off the floor and flew out of Felix's hand. He pinned her down, his knife arm squished between them. Her face was so close that her breath fogged his visor.

She opened her mouth to scream. Felix reared back and slammed the metal edge of his helmet into her nose. The back of her head bounced off the floor and her eyes rolled back.

Felix snatched up his bayonet and thrust it into the sniper's neck. The tip burst out of the other side just below her chin. He fell back on his haunches, the knife left in place.

"Ah! I didn't—didn't know!" He clamped his jaw shut. The sniper let out a wet gurgle and went limp. "Didn't know you were a girl. Shit."

The sniper rifle was on an improvised table, the barrel angled up on a tripod. The wooden stock had several rows of kill tallies carved into it.

Felix's instinctual guilt at killing a woman faded away as he did a quick count. He grabbed the body by the ankle and pulled it away from the table. He slid the visor to the top of his helmet and nestled the stock against his shoulder. The optics package on top was fairly modern, with enough zoom and image enhancement to be accurate out to at least two kilometers.

He fiddled with the controls until the picture stabilized. A Hegemony Flanker took cover behind a wall across a wide and open highway. Felix shook his head slightly in disapproval. Whoever that was must've known there was a sniper operating in the area. Knowing where the sightlines were to avoid exposure should've been communicated to everyone by now.

"Amateurs. You trying to get killed?" he muttered. Felix scanned the optics back and spotted a close grip of insurgents massing just across the highway. None had the outline of a Flanker or Cataphract, and the faint "X" of crossed bandoliers convinced him they were the enemy.

He hit a range-finder button and lined up the optics. He squeezed the trigger and the rifle slammed into his shoulder, nearly knocking him off balance.

"Son of a bitch." He rubbed a now sore shoulder and reset. The group of insurgents was taking fire from the Hegemony soldiers, a brand-new hole in a wall above their heads. Felix aimed again.

He watched the air curve behind the round as it passed through one insurgent's shoulder and hit another in the back. One of them spun around, then lifted a radio to his mouth.

A radio on the dead sniper's chest warbled. The speaker's voice was high-pitched and past the edge of panic.

"There's the officer." Felix adjusted his aim to the new target and shot again.

The bullet hit the insurgent with the radio in the thigh, blasting out a chunk of flesh. The man went down, his scream carrying through the radio for a few seconds. The rest of the insurgents rushed from cover toward the Hegemony lines. Felix inched the muzzle to one side and lined the crosshairs up on a man with a rocket-propelled grenade held in his arms. He tapped the range finder to adjust and aimed for center mass.

The sniper rifle bucked hard and when Felix reacquired the target, the man was in a fetal position, a dark patch of blood growing from his lower back. The launcher was on the ground rolling away from him.

A bullet struck the tower wall. Pulverized mortar and rock spat up in the optics. Felix ducked as more shots snapped through the air and *thwacked* against the tower.

"That how they always handle friendly fire?" He kicked the sniper rifle away from him and fired a single round into the optics mounted on top of the weapon. It shattered, stinging his hands and arms with fragments. The split battery sparked and fizzled as he popped the magazine out and removed one of the last bullets. He jammed it sideways into the open breech and kicked the bolt hard, shearing off the bullet and fouling the weapon for the next insurgent that found it.

Felix hurried down the stairs.

"Frag out!" Mason chucked a grenade over a high wall and ducked.

Noah scrunched against the blown-out wall he trusted his life to as a sudden blast rustled his entire body. The headache that adrenaline had tamped down returned, pounding against his temples and making his teeth ache.

He popped his head and shoulders over the craggy top of what remained of a business and spotted two insurgents stumbling out of the dust cloud kicked up by the explosion. A three-round burst hit one man in the back. He pitched forward, one leg scraping against the dirt. The next insurgent went down to a burst that blew out his throat and one side of his head.

Noah dropped again and scurried closer to Mason, who worked his open jaw from side to side.

"Got 'em." Noah tapped his brother on the shoulder.

"What?" Mason tapped the side of his helmet with the heel of his hand.

"I got—never mind." Noah checked the squad net and no one else was in contact. He flashed his round count and water level to Sergeant Corre and got a read receipt. More data feeds trickled in; the enemy seemed to have ended their current assault and pulled back to regroup. Not the first time that had happened in the last few hours.

"Holy shit, Noah," Mason said. "Did you do that?"

A pic of a dead insurgent lying on his side flashed in the corner of Noah's visor. The man had his hands stuffed between his legs, a deep red blotch covered his arms and crotch.

"Do what? No, I just got two more at our ten o'clock . . . damn." Noah swallowed hard.

"You shot him in the dick," Mason said. "I know they're trying to kill us and everything but . . . that's just cold for a kid who's on his first day in the shit."

"I didn't—" Noah rolled his eyes. "He's not even in my sector of fire! *You* must've shot him in the dick."

"Uh-uh, he's like fifty yards away and I was using my last frag. No way my grenade blew his dick off from that far away. 'Least he bled out quick . . . sure as hell knew what happened to him while he was dying. Remind me not to piss you off anymore."

"It wasn't me! What . . . what does it even matter? Why aren't we more concerned about that rocket launcher that's out there in the street? One of them gets it and this nice wall's about as useful as toilet paper the next time they attack." Noah tapped his chest harness. "You got a spare mag? I'm getting low."

"I'm on my last one." Mason flicked his carbine up on its side. "We'll cycle back for resupply soon. . . . Let me ping Rochelle and see if they've got any mags. They don't want us running out while we're holding this spot. Watch your sector."

"I hope we get ammo before they come back." Noah slid his back against the wall towards the broken edge. "I gotta use harsh language . . . don't think they'll even understand me. Maybe just yell 'bang' or something."

Noah spun on the balls of his feet and did a combat peek around the edge of the wall.

Another Flanker helmet was looking right at him.

Noah fell back in shock, his arms extending out with his carbine as he let loose a flood of consonants.

"Don't fucking shoot me! Friendly! Friendly!" came from the other side of the wall. Mason hurried over, carbine at his shoulder. Noah fell on his back, weapon pointed between his knees at the wall.

A pair of dirty hands popped over the edge.

"Friendly!" Felix shouted again.

"P-prove it!" Mason lifted his carbine higher, ready to lean over the wall and end the new arrival.

"Is 'God damn it don't shoot me' not enough? I've got my carbine slung over my back, but the Flags are still out there. Can I come over to your side of that nice and thick-looking wall without any new holes in me? I've had a shitty day as it is," Felix said.

Mason and Noah glanced at each other and shrugged at the same time.

"Fine, come around, keep your hands up," Mason said.

Noah shimmied backwards, carbine still pointed between his knees at the wall.

Felix kept his hands high and spun around the edge of the wall. He leaned against it and sank down. He lowered his hands to shoulder height, his chest heaving.

"Name. Unit. Sing the first half of the anthem." Mason kept his weapon trained on him.

"PFC Felix, one each. Thirty-seventh Syddan Dragoons, Second Battalion, Bastard Company. Ugh . . ." He cleared his throat. "He-gem-ony my heart. Hear unto me they voice . . . raise to the highest our—"

"Stop, stop, you can't sing worth a shit." Mason lowered his weapon. "Just 'Felix'? They don't have last names on wherever?"

Felix let one hand drop to his side and slid his visor up and wiped grime out from the side of his eyes.

"Last names are for paperwork. It's Ibensen if you care that much. I'm just Felix to everyone. You guys sound funny. Where you from?"

"Bretton." Noah shifted to one knee. "What were you doing out there with the Flags?"

"My convoy got ambushed way . . ." Felix waved a hand to one side, "way the hell over there. Route 14 near Shimshar Township. I've been on the run ever since. This city's supposed to be secure. What happened?"

"Buddy, we just got here." Mason activated his forearm screen and wagged a finger at Noah. "Keep him talking. Let me send this up."

"We made planetfall earlier today. Or yesterday. Or the day before—it's been a blur," Noah said. "Flags launched an attack with the lunar eclipse, and we've been holding on by our fingernails since we got here. Lots of casualties."

"You're all that green? Explains why one of you doesn't know how to take cover when there was a sniper. I took out the nest for you, you're welcome, hit a couple Flags with the rifle while I was at it." Felix half reached back for his carbine. "You mind? She's diggin' in my back."

"Yeah, fine," Noah said. "Wait, you were hitting them from that tower? I think you shot one of 'em in the dick."

Felix blinked hard.

"I did what?" he asked.

Noah found Felix's helm on the near-IR net and sent him a picture of the dead insurgent with the fatal groin wound.

"Oh shit . . . no." Felix covered his mouth. "I was aiming center mass on his back and the bullet must've dropped with the distance from where I was shooting. I thought I hit him where we have our main battery packs." He reached back and touched his lower back.

"Mason, *this* guy's the dick shooter. Wasn't me," Noah said.

"Look, I wasn't aiming for his dick. Just sort of happened. And I killed him before he could frag the both of you. You're welcome." Felix laid his carbine on his lap. "Not to impose, but you got any food?"

"Huh? Yeah, I got something," Noah reached into his pouch and pulled out a packet of *tong* jerky and held it out to Felix.

Felix looked at the offering, his lips twitching. He picked up a small square and lifted it slightly in thanks and salute.

"Maybe I am in hell and that Antares just didn't think I was worth saving." He looked away.

"Okay," Mason slapped his thigh, "Sarge wants us to bring him back to the platoon rally point for debrief. First Squad's coming to relieve us in a second. Wow, you really put a sniper shot through that insurgent's asshole to pee hole? Glad you're on our side."

"I wasn't *trying* to blow his dick off. Like I said . . . just sort of happened." Felix shrugged. "Hold on, I'm in Tabuk, right?"

"Uh . . . probably?" Mason frowned. "You're with friendlies. That's what matters, right?"

"For sure and no one's shot me in the dick. Yet. Not everyone's got that luxury." Felix got to his feet as more Flankers approached.

Corre took steady steps down a concrete staircase. Cataphract suits massed several hundred pounds, and battle-damaged structures had a bad habit of failing under the concentrated weight. He entered a basement without incident and found Mason and Noah standing on either side of a pale-skinned, bald Flanker with a reddish beard sitting in front of Sergeant First Class Malo. The stranger munched on a steaming cup of instant noodles, mumbling to the platoon sergeant.

Boyle stood against the wall, his breastplate and helm open.

The company communications soldier, Servat, had his backpack off and was busy attaching wires from fresh holes in the ceiling to the pack.

"There's a hose in the far corner," Boyle said. "Fresh-ish water, but the pressure ain't gonna last."

"Thank Saint Robin." Corre went to a spigot with a ratty hose next to it and dismounted from his Cataphract suit.

The bald Flanker scrunched his nose and looked at Corre as he brushed brown lumps off his bodysuit and into an uncovered drain on the floor.

"It's not my shit." Corre screwed the hose on and washed himself off.

"Then whose shit . . . is it?" Felix asked. He rolled noodles around his mouth and kept eating.

Corre grumbled, as the rank smell of the water out of the hose wasn't going to do much to improve the aroma in his suit.

"Mason and Noah found this stray out in the gray zone," Malo said. "Survivor of a unit that got ambushed a ways from here. He's been on the ground for how long? A year?"

"Fifteen months," Felix said. "Are you guys supposed to be our relief? We should've been home for Christmas."

"It's been a bit of catch-as-catch-can since we landed," Malo said. "Servat, you got the LT yet?"

"Negative." Servat held a speaker from a headset against an ear. "Nothing on the local nets either. My ciphers are still pinging green off the re-trans servers. I don't know why we're not getting anything."

"Where's Lieutenant Govrien?" Corre asked. "Thought he'd be back from whatever the colonel wanted him for by now. They pinning captain on him or something?"

"Still with Jematé from last word we got." Malo shrugged. "Felix here's pretty resourceful. Managed to sneak through enemy lines and get right in Noah's face."

"He shot one of them in the dick." Mason nodded emphatically.

Corre lowered the hose as his brows raised.

"Not on purpose." Felix lowered his noodle cup. "What is it with you Bretton guys and dicks? Are you like, obsessed with them or something? Everyone that's come in the room, you've pointed at me and told them I'm a dick shooter. There's more to me than that, just so you know."

"Hold on, why *did* you shoot someone in the dick?" Corre asked.

"Damn it!" Felix dropped his plastic spoon into the cup. "I was on a sniper rifle I wasn't familiar with and I had the choice to shoot a Flag with it—and blow his dick off in the process by complete accident— or let him blow way more off Mason and Noah than just their dicks. Okay? How about a thank you? Maybe a unit coin if you Brettons do that. Unless there's a dick on it. I don't want to have to explain why I'm walking around with a dick coin like those weirdos from Agrios Sector units have on them for luck."

"I think we're done discussing that." Malo gave Mason the look that only senior non-commissioned officers can to the Flanker to make his point. Mason shrank back slightly. "To be a bit more useful, Felix here saw the Flags moving battalions' worth of soldiers east of the city. I think we've only seen the beginning of the attacks. Problem is we can't get anyone at battalion on the horn to pass up the intel and I don't even know where to send a runner."

"Heh, what're we supposed to do without battalion telling us when we can shit?" Corre sprayed a brown lump into the drain.

"Got something." Servat pumped a fist. "It's on the breakthrough channel . . . coming in off satellites and every repeater I can tap into . . . Weird. Let me pass it through."

A holo emitter on his backpack cast a light through a cover. Servat flipped a bit of fabric up and a news broadcast desk with two pristine anchors appeared in the middle of the basement. Between them was a Dahrien insurgent, red sashes crossed over his chest and a pair of Hegemony sidearms on either hip. The man had the thousand-yard stare of a combat veteran and a face pockmarked by old wounds.

"—and I'm Chad Storm," the male anchor said. Vanessa Blanco, sitting on the other side of the insurgent, beamed a smile to the camera.

"In breaking news," Chad tapped a small pile of papers in his hands against the desk and an image of the destroyed *Highest* appeared in front of him, "the Hegemony has destroyed—is destroyed—loyalty programming violation number eight-eight-one. Filler loop activated."

"What is this?" Malo took a step towards the holo. He looked back at Felix, who shrugged. "This some sort of sick joke?"

"Ciphers read green, platoon sergeant," Servat said.

"That's right Chad," Vanessa extended her chest out, revealing more cleavage, "the complete and total erasure of the Hegemony has been announced by Marshal Telemachus, long may he reign. All military forces are hereby ordered to fall back to the nearest void port for loyalty oaths and reassignment to-to-to-to-to . . ." Her face froze but her voice repeated the same word over and over again until the insurgent pulled out a pistol and shot her in the temple.

Vanessa Blanco's cranium exploded into plastic and burning hair. Her face hinged forward, revealing animatronics within.

"That's great stuff," Chad Storm continued. "Now for sports."

Another bullet revealed the other anchor was just as robotic as the first.

The insurgent set his pistol on the desk and stared into the camera.

"Occupiers," he said, his accent thick, "your Hegemony is dead. I am General Bonifacio. We have taken control of the territory around Malakal City and most of the buildings around your 'Central.' No help will come from there. There is no more reason for you to fight. You will unconditionally surrender to the nearest Rightly Guided Forces of the Red Flag immediately. Those of you who have massacred my people will receive . . . justice. Those of you who are innocent will be spared and put to work repairing the cities and countryside that your occupation has destroyed. You will be our prisoners until such time as we see fit to release you. This is your only chance to survive. Any Hegemony soldier or civilian not in our custody by nightfall Malakal time will be killed on sight. Surrender. Now. There is no Hegemony anymore. No one is coming to save you, but I will show mercy."

Bonifacio leaned to one side and swiped his fingertips across his throat.

The broadcast ended.

The basement was deadly silent for several heartbeats.

"That's . . . got to be fake," Noah stammered. "The Hegemony can't just *end*. This can't happen."

"It's not AI-generated." Servat looked up from his forearm screen. "There'd be attribution coding in the file headers. I'm telling you it's real. All of it."

"We don't want to surrender." Felix jumped to his feet, his face going pale. "Not to those animals. You all just got here but you don't know what they'll do to us." He rubbed the top of his head where the insurgents normally scalped prisoners.

"They'll string us up and slice us across the stomach," Corre said. "I've seen it."

Mason leaned forward suddenly and vomited.

"Everyone just . . . stay fucking calm!" Malo shouted. "No one fucking panic! I need to—shit. Every squad leader is trying to break through. Hold on." He touched his earbud.

"Servat, get someone else on the radio," Boyle said. "Anyone. There's got to be an explanation for this. Marshal Telemachus is a hero of the Hegemony. I fought for him on Colima, he wouldn't do something like this . . . he wouldn't."

Corre turned the water pressure higher on his hose and washed out the last of his suit.

"Battalion!" Servat tapped a code into his forearm screen. "Major Perrin's on the command override channel."

Corre's earbud clicked as the holo changed to a drone view of a burnt-out building, smoke and dust still curling around the wreckage.

"Men of Bretton," Perrin said through Corre's earbud. The rest of the soldiers in the basement except for Felix cocked their heads slightly to listen. "The transmission we just received is valid. The last word I received from Colonel Jematé was from the building you see on the screen. It was attacked and destroyed. There has been no word from the colonel or anyone else that was with him. I must assume they have been killed in action. May the Saint receive their souls," Perrin's voice cracked and he cleared his throat, "—receive their souls and comfort them as ones worthy of rest. I am assuming command of the battalion.

"There is cause for hope. Colonel Lambert of the Territorial Logistics Corps sent news of the *Highest*'s destruction and the death of the Most High council to our headquarters less than an hour ago. He has a plan . . . one with a slim chance of success—to evacuate out battalion off of Dahrien and get us back home aboard the *Izmir*. I've used the lead time to plan our route from here to a small void port at Fort Triumph."

The holo changed to a map; an orange highlighted route from the city to a "V" within a circle nestled in a valley flashed on and off.

"We must secure the void port for the *Izmir* and the fuel stores there. Then we will get the hell off this planet," Perrin said. "While the rest of friendly forces in the city are . . . processing this information, we must act. We will take advantage of the confusion and march toward Fort Triumph immediately. Take only food, ammunition and power packs. All other equipment is forfeit. Colonel Jematé's last command to me was to get us home, and I will obey that order as a man of Bretton, an officer in the service of hearth and home and as a son of the Hegemony . . . what the Hegemony once was.

"Fall back from your current positions and into the march order transmitted time now," Perrin said.

There was a *ding* inside Corre's armor as a file was delivered.

"We step off for the *Izmir* in ten minutes," the major said. "I do not wish to leave anyone behind, but this is a day full of regrets. Perrin, out."

Corre's earbud clicked off.

"Hello?" Felix raised a hand.

"You heard the major," Malo said. "Everyone grab enough ammo and batteries for the march. No, take all the packs out of here and we'll pass it out on the move. Move your asses!"

"Hello!" Felix stood and waved his hand over his head.

Corre opened his radio and spoke with Sergeant Rochelle quickly, then climbed into his moist and musty Cataphract armor.

"What do we do with him, Sarge?" Mason spat out the last of what he'd thrown up to the floor and canted his head at Felix.

"Take him with us if he wants to go," Corre said. "We'll have room on the *Izmir*."

"Hey, dick lovers!" Felix shouted. This got the room's attention. "I didn't catch all of that because I'm not on your net." He pointed a finger at his earbud. "But if you're trying to get to the void port at Triumph you do *not* want to take that route through the countryside. Whole place is Flag country. Has been for months. You'll get ambushed every time you turn a corner and they've got the road mined seven ways from Sunday."

"None of that was on the map," Malo said as he picked up a satchel full of batteries.

"Do you want to believe a map or the guy whose unit fought and lost that whole sector? You think I'm making this up?" Felix tossed his hands in the air.

"I can get the major on the net." Servat held up a microphone handset.

"No time." Malo handed a bandolier of grenades to Felix. "I don't want the good idea fairy on the net while we've got a viable purpose and a mission. Temporarily viable. Corre, take the new guy straight to Perrin. The route out of the city's still clear and we won't get to the route he says is bad for hours. The major can put a decent plan together this fast, he can put another one together too."

"Roger. Moving." Corre buttoned up his Cataphract armor. "Second squad, fall in on me. We need to move fast."

CHAPTER 19

Corre and Boyle marched on either side of a road leading out of Tabuk City. The city had gone from prefab one- and two-story buildings to dusty fields within a few miles of their last position. Inside the city had been eerily quiet as they left. The insurgents kept to their commander's word to cease attacks until sundown. They'd heard sporadic gun fire behind Hegemony lines, former Hegemony, at any rate.

Corre didn't know what to label things that weren't Bretton or insurgent anymore.

None of the Hegemony soldiers they'd come across had tried to stop them or attacked. Having what remained of the battalion in a coherent marching formation with overhead drone cover and plenty of armed and dangerous Cataphract armor in a cordon around the Flankers and wounded gave off enough of a "don't fuck around" vibe that no one tried to find out what the Brettons were willing to do to protect themselves.

Felix trotted away from Major Perrin and fiddled with a brand-new earbud. He moved with a more natural gait than anyone else in the column as he lacked a Flanker's exo-skeleton.

"Hey, Sergeant Corre." Felix popped his helmet on, the visor raised to the top. "Your major said I can pick a squad. It cool if I'm with you?"

"Fine, you're in Tallec's fire team. Mason Tallec. Noah Tallec's his little brother. You've met them. What all did you say to the major?"

"I showed him a better route to the void port. Not a shorter one. One with a lot less Flags between us and there," Felix said.

"How sure of that are you? Things have been pretty fluid lately. Last time I went to bed there was a Hegemony keeping the peace across the stars. Now, I don't know what's happening," Corre said.

"Well," Felix scratched his face, "we seeded Dagger nests south of the route we were going to take. All of them were pinging green and active when my convoy crossed the line of departure yesterday. Flags know better than to go near them unless they're making a serious push. But if I was the Flag commander in that area and the Hegemony just went tits up...I wouldn't assume the Daggers magically turned themselves off."

"What would that Flag commander be doing right now?" Corre asked.

"Getting shitfaced and fuckin' a pig in celebration? Definitely not being brave when we're supposed to be surrendering," Felix said. "I've been here awhile, sergeant. I gave up on the idea of winning pretty quick. But I didn't think we'd out-and-out lose. All Father, hear my prayer."

"Lots in doubt right now," Corre said. "Where you from? I don't think I've ever served with anyone like you."

"Syddan. At least, that's where I was drafted out of. Born there but void-raised on a longship-class freighter with my clan. We pulled into the skyhook over Syddan and I ran into the one Hegemony draft officer that couldn't be bribed." Felix took a deep breath and forced it out quickly. "Some luck, eh."

"Where the hell is Syddan? It anywhere near the Gallia sector?" Corre asked.

"No, Tirana sector. Yggdrasil system," Felix said.

"That's not on the way back to Bretton. Nowhere even close," Corre said. "You understand that's where we're going. Our home. You come with us, that's where you'll end up."

"Eh, like I said, I'm void-raised. My clan runs trade routes through the Hegemony...or we did. They'll probably set sail for home once they get the word everything's gone to bilge. I can book passage home or find one of our ships out there. They won't ever come to Dahrien, that's for sure. Nothing here worth the trade or the risk."

"What did Major Perrin say about getting you home?" Corre asked.

"Gave me his word as a man of Bretton that he'd help me. That's better than taking my chances here. Not that I don't believe him," Felix said. "But...would *you* stay here?"

"Nope," Corre said. "What Flanker certifications do you have?"

"Basic ranks one through six. Tested out of the Hegemony tech assessments. I couldn't pass the land navigation quals for sergeant." Felix chuckled at Corre's look. "What? I'm a spacer. I can plot a ship route anywhere in settled space just off pulsars, but you ask me to do anything more than read a map and I get confused."

"You're value-added already," Corre said. "Bretton's a voluntary analog world. We work with our hands for everything we can, rely upon ourselves for our needs. All of us can use modern tech, but we may not know how it works."

"You're from one of those planets that doesn't use robo-labor?" Felix asked.

"We'll use them for more dangerous work and only after the church approves. 'To work is to know the Lord,' as Saint Robin taught. But we've all learned how to be soldiers from the same manual. Though it sounds like you've got more combat time here than the rest of us combined. Don't be afraid to speak up if we're about to do something out of ignorance that'll get us killed or injured, understand?"

"Roger, sergeant." Felix nodded. "Sorry for calling you all 'dick lovers.'"

"Did you ... really shoot a man in the crotch?" Corre asked.

"Yes, but not on purpose. It was an unintentional dick shooting."

"Fair enough. Tell me more about the Flags' use of mines. Can a Dagger with a sensor suite pick them up?"

Noah hiked his carbine higher on his chest, clutching it almost at the ready against his chest plate. He scanned the roadside off to the right, noting trash and dirt mounds next to dried-out patches of fields and a canal running parallel to the road. The pack full of power rods on his back hadn't been secured properly and swung like a heavy pendulum.

Boyle walked slowly in his Cataphract armor a few steps away from him, his rotary cannon spinning back and forth every couple of steps.

Mason lengthened his stride from behind Noah and caught up to him.

"You good?" Mason asked.

"Are *you* good?" Noah smirked. "I haven't seen you barf like that since grandpa died."

"Not my finest moment. All of this is a bit much to take in all at once. Don't tell me you're already the perfect Stoic the way everyone's supposed to be back home," Mason said.

"Mason...I've barely slept in days. I've been shot at, lost friends, killed men and we've taken way more casualties than I want to think about. Now the Hegemony's gone and we're supposed to believe Major Perrin and that civilian colonel that's always fussing about gear are going to get us home. Maybe a pixie will fall from the sky with a note saying my pox is back and I'm contagious again." Noah put a hitch in his step to shift his gear higher up on his shoulders.

"It didn't kill you the first time you had it. Won't kill you the second." Mason looked away.

"Ah...I'm sorry, Mason. Shouldn't have said that. When Natalie and your girls—"

"You gonna keep humping your gear or do I need to carry it for you for a bit?" Mason snapped.

"Can you tie it down? My noise and light discipline is horrible right now," Noah said.

"I lash it down and what happens if we're in contact? You want that nice big target on your ass? We're on an open road flanked by Cataphracts. Bet the Flags could see us from orbit if they had the satellites...You worried about Mom? I'm worried about Mom," Mason said.

"Yeah." Noah choked down a sob. "Why did she have to cry like that when we marched out under the Hero's Boughs? She didn't do that when you left the first time."

"She still had Dad and you with her. Now she's got our paychecks and the church-approved maid bot for the house. Except she's not going to have our paychecks anymore, is she? The Hegemony made the deposits." Mason rolled a shoulder and adjusted the strap holding a sack with an ammo can in it. "Governor Engelier promised to take care of our families while we're gone. I believe him. He'd better or he'll end up like Governor Witt after the battalions came home from the Alliance War..."

"It's amazing what burning a politician at the stake does for the public good," Noah finished the Bretton joke. "What's going to happen back home? To the whole Gallia sector?"

"Maybe we worry about the fifty-meter target before the one out at three hundred," Mason said.

"We're on a road march, Mason, this is the most boring thing Flankers do and I'd rather not think about how we're up to our necks in shit before it gets up to our noses, okay?"

"Just think about baseball. That always works . . . I don't know, but the other systems settled by Saint Robin's pilgrimage won't be in any hurry to bow down to Marshal Telemachus. Armorica, Devon, Nantes . . . we're all one people. Not like those heretics in the Hudson cluster. Even then, nobody liked the Gallia sector governor. Bet he'll skip town for Union space with all the money he's been embezzling, if he's smart."

"But Bretton will be okay on its own? Should be . . ." Noah said.

"Good thing Saint Robin demands we be self-sufficient in everything we can. We grow enough food and have the foundries to keep everything running without imports. The miners out in the Cornwall system are going to be in trouble if the trade lanes collapse. Which they probably will," Mason said. "Or not. Nothing like this has ever happened since the Diaspora. We had the Hegemony to keep all the sectors in line and cooperating with each other. Not no more."

"Hudson would just love to get their hands on the Saint's bones, wouldn't they? There would've been a war for them if the Hegemony hadn't stepped in," Noah said.

"Hudson's full of blustering idiots. It's the Maghreb and Deseret sectors I'm worried about. They hate each other. Can't even have their levy units on the same planet most of the time. They'll go out of their way to arrange 'friendly fire' incidents. Nazare's had disputes with Maghreb as well. The Tirana sector never wanted to be part of the Hegemony to begin with. They had to have their arm twisted to join up for protection against the Alliance." Mason sighed.

"I'm not making things better, am I?" Noah looked off in the distance as a small truck appeared on a side road.

"No, you're not. Shut up already. At least we're going home. Bit sooner than expected but this planet's a shithole as it is." Mason popped his visor and spat on the road. "But we've got to stay together, Noah. Not just you and me 'cause we're brothers, but the whole battalion. Whoever tries to survive onesey-twosey will get eaten by the next bigger mob they come across."

"Wasn't that the reason for the Hegemony? That ain't working out, is it?" Noah asked.

"I failed civics. But the Most High are all dead and I'm still kicking, so maybe I've got a better grasp of the fundamentals than they did." Mason looked over his shoulder as Felix jogged up the road to them.

"Hi," Felix said. He stood barely to the brothers' shoulders and seemed almost juvenile without his Flanker's exo-skeleton across his shoulders and down to his feet. "Sarge is done talking to me, what's my sector?"

"You've got even less protection than us and we're hiding behind the Cataphract's skirts," Mason said. "What happened to your rig, anyway?"

"Tossed it off a cliff after it lost power. Made sense at the time," Felix said. "So you guys are from an analog planet, right?"

"Wow, he didn't accuse us of being in a cult." Noah chuckled. "This is better than going on a mission, let me tell you."

"Our way of life isn't a tourist attraction," Mason said. "Sometimes off-worlders will show up on a market street ogling us as we work the looms or bakeries. There was some celebrity that tried to live like us for a few weeks for a Net show and she didn't last a single shift on the ovens."

"Bakeries?" Felix tensed up. "What kind of bread?"

"You that hungry?" Mason asked. "Go talk to Boyle, his family runs a place. They do good kouign-amann and their gâteau is okay if you like it way too salty."

"I heard that, you heathen." Boyle shook an armor shod fist at him. "We make it with proper butter and sea salt caramel the way God intended."

"I only like the churri ones your sister makes." Mason waved a dismissive hand at him.

"She almost got kicked out of the guild for those. Don't ask for any when we get home," Boyle said.

"That's all . . . bread?" Felix asked.

"Of course, what do you think bread is?" Noah and Mason traded confused looks.

Felix held his hands about two feet apart.

"I was on shore leave once. Had a bread that was about this big. Crunchy outside, slight sour smell to it. Think it was called a baggy-eat," Felix said.

"Baguette," Boyle said. "Whole other discussion. Well, not really, as there's only one right way to make them."

"Agreed." Mason nodded emphatically.

"Tallec," Corre's voice said through their earbuds. *"Does our scout speak the local dialect?"*

"I really need a new helmet with a working mic," Felix said. "Tell him I speak a little. Basic stuff. 'How much is that? Go away or I'll shoot you.' The usual."

"I monitored. Escort him up, Major needs some language support," Corre said. *"Double time it."*

"Shit, I should've said 'no.' I've just volunteered for a bunch of bullshit, didn't I?" Felix's shoulders drooped.

"Yeah . . . well, at least you're smarter than Noah." Mason jerked a thumb at his brother. "He voluntarily enlisted."

"On purpose?" Felix narrowed his eyes at Noah.

"Isn't that what 'volunteered' means? They were gonna draft me anyway," Noah said.

"You've moving like pond water. Step it out," Corre ordered.

Felix trotted to a group massed in the middle of the road. Flankers and a pair of Cataphracts formed a semi-circle around Major Perrin and Sergeant Malo. The two spoke with a Dahrien woman who was on her knees, an infant wrapped against her chest and a toddler at her side, clutching her arm.

The woman wailed and tried to grab Perrin by the hand, but he kept pulling away. A small shack with an open door stood amongst thin crops near the shoulder. The major had his helm off and tucked beneath one arm.

"Finally," Perrin said as Felix approached. "Felix, is it? Ask her if she knows anything about insurgent activity ahead of us."

"Kapayap, kapayap," Felix said, and the woman's gaze snapped to him. She looked him over and wiped tears from her eyes. The toddler was of mixed race, his skin and eyes lighter than the Dahrien he'd seen.

Felix's eyes went up to the left and he stammered out a question.

The woman shook her head then reached for Perrin again, pleading with him.

"Well?" Perrin asked.

"Ugh, she said she stays here and doesn't go to the mountains," Felix said. "That's pretty standard here, sir. None of them know anything unless it was one of us that damaged their property or killed one of their pigs. Then they have all the details because that'll get them paid."

"If she's not going to be helpful, then tell her she can go back to her house,"

"*Umlasa. Kama, kama.*" Felix tried to shoo her away.

The toddler pointed at Felix and said something to his mother. The woman looked at him and put one hand against the baby swaddled against her chest. She spoke slowly.

"Sir, she ... says the Flags will kill her because she has Hegemony children. She wants to come with us. Says she'll cook, clean ... other stuff just for you." Felix grew uncomfortable.

The Bretton marched on around them.

"No, we can't. Impossible," Perrin said. "Tell her to get off the road for her own safety."

"Sir." Malo raised a hand slightly. "What if she's telling the truth? We can't just leave her here. The Flags are animals."

Perrin pointed two fingers at Felix.

"This true? The insurgents target women and children?" the major asked.

"Well, there's rumors some families will go after a girl if she has relations with one of us. Outside of ... approved facilities. Working girls work for the clans. They're not as concerned about their honor when there's money flowing up the chain," Felix said. "But them going after kids? No. At least, I've never heard about it."

"Does she know about the current state of the Hegemony?" Perrin asked.

Felix gave Perrin a hard look, then stammered out a question.

The mother mimed an explosion.

"Then she's just scared. She doesn't have an active threat against her." Perrin lifted his helmet.

The woman broke out in sobs and bent forward, her forehead against Perrin's boots.

"Sir ... please," Malo said. "Most of us have wives and children back home."

"Sergeant," Perrin inched away from the woman who'd gone nearly prostrate, only keeping the infant off the road, "what if we bring her along? Do you know how much fighting is ahead of us?"

"I do not, sir." Malo straightened up.

"Not only would we put her at risk, but there are likely more civilians between us and the void port. What if we take in all that want off this world? How many will be there when we embark? Because if we take her and her children, we take all we come across. There will likely be more than the ship can carry and then what am I to do? What are any of us to do?" Perrin asked.

Malo's jaw tightened.

"I would appreciate an answer, sergeant," Perrin said.

"Then we could only take as many as the ship's life support will allow," Malo said.

"And then? How much food is aboard the *Izmir*? Will that last until we're home? And how do I choose who comes aboard and who doesn't?" Perrin took a step towards Malo. "I must make an awful decision now so I don't have to make a worse one later. It isn't fair. It isn't right . . . but it is what it is and I can't change that."

He put his helm on and locked it to the ring around his neck.

The mother reared back on her ankles and clutched her children against her, wailing and pleading.

"Here." Perrin reached into a pouch on the back of his belt and held out a plastic-wrapped pack of caramels and folded bills held together in a clip. Felix recognized Central script, issued to the Hegemony military as currency.

She looked at the offering like it had come out of a toilet.

"Not everyone's heard the news," Perrin said. "Perhaps she can trade it for something of value before the governance . . . shifts. I have nothing else to give her. Get her off the road now or I'll have to make an even more difficult decision."

"*Gimoh, kama kama.*" Felix took the script and candies from Perrin and pressed it against the woman's shoulder. She snatched it away and stuffed it into her blouse. She turned her head away and put an arm over her son's shoulders and shuffled off the road.

"You disagree, sergeant?" Perrin asked Malo.

"Negative, sir. I don't think we'll know what the right decisions are for a long time. Just have to do the best we can with what we know now," the platoon sergeant said.

"And the consequences of those decisions are mine alone. God guide me. God forgive me." Perrin checked the optics on his carbine and slapped the bottom of the loaded magazine. "Thank you, Corporal Felix, fall back in."

Perrin reached into a pocket and handed Felix a rank tab; one corner was stained red.

Felix accepted the promotion and almost saluted. Any sniper watching would likely have figured out Perrin was important just by how he was surrounded, but removing all doubt as to Perrin's rank would've been amateurish and likely not have ingratiated him into his new unit.

"Roger, sir." Felix nodded quickly.

He, Mason and Noah jogged back to the rest of the squad.

No one spoke of what happened.

Boyle zoomed in on a bend in the road. The terrain had elevated slightly several kilometers back, becoming rocky and forested. His squad had cycled to the fore of the entire battalion, putting him and Corre at the tip of the spear.

Also the first ones into danger, which he was well aware of.

"Scope's clear," Corre said as he swept his Gatling cannon along the left side of the road.

"Which doesn't mean much." Boyle switched to infrared and spotted a hot plume of air in the distance. "I'm launching a Pigeon. Haven't had a blip on the EM detector for hours. Let's see what's over there."

"Go," Corre said.

Boyle focused his vision on a drop-down menu and his helm opened it for him. He entered in a reconnaissance mission code and traced out a search area on his visor's map. The Flankers had the privilege of using their fingers on their forearm screens; Cataphracts had to make do with facial tics and eye movement to give orders to their subsystems.

The heavy armor plate on his back jostled as a drone spat out of its housing into a high arc. Repulsor rings snapped out and it shot over the treetops. Video beamed back to Boyle and Corre as it closed in on the heat source.

"Do I patch this back to Malo or who?" Boyle asked. "LT's dead. So's the captain. You think we'll get field promotions?"

"How about you worry about what's over the next hill and not if we've got to sew on new rank," Corre said. "You want my job that bad?"

"No, Sarge, but maybe there'll be back pay when all's said and—ah, shit." Boyle's mouth went dry.

A destroyed Wolverine tank was half-on, half-off the road. The hatches were open and spewing smoke, a broken tread traced behind the vehicle like a steel ribbon.

"I don't see any obvious damage . . . there, blast seat." Corre pinged a temperature gradient in the center of the road close to a smattering of broken tread links.

"It hit a mine or the Flags pressed a button to set the bomb off?" Boyle asked. "Neither option's good for us. Got a long way to the void port."

"Malo wants us to get closer," Corre said. "Have the Pigeon spiral out. Better we spot any assholes out there before they spot us."

"Roger, she's on auto." Boyle blinked in the new instructions and the drone flew an ever-widening circle around the destroyed tank. The Cataphracts continued up a steep incline in the road, rushing over the crest.

The tank's armor pinged as heat from melting battery packs spread through the wreck. Rust had spread like a rash over the right side of the tank where the paint had melted away. Boyle rushed up to the front of the vehicle, ignoring the heat pulsing through his suit. He searched the surrounding forest, finger twitching against the trigger of his rotary cannon.

"Squasher got it." Corre kicked at a crater almost a foot deep behind the tank. A half-sphere flipped out and skidded across the dirt road. "Warhead mashes against the battery packs and blows spall into the crew compartment. No point in looking inside. Nobody survives that."

"See a detonator? Wire?" Boyle asked.

"Nothing. Probably seismic trigger or magnetic. Good news is we're not big enough to set one of those— Hold up." Corre pointed at the shoulder. "More tank tracks going around the wreck. There's another one out here."

"This one's still burning. How long you think since it was hit?" Boyle asked.

"They'll normally cook off for a couple of hours. No real hot spot in the crater so we're probably at the longer end of that estimate," Corre said. "Sure could use a Wolverine with us."

"The major wouldn't take a mother and kids but a Wolverine's welcome? I didn't go on a mission, but I remember something from church about greater goods not excusing lesser evils," Boyle said.

"I *did* my mission . . . and this isn't my first time in the thick of it either. Maybe that lady and her kids will be in danger. One of our tanks and crews? No chance. But there's another tank out here." Corre shared a zoomed-in pic of the map with Boyle. There was a fork in the road a few kilometers ahead. The void port wasn't far from the junction.

"If I was a fuckwit of a terrorist, I'd have more mines at that intersection," Boyle said.

"Which would make you not a fuckwit. And if the other tank commander's got an IQ higher than room temperature he'll think the same thing and look for another way to the void port."

"Assuming that's where they were going." Boyle zoomed out on the map. "Has to be. Wolverines don't have a hell of a lot of range. There's nothing else out here."

"Likely." Corre's head cocked slightly. "Malo says to keep moving. We've got two more klicks before another platoon cycles forward."

"It's going to be a fun march, I can tell," Boyle said.

"I'm calling the Flankers up. They're good in this terrain." Corre pointed down the road and swung it forward.

CHAPTER 20

"I've got eyes on." Mason kept one shoulder tight against a thick tree and slid his carbine along a root arcing up from the dirt. He was on a hilltop with an elevated position over the intersection leading to the void port. Taking up the most obvious observation point on the key terrain was a poor tactical decision, but he didn't have time to find the perfect solution.

His optics zoomed in, and he sent pic captures back to Corre and Rochelle. The other Flanker sergeant and his two men were on the downward slope behind him, waiting to bound forward.

"No activity," Noah said from a few feet away. He was prone, only the top of his helm and eyes peeking over the crest. "How'd we get this tasking? Thought we were supposed to be cycled back."

"Shut up," Mason hissed. "We've got the local Flanker in our squad. Guess the chain of command wants his experience up here. What're you going to do, write our Hegemony congressional rep?"

"Maybe I will. I've heard that can—oh wait . . . right," Noah said. "Felix, what're we looking at?"

Felix was further down the steep hillside. He was propped up on his side, breathing hard. Without the exo-skeleton to provide strength augmentation he'd been running off pure muscle power.

"It's . . . it's . . . a road. God damn I . . . shouldn't have thrown my exo away," Felix struggled to say.

"So glad you're here. Very value-added." Mason shook his head. "Rochelle, we've got overwatch. Bound up and get the scans in on the road, make sure it's not mined."

"*Moving,*" Rochelle sent over the radio.

"You see tank tracks anywhere on the road?" Noah asked. "I can't see any."

"Road's paved at the intersection. Way too much foliage in the way on the unpaved part," Mason said. "No Wolverine's moving off-road through here."

"So, then where's that other tank?" Noah asked. "Because we didn't see any sign of it coming up here."

"We weren't on the road either. You think it's hiding under a bush somewhere waiting to jump out and say 'boo'? Just watch your sector." Mason shook his head.

His visor superimposed the position of Rochelle and his Flankers, Herve and Saluan, as they crept through the underbrush toward the intersection. Mason took a long sip from his water nub all the while trying not to think about how many times his suit had recycled his sweat and other waste to make it. The slightly salty taste was supposed to be an electrolyte compound added to the purification process, but anyone that had been in a Flanker in the field had doubts and suspicions of that claim.

The icons over the three other Flankers stopped moving.

"Rochelle, problem?" Mason asked.

"Saluan tripped a wire . . . don't know what it was connected to," Rochelle sent back. "Might be an old booby trap. This something the Flags use?"

"Usually just a frag grenade," Felix said. "It was shin-level, right?"

"Negative. Chest. Strung up between a bunch of branches," Rochelle said.

"New one." Felix shrugged. "Maybe hunters. There's some of those big dogs with horns on 'em out here that used to bring off-world tourism. They'd kill 'em and keep the heads."

"You mean 'deer'?" Noah asked. "Maybe elk or *hirvi*?"

"Big enough you can ride them. Dogs with hooves instead of paws. I'm a spacer and I don't know all the animals you dirtsiders deal with," Felix said.

"Rochelle, continue mission." Mason slapped his thigh twice to quiet the other two.

"But if this planet has big dogs with antlers . . . I don't know if that'd be awesome or horrible," Noah said. "Wasn't there some planet in the Deseret sector with rabbits like that? Jack-a-whomps or something?"

"Just regular rabbits here," Felix said. "Flags love them in a stew."

"Will you two shut the—"

An electromagnetic detection alert blinked on Mason's visor. He sent it back to the Cataphracts as flash traffic and turned his attention to the skies. Something dark zipped between treetops near the intersection.

Flocks of birds took to the sky, squawking and screeching.

"Rochelle hold." Mason lowered himself against the crest. "Radio silent. I think there's a drone."

The three icons for Rochelle's fire team blinked off. A sudden buzz roared up behind them. Mason tensed up but didn't move. The Shrikes launched by Corre and Boyle were there to intercept any enemy drones, but they were protecting Mason's team and not Rochelle's.

More birds were startled out of a treetop.

"What kind is it?" Noah whispered loudly.

"Not sure," Mason said. "If it was automated the Shrikes would've nabbed it by now . . . might be first-person control, those are a bitch to intercept. I'm going to lure it out."

"Say again?" Noah turned his head sharply to Mason.

Mason leaned back onto his feet and raised his carbine. He fired a single shot at the last tree that had any movement and sidestepped away from Noah. Something jumped out and landed on a thick branch. It scuttled towards the trunk.

Mason shot again and blew off a hunk of bark, exposing white wood beneath.

"Tell them to run! Tell them to run!" Felix shouted.

"Rochelle! Fall back, now!" Mason ordered as he and Noah both opened fire on a dark green shape moving down the tree trunk. It crawled to the other side, protecting itself from fire.

"Going manual," Corre sent over the radio. The Shrike drones overhead flew forward.

The enemy drone leapt off the tree and took flight. It arced up and dove at Rochelle's last position. The two Shrikes darted at it, but missed. Both burst into brief domes of flame and shrapnel in the undergrowth.

The enemy drone exploded with a crack like lightning. A wall of overpressure slammed into Mason and knocked him back. He careened off a tree and landed hard on a carpet of sharp rocks. He rolled down the hillside, his ears ringing and head aching.

Felix grabbed him by the carry handle on the back of his harness and stopped his descent.

"Ah! Ahhh!" Noah threw his helmet away and sank to his knees, hands over his ears.

Even with the protection from his helmet, the thermobaric explosion had rendered Mason's ears nearly useless. His eardrums rang painfully, an unending 'reeeee' stabbing into his brain.

Felix pulled Mason's arm away from his head and mashed a button on his forearm screen. There was a sudden pinch against Mason's neck and the pain in his ears died out. Mason flipped his visor up and retched out a thin green line of mucus.

He fell to the hillside, breathing heavily for a few seconds. He raised his head and found Felix with Noah, patting him on the back as his brother spat out his stomach's contents.

"Roche . . . Rochelle come back," Mason said over an open channel. No response.

"Mason, you hurt?" Corre asked. "We're moving up."

"Got our bell rung by a thermobaric." Mason crawled up the hillside. "We weren't the target. No word from Rochelle. Senomis administered to me and Noah . . . and the new guy."

His muscles went to rubber as the Senomis drug coursed through his system. The drug would counteract the concussive effects but had awful side effects as adrenaline subsided from their bloodstreams.

Mason rolled to his back next to Noah. His legs twitched and kicked of their own accord. Noah had to hold one arm against his chest to keep it from flopping about.

"Why aren't you—why aren't you all fucked up too?" Noah asked Felix.

"Did you know you can build up an immunity to Senomis?" Felix asked. "I don't recommend it. Not everyone's brain rots from it, but some do. Enough do."

Corre and Boyle stomped past them lower on the hill and moved toward Rochelle and his team's last known position.

Mason rinsed his mouth out with water as his legs stopped twitching. His feet still felt like they were being stung by pins and needles by the time Corre returned. The sergeant had three bloody dog tags hanging from a cord on his armor.

"We hold here," Corre said. "Perrin's working up a new plan. Felix, there any other surprises out there for us?"

"The poppers . . . I heard about them being used up north, not out here. Sorry," Felix said. "Those things are rare and expensive. It costs the Flags less to just lose fighters than use those drones."

"Alright, we squat and hold," Corre said. "Saint receive and protect our brothers. May they rest."

"May they rest," Noah said.

Mason rolled to his side and retched again.

"Then find me another route to the Fort Triumph." Perrin put his hands on his hips and scowled at a holo projection off Roux's pack. Most of the battalion was spread out along the road. Squads and fire teams grouped up for maintenance and to eat in one of the few pauses they'd had since leaving Tabuk City.

The comms soldier cocked his head to one side, his brows furrowed.

"Message for you, sir." Roux held up a handset. "It's pinging through the repeater network. It can't be traced back to us."

"How do you know it's for me?" Perrin took the handset.

"It's for 'Hegemony commander southeast of Fort Triumph.'" Roux double-checked his forearm screen. "Just a recording. We won't ping back."

"Play it." Perrin put the handset to his ear.

"Hegemony man," a locally accented voice said. "Or one-time Hegemony man. No Hegemony now. I have Fort Triumph under my control. The last commander didn't want to surrender, but he's not in charge of anything now. I follow General Bonifacio. He says give you to nightfall, I give you to nightfall. You come closer with weapons and no deal. You come with empty hands held high and you'll be better off than the crabs who wanted to fight. Come quick or I'll come find you when time runs out."

The message clicked off.

"Well . . . fuck!" Roux tossed his hands up. "Just can't get a break, can we? We land on this shithole and immediately get thrown into the fire. Then we get hit—"

Perring grabbed him by the front of his flack vest and gave him a hard shake.

"What if the men see you like this?" Perrin hissed. "Like it or not, I am the commander now and if it looks like I am panicking—or letting anyone's discipline slip into panic around me—then what will happen to everyone else, eh?"

"S-sorry sir." Roux swallowed hard.

"Panic is like shit. It gets worse as it rolls downhill," Perrin said. "Forgive the vulgarity. The men look at me and see an officer that's calm, cool and collected and what will they think?"

"You don't understand the situation?" Roux's brow furrowed.

"Yes, exactly—wait, no." Perrin let him go. "If they see me as a point of calm, hear reasonable and well-articulated orders over the radio, then they know their chain of command has the situation well under control. No matter how truthful that belief may be. Now, this enemy commander's handed me something of a wrinkle to the plan, but the plan can change. At least we've got until nightfall until the enemy reacts, which means we have the initiative!"

Perrin gave the handset back.

"I need some reconnaissance. How many Pigeon drones do we have left in the battalion?"

CHAPTER 21

Noah moved through jungle. He kept the contrast on his visor high to spot trip wires. Mason was a few steps away and Felix behind them. The squad's two Cataphracts followed along a few dozen yards behind them.

"What the hell are we looking for?" Noah asked.

"Some other way to the Fort," Mason said. "Major wants us to infiltrate in if we can. Keep the Flags from damaging the port before we can use it."

"The TEUs are worth a lot just for power plants," Felix said. "Capturing the place was probably a cash grab more than anything else. They don't want to destroy it, not when they'll need it. Doubt any deliveries are coming in from off world anytime soon."

"Don't they keep that stuff in vaults under the tarmac? How're they even going to get it without the right codes?" Noah asked.

"I've never met a safe that was immune to an angle grinder," Boyle said over the radio.

"Stop jaw-jacking and pay attention," Corre chided them all. "Bad enough we're out here with no overhead recon drones after the major recalled them all."

"Just some face-first recon by Flankers," Felix said. "My last commander did the same."

Noah stepped through a bush and his boot crunched down on tall reeds. The smell of sap carried through his helmet. He looked up the hillside and found a trail of ground-up foliage. He looked down and did a double take.

"Whoa, got something here." Noah turned left and followed the bulldozed path to an embankment. A Wolverine tank had come to a stop with the rear sunk into a muddy stream. The front edge of the treads had sunk into the grassy edge of the dropoff, and the turret turned to one side, as if aiming at something upstream. The hull was undamaged, but all the hatches were open.

"Huh." Mason joined Noah on the edge and looked up the way it had slid down. "So there *was* another tank. Looks like it slid off the road."

"And the crew just left it there?" Noah asked. "That doesn't make any—gah!"

Noah backed into his brother.

Hanging from trees were five men, all pale of skin. Their wrists were bound to branches with chains, their throats slit and heads scalped.

"Well, that's what happened to the crew," Mason said. "Maybe there's something worth salvaging inside?"

"Wolverines carry six," Felix said. "Might be another stray around here. Unless they ate him."

"They do that *too*?" Noah backpedaled against Mason. Mason twisted around and let his brother fall on his backside.

"Mason, get in there and see if any of the drones are still in the launchers," Corre said as he emerged from the jungle. "These are supposed to have a decent complement of Pigeons and Shrikes."

"Roger, Sarge ... Felix. Get in there." Mason waved the other Flanker forward.

"But he told you—"

"I'm not dumping my exo to fit in there when you don't even have yours. Move it, new guy." Mason waved again.

"Why am I getting 'new guy'd' when as a newly minted corporal I—you know what, I'm not going to fight your logic." Felix handed over his carbine and climbed onto the front of the tank. He slid down to the driver's hatch on the front and looked inside.

"Huh, no driver's seat, just power rod housings. All empty, of course. Weird." Felix looked up at the growing twilight, then popped a small flashlight off his belt. He climbed onto the turret and gave the tank commander's hatch a tug. He glanced inside.

"Hey, Sarge, if the Flags were smart enough to take the power rods, they probably got the drones too," Felix said.

"Quit goldbricking and get in there." Corre waved a heavy mitt at him.

"I'm just saying." Felix put two fingers to his forehead and turned his palm up to the sky. He dropped into the turret and clicked on his flashlight.

The inside of the Wolverine was surprisingly spacious. The gunner's seat was built into the turret next to the main gun's breech; another seat with more optics and control handles for machine guns was on the other side.

In the main hull was enough room for a shorter man like Felix to stand up. Two control stations with holo emitters built into the metal sides were powered off; a fifth place next to sliding ammo lockers had trash and bloody bandages piled on it.

A matte-black hump ran along the bottom of the hull, gouges and dents all along the edges.

"This is fine," Felix said to himself as he dropped down. "Tanks don't get haunted. It's fine."

He kicked the bandages away, gagging at the heavy copper scent. He shined his light along the walls until he found three pneumatic tubes angled away from one of the control stations that ran up the inside of the hull and to the rear of the tank.

"Bingo." Felix sat in the chair and felt something moist seep into his pants. He flipped a hatch on one of the tubes up. Empty. The next one had a red and white striped cylinder inside of it.

"What's this?" He pulled it out and another sprang into its place from a magazine beneath his chair. He adjusted the light on the cylinder but couldn't read the text. He flipped it over and angled the cylinder away, attempting to read the rainbow-hued font that refused to stay lit.

"Watch this be one of those poison gas canisters the Flags always claim we use. Wouldn't that be just my luck—"

Thunk.

The bulge down the center of the hull spun slowly with a guttural rattle of gears. The edge came over the top, revealing a ghastly white figure.

Felix let out a screech and sprang up. His head struck the low hull and stars shot across his eyes. He dropped the cylinder, arms flailing in front of him as the flashlight spun around and around on the deck.

A ghost rose up from the tomb. He got glimpses of it coming for him as the light moved like a beacon. Its head was bulbous with a long, hollow tongue.

"Mommy!" Felix swiped at it as blood ran down his face.

"What the hell is wrong with you?" a young woman asked. The light stopped spinning as the ghost took up the flashlight and shined it at Felix's face. "Name. Unit. Answer before I designate you as a hostile combatant."

"F-F-Felix!" He held his arms up in front of his face. "Private firs-corporal? Corporal! Unit is…umm, Bretton. The Bretton something-th. Don't eat my soul, please!"

"Your answers are inadequate." There was the sound of a pistol being racked.

"Hey!" Mason called out from the turret hatch. Fresh light shined into the hull. "Felix, who the hell is that?"

"Ghost. Ghost!" Felix pressed himself into the corner and slapped a hand against the cut on his head.

"I am no imaginary creature. Identify yourselves!" she shouted.

"How about you point that pea shooter somewhere safe before we talk," Mason responded.

Felix lowered his other hand. The "ghost" was a woman in an eggshell-colored body glove. A helmet with attached air mask was on the deck next to her. Her skin was the color of ivory, her eyes a glacial blue. Platinum blonde hair matted with sweat came down to her jawline. She wasn't the curviest woman he'd ever seen, but she was proportioned nicely. Small gold tattoos on her cheek and neck reflected the light.

"Coriaria 14, Sibirica gene line. Aleph Troop, Argent Squadron, Hegemony Cavalry. Designate yourself!" she yelled back.

"Bretton Eleventh Infantry…we're all on the same side. Let's calm down," Mason said. "You're a Skien?"

"I will not repeat myself nor use slurs," she said. "Are you in contact with my squadron? I require wrecker support to get out of this position."

"Do you have a med pack?" Felix asked. "The bleeding won't stop. Good thing I've still got some Senomis in my system or I'd be right out…still hurts."

"Left side of the Droner chair. Next to the calf area," she said. She rubbed the neckline of her bodysuit. "My hydration levels are unsat."

She smacked dry lips.

"Hold on, I'm coming down there," Mason said.

". . . lost sufficient power . . ." The woman chomped down on a bit of *tong* jerky and kept talking as she chewed. ". . . for me to move again. Hostiles arrived while the rest of the men were outside attempting to cut down trees for traction."

Noah and Mason sat across from her as she ate and gulped down water through a tube from the hydration blister that had been on Mason's back. Noah pressed a bandage against Felix's wound and there was a smell of cooking flesh as the sutures took hold.

"Ow ow ow!" Felix smacked Noah's hands away.

"I went back to my chamber." She stomped a boot against the open cylinder in the floor. "The enemy lacked the correct tools to open it. They were unable to read the extraction instructions printed on the side."

"How long ago was that?" Corre asked from the hatch. The Cataphract armor was far too big for him to fit into the Wolverine.

"I . . . do not know." She took another bite and chewed with her mouth open. "The chamber has a number of pharmaceuticals that numb my biological systems. I was . . . generous with them. I did maintain a reserve should self-termination become necessary to prevent capture."

"Not the worst idea," Felix said.

"I need a shower." She adjusted her bodysuit and scrunched her eyes shut. "My corporeal areas are . . . itchy."

"Can we get this tank moving again?" Corre asked. "Because if not, we've still got our own mission. You can come with us, beats waiting out here for the Flags to get you."

"I cannot abandon my post," she said flatly. "My power reserves are inadequate for motion. The enemy stole my motive power supply. I cannot move without a replacement."

"Okay, that's overcomplicated," Mason said. "We can't leave you here and no one has a 'motive supply' in an infantry unit. So how about you just climb out and—"

He reached for her arm. She slapped him away and inched towards the chamber.

"I cannot abandon my post," she said firmly. "My gene-code forbids it. I will not be found wanting by the examiners."

"We could use a tank, right?" Noah asked. "The ammo lockers are still sealed, so there's plenty of rounds. Maybe we can jerry-rig this motive thing she's talking about."

"Sarge?" Mason looked up at Corre.

"I'm no tread head," Corre said. "What's this 'motive' supposed to do? Or even look like?"

The woman pointed to the power pack on Mason's back.

"I need eleven power rods in the front casing," she said. "That will re-fire the reactor and I can move again."

"Oh, why didn't you say so?" Noah beamed. "We've got plenty of power rods. I left a pack full of them on the turret."

"We've got six up here," Corre said. "I'll have to—what did you say your name was again?"

"Coriaria 14, Sibirica gene line. Aleph Troop, Argent Squadron, Hegemony Cavalry." She took another bite of the spicy jerky.

"That's a mouthful. What did your crew call you?" Corre asked.

"Pilot. We are our positions," she said. "I cannot operate alone. I need the rest of the stations manned."

Noah looked around the inside of the tank, then raised his hand.

"Can I shoot the big gun?"

"No!" Mason and Corre shouted at the same time.

"Pilot—no name, really—Pilot, I'm going to dismount my armor and use the power rods to get you going again," Corre said. "Boyle will hook up the winch and line on the front of the tank to a big enough tree. Felix! Get in that seat you've already bled all over."

Felix gave him a thumbs up.

"Mason, on the seat on the other side of Pilot's box. Noah, ammo bitch. *I'll* take the main gun. Boyle will take the other gunner slot. I've got to box up and lash my shit down. Move it!" Corre turned away from the hatch.

"Why do I have to be ammo bitch? Felix is the new guy!" Noah tossed his hands up and smacked a knuckle against the ceiling.

"That's Corporal Felix to you." Felix wagged a finger.

"Where do you go?" Mason asked the pilot. "The driver's compartment doesn't have controls or even a seat."

"My chamber." She slid into the cylinder and put the headset and mask on. "I see through cameras mounted all around me. Keep your current headgear as I can tap your comms and additional concussions will impact combat effectiveness."

The cylinder rotated around, locking her into place.

"No way am I ever driving," Felix said. "Nope. Never."

"You lack the cerebral implants to interface with the drive systems," she said through their helmets. "Take up positions and perform ready checks. There's still enough ambient power from the main banks for the screens."

"What . . . what am I doing here?" Felix's hands hovered over the controls. A holo screen flickered to life. Drone counts flickered in a field and cameras arrayed around the tank piped in their feeds.

An electric shock zapped him through the seat.

"Ow! Thor's balls, what was that?" Felix leaned forward and rubbed the seat of his pants.

"Replace the Hedgehog drone to its proper housing. Unauthorized storage is a violation of Standard Operation Manual chapter 16, section 9, subparagraph—"

"Did you shock me?" Felix sat back down slowly.

"Non-tissue-damaging corrective procedures are required as per SOM chapter 2. Previous Drone operators are aware of performance requirements," she said through his helmet.

"I literally just sat down! Give me a minute to figure out where the buttons are before you do that again," Felix said.

"Ow! What the hell?" Noah shouted.

"Your work area has an unacceptable amount of flammable material," she said. "As per SOM chapter 8—"

"What is your problem?" Noah poked his chair. "Do you think we just magically know what we're supposed to do? We're Flankers. Grunts that run around, spot targets and eat bullets. We're not tread heads."

"It is my duty as Pilot to enforce discipline among the rest of my positions," she said.

"She *is* a Skien." Felix shook his head. "I didn't think she was *that* sort of a Skien."

"How do your officers maintain discipline without frequent applications of corporal punishment?" she asked.

"Training and leadership lead to discipline," Mason said. "We're men, not dogs you can ring a bell to train or cattle to prod. Stop with the shock treatment and tell us how we're supposed to run this thing."

The Pilot was silent.

"She still in there?" Noah asked as he gathered up bandages and trash.

"I am unfamiliar with disagreement from my stations. I do not know what to do," she said finally.

Noah pushed the garbage out of the top hatch and got out of the way when Corre dropped a foot through. The sergeant was in his still-soiled body glove, his auxiliary pistol strapped to one thigh.

Felix sniffed at the air and crinkled his nose at Corre.

Corre double-tapped an earbud.

"Radio check . . . good." He climbed into the main gunner's seat, which was at a low angle, with his legs extended out into the front of the turret. He put on a headset and a holo activated on a visor across his eyes.

"Main gunner, the other positions are refusing corrective actions," she said.

"She zapped my ass," Felix said. "No good reason."

"What? All of you stop whining and figure out your stations before you get my boot in your ass. You think we're in here for fun?" Corre asked. "Pilot, the power rods are installed and my Cataphract gear is lashed down on the back of the tank. Can you get her going or did I get undressed for nothing?"

"There is a distinct lack of protest at the promise of footwear applied to rectal sphincters, yet a minor electric shock to teach compliance is unacceptable. I do not understand natties," she said.

A thrum went through the tank and more holo screens came online. Felix replaced the drone into the launch tube. He turned dials within the holo screens, glancing over the different types still loaded up. He touched one field and dragged it to a box at the top of the screen.

The pneumatic tube next to him chugged.

"Oops." Felix covered his mouth.

"Why did you dump a rusty?" Sergeant Boyle asked over the radio. "Now all my IR's washed out."

On Felix's screens, a cloud of particles and thin smoke spread over the tank from above. A shock pinched the back of his thighs.

"Ow! Okay, okay I deserved that one," Felix said. "Is there . . . a manual?"

"I am cross-trained in all positions," Pilot said. "I will assume complete incompetence from you all and direct each of you without my goads. Is that acceptable?"

"Buttons aren't toys, Felix!" Mason shouted.

"Should I open the ammo locker?" Noah asked.

"No!" everyone else in the tank shouted.

"Just keep telling us what to do," Corre said. "Driving is the hardest part, I imagine, and you've got that covered."

"I am waiting for the anti-personnel gunner to attach my winch line," Pilot said. A vid feed of Boyle dragging a thick metal wire with a hook toward a massive tree appeared on all the holos.

"Power levels are optimal. Ammo, slide the closest door to you up and hold it in place until the mag locks engage. You can lose digits to an unsecured blast door," Pilot said.

"Roger." Noah grunted as he pressed the door up. There was a solid *thunk* and he took his hands away slowly. Inside the locker were dozens of strike faces for large caliber rounds, each the size of his palm.

"Remove the upper rightmost munition, blue-colored base, DPAT round," she said.

Noah slid the round out and held it in the crook of his elbows. The warhead was smooth and brass-colored at the tip; the body widened into a matte black that was rough to the touch.

"Damn thing's heavy," he said. "Why didn't the Flags take these?"

"They were unable to defeat the mag locks," Pilot said. "Also, main gun rounds are known to spontaneously combust when exposed to shock or high temperatures. Do not drop it."

Noah clutched it to his chest.

"Gunner, open the breech. Flip the *red* handle," she said.

Corre pulled a handle back and a metal flap snapped down on the back of the main gun.

Noah shoved the round in, pushing it forward with the knuckles of his fist. He lifted his hand just before the breech snapped shut with enough speed to have severed a finger. Noah looked at Corre in shock and counted his fingertips.

"The breech lock is automated," Pilot said. "Loader, familiarize yourself with the ammo types."

"What else is automated?" Noah went back to the ammo locker.

"The blast door will fall automatically should the battery packs be damaged. There is a point-six-four second warning sound," she said.

"This is not exactly how I thought I'd end the day." Corre lifted the visor goggles up. "Anyone tell her what's happening?"

"My orders are to evacuate this asset to Fort Triumph," she said. "They have not been rescinded by a field grade or above officer."

"Good news, that's what we're trying to do," Corre said. "The finer details can wait.... This tank have a name? Last armored unit I served with had names stenciled on the barrels."

"What reason? My designation is embedded in all transmissions," Pilot said.

"Luck," Mason said. "It's bad luck to go into battle in a ship or anything without a name."

"This is true." Felix wagged a finger close to his head. "We had one hell of a christening when my clan's ship left the docks. Dozens of pigs, wine...so much wine. I don't remember much after that."

"My designation is Coriaria 14, Sibirica gene line. Aleph Troop, Argent Squadron, Hegemony Cavalry," she said.

"That's a mouthful." Corre shook his head. "There's already one 'Corre' here and I'm not giving it up. Noah...give her a name. You've been luckier than most of us so far."

"Really," Noah deadpanned. "Sure, Sarge..." He looked at Mason and mouthed a name. Mason shook his head ever so gently. "Then, let's go with something from the old tongue. Ta'essa. The diminutive is normally used, though Sister Tricia hated when we used that at weekly seminary school. So she'd be Tessa."

"Ta'essa before God, Tessa to everyone else," Corre said. "Go with it."

"Huh, not bad," Boyle said over the radio. "Got Tessa hooked up."

"I don't need a name. I have my position," she said.

"Well, we're still a bunch of grunts and we don't call each other by our position," Corre said. "So we're going to call you Tessa."

"This is not in the manual," Tessa said. "Winch engaged. Moving."

The tank lurched forward, treads spinning. The winch whined as the Wolverine tipped forward. The treads bit into the ground and inched forward. More of the treads secured purchase and the entire tank chugged up the hillside.

"It feels good to move again," Tessa said. "Ammo, balance out the torsion compensators before the number three axle overheats."

Noah lifted a finger to a holo screen and moved it about like he was about to poke a fly.

"Is that ... the blue—"

"Green! Open the green field and move the slider to the left!" Tessa shouted.

"Oh, that one. Do I long press it or double—ow! Again with the shocks?"

Noah rubbed an eye and went back to memorizing the types of main gun rounds. The DPAT (Dual Purpose Anti-Tank) round he'd loaded earlier was the most numerous. The white-colored 99-S were something called "sabots" that didn't make sense to him but were on the other side of the locker from the DPATs. In between were shells with green baseplates, 99-Fs, for anti-personnel targets. There were three shells with neon baseplates that he was told not to touch.

The other locker had ammo canisters for the machine gun mounted on the turret that would be fired by Boyle. The Cataphract had dropped his armor for the other gunner's seat and was snoozing in the reclined chair. Felix and Mason both had nestled into a corner and had also dozed off.

"Hey, Tessa?" Noah rapped a knuckle on her chamber.

"Don't do that. I can hear you through your comms just fine," she said.

"Sorry ... don't you sleep?" He pulled an ammo case from the second locker and found it was full of drone canisters. He rummaged through them, sorting them out by color.

"Not precisely. I can rest segments of my brain and body at will, which keeps me alert and ready to respond to sudden changes in battlefield conditions. I do not go completely offline like you natties."

"Must be nice," he said. "I'm so tired that I can't sleep. That ever happened to you? Can it? My body might still be on shipboard time. It still thinks it's the middle of the day. Maybe it's the anti-concussion drug. My ears are still ringing a little bit."

"You are blathering. There is no tactical or operational importance to your words," she said.

"What? You tankers never just make idle conversation?" He sat on a chair that folded down from the inner hull.

"That is not our purpose," she said.

"I'm not trying to be rude . . . but what . . . how'd you end up like this? Even the Hegemony High Guard aren't so uptight all the time."

"Am I the first gene-perfect soldier you've ever met?" she asked.

"I've seen a couple . . . never talked to one before or had her zap me in the ass. That came out wrong. I mean—"

"We are purpose-bred to serve the Hegemony in whatever manner we are required. Some of us are more natty in our disposition. Supreme Marshal Telemachus was not raised in a crèche, he is of the Skien but he is most like you natties. I hope to one day fall under his glorious command."

"Yeah, he's pretty normal for a human being." A half smile tugged against Noah's face. "So, what did you do before you were assigned to all-those-words Cavalry? Where were you born?"

"There is no 'before.' The location of my crèche is irrelevant. I exist to pilot this tank with my other stations."

"Sorry about them. Casualties have been pretty bad all over the place," Noah said.

"Irrelevant. Stations have been replaced on seven different occasions due to system failure or casualties. The Ammo station was the sole survivor of a crew that participated in the Mekan Cleansing earlier this year. His pips extended from jaw to waistline. He was efficient at his station. Much more so than you."

"Hey, I just got started. . . . What was the 'Mekan Cleansing'?"

"Marshal Van Wyck ordered the eradication of Mekan City following an anti-Hegemony protest and riot on Foundation Day. Skien units were selected for that mission as we do not have the biological or instinctive dampeners against eliminating other humans. Ammo received partial kill credit on several thousand targets, hence his envious pip count," Tessa said.

"Wait. What? An entire city?" Noah sat up straighter.

"Complete eradication. I arrived dirtside months later. Skien employment elsewhere on the planet became problematic after Mekan as the Flags—any local citizen, actually—were incentivized to attack us. Less than optimal."

"And you're okay with that? Saint's Bones, no wonder they hate us so much."

"I do not render opinions on orders. That is not my purpose," she said.

"We're only supposed to follow lawful orders. That was an important class at Basic."

"How can an order be 'lawful' or not? Orders are to be obeyed, not subjected to additional scrutiny," she said. "This is an improvement bred into Skiens over natties like you. There is a reason we are the preferred soldiers of the Most High council."

"That's sort of confusing, with what Telemachus did and all." Noah leaned back and closed his eyes.

"Do Naturals like you process orders differently? What matrix do you filter commands through?" she asked.

"I am way too tired for this, but I brought it on myself," Noah said. "We swear to obey lawful orders. Orders that are allowed by the Interstellar Laws of Warfare that the Hegemony's a part of... huh, wonder how that works now. But before I left home, my father and my Bishop got all us first-timers together and told us that wars end. Battles don't last forever. We're going to come home eventually and we have to do it with our heads held high. A man commits a crime to survive or because he thinks he can get away with it... there's a reckoning. You darken your soul and that mark just festers over the years. The guilt will get worse and worse, and you can't un-fire a gun, can't bring someone back. Maybe you get through this life without consequences, but there's judgment waiting for you in the next."

"That is needlessly inefficient," she said. "Considering every order against some sort of religious or ethical standard will reduce reaction time and put other stations in danger."

"Getting told to toe the line and take a hill doesn't take a lot of consideration, Tessa. But we get told to mow down a village full of civvies and that's when we've got to make some harder choices. But Colonel Jematé's not the kind—wasn't the kind—to do that. Neither's Major Perrin."

"Curious," she said after a few seconds.

"Not to me. Now everything's one big shit show and we've got to watch every second of it." Noah lowered the blast door as gently as he could and leaned his head against it. He closed his eyes as his legs and hands twitched of their own accord as he slowly drifted towards sleep.

The top hatch slammed open.

"On your feet, look alive!" Corre said as he dropped down. The rest of the tank groaned as they shifted out of sleep. Noah gave his squad leader the ugliest look he could without Corre noticing it.

Corre wore a fresh body glove and somehow had found the time to shave.

"Operations order for the attack on the void port is out." Corre slid into the main gunner's seat. He punched a button on the underside of the turret and the hatch hinged shut.

"We cross the line of departure in ten minutes...son of a bitch, can't believe he did that to me," Corre grumbled as he donned his headset.

"Who did what, Sarge?" Boyle asked from the other side of the main gun.

"God damn—I mean Major Perrin acquired my Cataphract armor for himself to lead the attack. Said I didn't need it while I'm in Ta'essa here. His logic checks out, but you don't *do* that to another infantryman," Corre said.

"Activating all systems. Start checklists on all your screens," Tessa said. "You all should have them memorized by now. Choosing to sleep instead of learning basic station skills would be a goad-able offense if you were Skien soldiers."

"What? You weren't sleeping in there?" Mason leaned over and rapped a knuckle on her chamber.

"Stop doing that! And sleep is for the weak," she said.

"Don't worry about it, Sarge," Boyle said as the machine gun next to him rose out of the turret. Armor plating closed around the hydraulic cylinder as it spun and rose slowly, testing out the machine gun's sweep and angle to cover targets around the tank. "I'll maintain the squad's honor in the Cataphract/Flanker team."

"Perrin got one whiff of my suit and he took yours too," Corre said.

"That son of a bitch!" Boyle kicked a pedal against his foot and the turret slowed to the left.

"We can whine about it later," Corre said. "Mission's pretty straightforward. Infantry advance to fix the defenders in the maintenance hangars and the control tower. Second company—what's left of it—will set up a blocking position at the end of the runway and keep any Flags from rushing in to help at the village on the other side of the mesa. Major's concerned they might have vehicles on alert there for a counterattack, which is where we come in. Soon as they've got the target facilities under control, we roll up and establish fire superiority over the airfield."

"That is poor tactical employment," Tessa said. "We should be the first element to make contact as we can bring the most firepower to bear. Further, our survivability has a higher survivability index over the crunchies."

"The who?" Boyle looked over the side of his cradle at Tessa's chamber.

"The infantry. Flags make the most amusing noises when run over by my treads. While they are rarely as well-protected as Cataphracts, I have speculated that the sound made by—"

"Good God," Mason said. "Are all Skiens like her?"

"I think she's one of the tamer ones," Noah said.

"No, all tankers are like that, trust me," Felix said. "Flags probably have hooptie-trucks in that village."

He shared a map with a time track of five minutes from the village to void port with the other stations.

"The doctrinally correct term is 'technical vehicle,'" Tessa said.

"The navigation menus aren't that different from the Flanker UI," he said. "At least something's easy in this thing. Hey, Tessa, how do I launch the mortar drones again?"

"You long press the munitions selection screen, drag and drop the appropriate munition to the ready queue and either make a direction and distance fire mission with time-of-flight adjustment for an airburst or—"

"Figure it out on the way to the fight." Corre cringed hard as he said that. "Discovery learning is not supposed to be happening on the way to contact. Let's hope whoever's supposed to crew the hooopties is too drunk from winning when the commander at the void port pushes the 'oh shit oh fuck' button."

The tank rumbled forward.

"Power levels are dropping pretty fast," Noah said, pointing to a holo. "I don't think the power rods are going to keep us going for that long."

"We have a max effective driving range of nineteen kilometers," Tessa said. "I suggest using the manual turret slew gears to save power."

"Oh, that's what this little wheel thing is for." Boyle tapped a ring next to his fire controls.

"Men, we've got one shot at this," Corre said. "There's no reason to hold back. We get aboard the *Izmir* or we die here. Heard?"

"Heard," the rest of the former infantrymen said.

"I cannot abandon my post," Tessa said.

"Then you'd better tell us how to work all this stuff well enough to kill our way home," Corre said.

"Yeah, what's this 'extermination blossom' field for?" Felix traced a circle on one of the holo screens. "It's locked for some reason."

"Buttons are *not* toys, Felix," Mason shouted.

"I wasn't going to press it . . . I'm just curious what it does," Felix said.

"I want to know, too," Noah craned his neck up.

"If any details of this action are transmitted back to my crèche, my gene line will be terminated," Tessa sighed. "All of you shut up and listen to me . . ."

CHAPTER 22

Major Perrin swung his Gatling cannon from side to side, testing the balance servos in his Cataphract's knees and shoulders. As the battalion's operations officer, he didn't need this equipment to do his job of managing the commander's plan to win the battle. As the commanding officer, he needed to lead from the front.

The sun had nearly set, casting golden light through the sparse jungle this close to the void port.

"All companies on the ready line," Roux reported from a few steps away. The communications soldier wore the second Cataphract suit acquired from the squad now inside the Wolverine tank. The suit that smelled like someone had lost control of their bowels in it.

Rank had to have some privileges.

"Open a battalion-wide channel," Perrin said. There was a click in his ear and a blinking cursor on his visor once Roux had done as ordered.

"Men of Bretton... this attack is a no-fail mission. Our Hegemony has fallen and Dahrien rejects our presence. While we are not guilty of the crimes they accuse us of... our innocence proves nothing. Many will use this time of crisis to seize what they can, to spill blood in revenge when there is no authority to punish such evil. But we are of Bretton, our actions are our honor and our honor comes from God's grace. We will honor Him through our bravery and skill of arms. I am not the man Colonel Jemate was, God receive him and comfort him, but his final order to me—to all of us—was to return home. Our home needs us. They need us there, to protect them from the chaos let loose on what is left of the Hegemony. As such, we either seize Fort Triumph or we die here, on Dahrien. To remain here gives us the choice of dying on our feet or being executed on our knees. I will not give up. Neither have any of you, my soldiers. My brothers. We left Bretton beneath the Hero's Boughs with our families and our people calling on us to return with honor. They have prayed for our return, and it would dishonor their pleas to God for us to do anything less than our utmost to wear their prayers upon our souls . . . and honor God's promise to them that we will return someday. We win here, now, and our families will see us march beneath the Boughs once again. The only way for us is forward. Forward through the fires of hell until we reach home.

"We must seize the airfield and the TEU fuel reserves intact," he continued. "Nothing else matters. We will receive no mercy from the Flags. Cry havoc, men of Bretton. Forward unto the breach. Let's go home."

Perrin looked back to Roux and the other Cataphracts in his assault element. Most crossed themselves, while others banged fists against heavy breastplates in agreement with him. He slammed his visor down and signaled the advance. His Cataphract broke into a steady jog, automatically calculating footsteps and short hops across the uneven terrain. He let the suit pilot itself as he monitored the rest of the battalion.

Individual Cataphract icons moved toward the void port on his visor map. The Flankers followed behind them, ready to assault the buildings once the more heavily armored soldiers had established fire control over the void port.

Anything not from Bretton moving around the target area wouldn't last long.

"Roux, contact the *Izmir*. Order her forward," Perrin said.

"Sir, wasn't the plan to wait *until* we had the void port secured?" Roux asked.

"We'll either have won the day or lost it by the time the ship can arrive," Perrin said. "I don't want to stay down here a minute more than needed. Call her forward."

"Roger, sir," the comms soldier said, and another channel opened on Perrin's visor.

The major waited until the leading Cataphract from Alpha Company crossed a dotted line on the map. Drones mounted on the

Cataphracts shot off the heavy suits and flew towards the void port. If the Flag commander had any doubts as toward Perrin's intentions, the mass of scout and attack drones would make the Brettons' intentions clear.

Hostile drone tracks appeared on his map and were quickly eliminated by friendly Shrikes. The counter-drone wave was less than Perrin had feared it would be, which meant the Flags had few drones to protect the void base with—or they were suckering him into a kill zone.

Either option was plausible. The second-guessing of the enemy leader knowing just how desperate Perrin's situation was versus the commander *not* knowing the *Izmir* was en route to evacuate them once he could seize the fuel reserves made calculations more difficult.

The Flag leader could simply fade back into the populace and live another day. Fighting to hold the fuel depot that wasn't going anywhere—so far as he knew—should be a losing proposition on its face. No one wanted to be the last soldier to die in a war, not when victory had been declared.

While Perrin could war-game the best possible scenario for the enemy commander based on what he assumed the enemy commander knew, assumptions had a bad habit of not conforming to reality. And while he assumed the other commander was not an idiot or a fanatic unwilling to do the smart thing, that assumption would be tested within the first few minutes of battle.

A sharp crack broke through the jungle. A wave of overpressure passed over him as a lightning-fast cloud in the humid air. His ears stung from the blast, but he kept moving.

"*Thermobaric drones in the trees,*" a platoon leader reported up. "*Permission for full Shrike employment.*"

"Granted." Perrin double-blinked at a pulsing box and his suit shuddered as the Shrike magazine on his back emptied. The small drones fanned out above him, slicing through leaves and branches as they formed a protective dome over his front line.

"All units, all units," Perrin sent on the command channel, "there's no efficiency rating on this mission. Expend all munitions and drones as you see fit."

The Shrikes would detect and home in on anything inorganic

moving through the jungle that wasn't a Flanker or a Cataphract and, unless the Flags had found a way to make their popper drones out of wood, his men would have significantly better protection.

A slew of Shrikes veered off ahead of him. A drone exploded high in the canopy, collapsing trees all around it and swatting most of Perrin's Shrikes out of the air. A giant groaned as hunks of bark and sap-thick wood cracked apart. A shadow grew over Perrin as thousands of branches and leathery fronds crashed down on him.

The impact knocked him aside and into a tight green cell of branches and wood pulp. Perrin cursed as he struggled to move his arms and shoulders. He spun up his Gatling cannon and blasted away towards the trunk, sending tree limbs flying about.

He stopped shooting and bashed through a log the width of his arm and stomped a path out of the emerald prison. The thermobaric grenade had cleared a decent gap through the jungle for him. His suit reconnected to the rest of the assault force and more data flowed into his visor.

Bravo Company had taken casualties during their advance, but were online and laying down fire across the void port.

Perrin negotiated his way through the smoldering debris and hurried up a slight ridge. Fort Triumph was already aflame. Bretton drones flashed in the firelight as they smashed through barracks windows and exploded. Tracer rounds spat through smaller hangars on the other side of the landing pads the size of baseball fields.

His visor's target finder put a spinning reticule on a vehicle as it raced up the other side of the mesa and turned sharply down the road ringing the port.

"Rocket, proximity fuse," he said. The launcher on his back snapped away from his armor and hinged over his shoulder. The warhead spun to the configuration he ordered and there was a pleasant *ding* in his ear.

"Fire!" he shouted.

Nothing.

The insurgents in the back of the truck leveled a high-caliber machine gun and shot wildly at the tree line where the Bretton Cataphracts were.

"Wait . . . Loose!" Perrin spat.

The rocket screamed out of the launcher and corkscrewed across the landing zones. It ignited a few yards away from the truck, spraying it with white-hot shrapnel that tore the vehicle and the fighters in it to pieces.

Perrin made a mental note that he wasn't a Flanker anymore and that Cataphracts had their own particular set of voice commands.

"Armor! Incoming armor!" Roux shouted in his earpiece.

More vehicles drove onto the mesa. Four Sabrah armored personnel carriers formed a firing line with practiced ease and advanced across the landing zones slowly, their turrets working methodically from one side towards Perrin.

"Ta'essa, get up here now!" Perrin said as he glanced at his empty rocket launcher. "Timeline's moved up. Get over here—"

He didn't see the shell that landed a few feet from him. He had a brief sensation of weightlessness, then he was on his back, staring up at a smoke-filled sky through a cracked visor. A mosquito buzz roared in his ears and for a moment, he had no idea where he was or what he was doing.

Perrin raised his left arm to brush a burning branch off his chest, but something sprayed out from the broken crablike plating over his forearm. Blood gushed out of a stump where his hand used to be, hissing and sizzling against the fire and overheated metal of his chest plate.

"Ah . . . there's a wrinkle." Perrin tried to focus on the white, bony stumps jutting from his ballistic sleeve.

"Sir? Sir!" He heard Roux chirp through his earpiece.

"The *Izmir* . . . tell her to . . . get you all out of here," Perrin slurred. His Cataphract systems activated tourniquet lines just below his elbow and a pinch against his neck heralded a drug-induced escape from the growing pain.

Perrin fought to stay conscious for a few more moments and failed.

"Advancing!" Tessa shouted through the rest of the crew's earbuds. The Wolverine lurched hard and accelerated up the road.

"Whoa whoa whoa!" Corre waved at her to stop from his firing cradle next to the main gun, which made sense if they were fighting as an infantry squad. As she was in her chamber, she couldn't see his hand gesture. "What's going on?"

"Uh, Major Perrin was just on the channel," Mason said. "Only got a fragment of the transmission but—"

"He accelerated the timetable," Tessa said. "We do not need to understand our orders to follow them."

"Tanks?" Mason leaned closer to a holo screen, squinting. "There are enemy tanks on the other side of the void port. Data's coming in fragmented with all the fires."

"What *kind* of tank?" Tessa demanded.

"How should I—"

"You double-tap the icon and it'll tell us! We have certain munitions for certain targets. How do you all not know this?" Tessa's words were laced with fury and consternation.

"We're infantry. Either the bullet kills what we shoot at or we don't shoot at it . . . Sabrahs!" Mason's fingers flitted in and out of the holo screen.

"I've got a DPAT loaded in the big gun." Noah put a hand to the ammo rack release. "Do we need a green one instead?"

"It is the *main* gun and the DPAT is sufficient for Sabrahs but not ideal. There's a higher chance of you fiddle-dicking the swap and killing us all should there be a hull breach," she said.

"'Fiddle-dicking'?" Boyle leaned over and glanced into the lower part of the turret.

"I heard Felix say it while he was playing with the infrared disruption drones," Tessa said. "We will crest the mesa in the next forty-five seconds. The front battery will be briefly exposed to a lethal shot. I am accelerating to mitigate the risk."

"Felix, watch your mou-owth!" Mason rocked back in his chair as the Wolverine jerked ahead. The tank angled up and the lower compartment crew flailed about for something to hold onto. The tank slammed back to level.

"Acquire a target!" Tessa shouted.

"Action front, armor fifteen hundred meters," Corre said. "Loose!"

The cannon shot back as the shell fired.

Corre found the four Sabrahs again—all had their turrets and hulls oriented towards the Cataphracts firing at them from the other side of the void port.

"Missed? I think I missed," Corre said. "One's turning towards us!"

"You have to target-lock with the double triggers," Tessa said. "Main gunner, give the command to—why must I do everything?—loader, sabot round. Now!"

"Sabot?" Noah lifted the blast door. "Green one?"

"White! Load a white one! Machine gunner, are you waiting for an invitation to be productive?" Tessa shouted.

Noah pulled a sabot round halfway from the ammo rack when a round struck the forward armor, rattling the tank. The sabot round tipped out of Noah's hands and bounced off Terra's chamber.

"Ah! Get it, get it!" Felix pushed the round away from him and it rolled back to Noah.

"I hate you all so much," Tessa said.

The machine gun chattered on the top side of the turret. Boyle turned the weapon from side to side, shooting quick bursts that sparked off the Sabrah armor.

Noah hefted the sabot round up and shoved it into the breech. He slammed it home and ducked back down.

"Double triggers? Ah ha!" Corre slewed the turret to one side. "Target lock, loose!"

The tank rocked again.

One of the Sabrahs to the left of the pack burst apart. The turret rode the flames into the air and smashed to the ground between the Wolverine and the rest of the APCs. The cannon on a Sabrah spat out brief flames as it chugged out smaller shells.

The road in front of the Wolverine erupted into broken concrete and dust.

"Loader, dazzler shell," Tessa said as the tank turned to the left and rolled into an unkempt field. "Neon. The neon-colored one."

"Thought I wasn't supposed to touch—anyway." Noah slid one of the rounds from the rack. The entire munition was one long canister, no bullet tip of a DPAT round or the enclosed spike of a sabot. He slammed it into the main gun breech.

"Ready a DPAT," Tessa said. "Main gunner, aim for the ground just ahead of the targets. The dazzler will disrupt their targeting sys—"

A shell struck the flank of the Wolverine. The inner hull bulged inwards, sending tiny slivers of metal bouncing around the crew.

"Son of a bitch, that stings!" Felix rubbed a shoulder; his fingers came away bloody.

"Loose!" Corre shouted. The dazzler let off a trail of spinning sparks that arced into the air and bounced off the tarmac of the landing zones before it thumped into the turret of a Sabrah. The tank lit up like a bonfire and veered hard to its right and crashed into another tank, throwing off its aim and sending cannon shells flying across the void port.

"Not ideal but acceptable," Tessa said.

"My auto-targeters are offline," Corre said.

"Acceptable! The firing solutions for the last target are in the system buffers, just manually aim and take out that Sabrah driving towards the burning hangar," Tessa said.

"Didn't know I could do that. Noah?" Corre slewed the turret toward the Sabrah darting towards the cover of a hangar, the side walls collapsing from the inferno inside of it. Corre led the target just a tad and fired. The shell followed a slight ballistic arc and glanced off the rear armor.

The Sabrah tilted up like it had been stepped on and veered straight into the burning hangar.

"That's bad for them, right?" Boyle asked.

"Do you want to drive in there?" Tessa asked.

"Do . . . we? I mean, no." Boyle nodded hard, then shook his head emphatically.

"DPAT loaded." Noah closed the breech.

Boyle fired the machine gun at the two burning Sabrahs as the crews jumped out. Bullets tore up the ground around the tanks and blew the insurgents to pieces.

"I prefer my Gau," Boyle said, "but at least I don't have to carry this honey." He gave the hydraulic base inside the turret a pat.

"Do you want to lose fingers?" Tessa asked. "Because that's how you lose fingers."

"Hey, we've got a big target coming up onto the mesa," Mason said. "I think Felix launched some drones while we were busy."

"No point in saving them for later." Felix tilted his palm away from his shoulder. "And the bleeding's not stopping, just so everyone knows."

Noah picked up a first aid kit and slid across the hull to Felix. He rummaged through the pack and found a metal tube with an angled head.

"What sort of target?" Tessa asked. "Do not keep secrets from the rest of us!"

"I've got a couple sensor dumps from the pigeon drones," Mason said. "But all the drones went to shit after the dazzler shell."

"Hold on, getting comms from Perrin." Corre slapped his thigh twice for attention and pressed his other hand against his headset. "Not Perrin ... the fuel dump's been secured but there's still enemy in the surrounding buildings. Flankers are clearing them—"

"That is an incoming Wolverine!" Tessa shouted as Mason shared images from the drones. "The DPAT round loaded up will barely scratch its paint."

"Noah!" Corre shouted at the loader.

"I can't stop the bleeding," Noah said as blood spurted out from Felix's shoulder and onto Tessa's chamber. "Give me a minute or we'll lose him."

"I'll get the round." Mason scrambled out of his seat and promptly slipped on Felix's blood. He landed hard over Tessa's chamber, knocking the wind out of him.

"You all are a fucking circus!" Tessa spun the tank, orienting the front towards the road leading up from the insurgent-controlled village where the other Wolverine was approaching from.

"Boyle, unloading procedure for the main gun is as follows ..." she said.

"Dismounts!" Boyle spun the machine gun to the left and opened fire on a building. "Got more coming up from the village."

"Tank. Tank!" Corre shouted as the Wolverine's prow came up the steep incline. He fired the DPAT round and watched the humid air heavy with burning motes from the dazzler shell swirl in its wake. The round struck the underside of the tank and ricocheted into the ground where it exploded into a cloud of dust and smoke.

"Not a kill shot." Tessa spun the body of the tank towards the main hangar, keeping the turret locked on the other Wolverine, and drove forward. "It would've been a kill shot but *someone's* still screwing around and not loading the target specific munition!"

Mason drew in a ragged breath, left arm clutching his ribs. He lifted the blast door and blinked hard at the ammo rack.

"I unloaded the gun for you!" Corre shouted and craned his head forward. "Where are we going? Don't we want our front towards the enemy?"

"The fuel depot is highly combustible," Tessa said. "I'm putting it between us and the other tank."

"You're what?" Corre asked.

"Felix! That drone I told you not to play with? Launch the extermination blossom at the tank and do it now," Tessa said.

"I was about to do that anyway." Felix's words slurred but he dragged and dropped an icon on the holo screen. His entire right arm was a red sleeve of blood. "Not going to die without a little . . . fun."

The pneumatic tube to Felix's left coughed hard, cracking one of the tubes. The tank rolled behind the fuel depot and came to a jerking halt.

"White one?" Mason asked.

"Yes. Yes!" Tessa shouted.

"If that other tank hits the fuel depot, we're all going up in a big white flash of light," Boyle said. "Do we have literally any other options for cover?"

"Felix, Shrike launch now now now," Tessa commanded.

Felix wobbled from side to side, then collapsed back into Noah's arms.

"He's lost too much blood," Noah said.

"Launch the Shrikes before the other Wolverine's drones can get us!" Tessa shouted. "It's the only way he can attack us without blowing the entire mesa to hell."

Noah's hand hesitated over the screen for a moment and then quickly snapped from side to side.

"Did you just fire everything?" Tessa asked.

"I have to stop the bleeding!" Noah pulled Felix from his seat and laid him out next to Tessa's chamber.

"Time of flight for the exterminator is closing to zero. Gunner, ready on manual, the dazzler's affecting them just as much as us," she said.

"Set," Corre said.

The tank reversed, exposing itself to the other Wolverine as the extermination shell opened high over the battlefield and spun rapidly. Tiny submunitions rained out, blanketing the opposite side of the void port with small explosive rounds that burst at head level among the insurgent infantry swarming up from the village.

The cluster munitions bounced off the other Wolverine's hull and exploded inches off the armor, shattering sensor blisters and tearing away camera blocks.

"Fire. Fire!" Tessa shouted as the tank kept rolling backwards.

The turret rocked the tank from side to side as the sabot round crossed the battlefield ... and went right over the other Wolverine.

The enemy tank's turret turned to track them.

"Mason. Mason?" Corre slapped his thigh.

"Another white one." Mason rammed the shell into the breech with one arm and fell to his knees, groaning in pain.

Corre watched as the other turret froze. Tessa reversed the gears on the treads and their tank spun in place. angling the right flank towards the enemy. She kicked the tank forward just as the other Wolverine fired.

Corre watched the blur scream towards him. The shell careened off the front hull and exploded in the jungle behind them.

"I am out of miracles. Kill it!" Tessa shouted.

Corre aimed center mass on the other Wolverine and pressed the triggers. The sabot round pierced the turret ring and tore into the open ammo rack. The Wolverine erupted into fire, killing more insurgents as its hull fragments became gruesome shrapnel all around it.

The turret flipped end over end in the air. The broken main gun plunged into the ground, propping up the rest of the smoking turret into a grisly battlefield totem.

"Target destroyed," Tessa said. "Machine gunner, there are still crunchies out there."

"Holy shit, we're alive," Boyle said.

"Machine gunner, why aren't you killing them?" Tessa asked. A brief electric shock jolted Boyle back into action.

"I stopped the bleeding." Noah held up a pair of red clamps. "He needs IVs and an actual medic."

"Is there one aboard that ship?" Tessa asked.

"Ship?" Boyle looked up, his face full of pain but a glimmer of hope in his eyes.

The *Izmir* roared overhead.

CHAPTER 23

"This is such a mess." Mehmet stood behind the helmsman station on the *Izmir*'s bridge. The ship had set down on the landing pad closest to the fuel depot. Burning tanks and tufts of flame dotted the holo all around the ship. Lambert was just behind him, a headset held against his ear. Harris clutched his data keys to his chest.

"The void port is secure," Lambert said. "There's a drone perimeter set up and the insurgents are retreating."

"I don't think we need to say how volatile the fuel is during transfer," Harris said.

"My ship is most allergic to bullets as well," Mehmet said.

"Then let's take on fuel and my men as quickly as possible," Lambert said. "Harris . . . it's time for you to keep to your end of the bargain."

"Yes, indeed," Harris chuckled nervously. "Overriding the remote systems now."

He pulled a data key from the pouch and slid it into the port built into the base of his palm. His eyes rolled back, and his lips twitched and pulled against his teeth.

"Auto-fueling systems engaged," a digitized voice came from his mouth. "Upload of . . . 697 TEUs commencing."

The *Izmir* shuddered as fuel lines beneath the landing pad emerged from underground reservoirs and connected to the ship's tanks.

"*How* many?" Mehmet whirled around, his jaw open. "That's not what you promised, Harris! That's barely enough to get us out of the sector! Mr. Barnes, the club."

Barnes grunted and stomped towards them.

"No no no!" One of Harris' eyes unrolled and locked onto Mehmet. "It seems the locals managed to siphon off some of the fuel stores before we arrived...that or the now-dead commander was supplementing his income selling it to the insurgents. I can still deliver on my part of the bargain. We'll need to make a pit stop along the way to Bretton is all."

"Not the deal." Mehmet snapped his fingers twice and Barnes put a heavy, warty hand on Harris' shoulder.

"We can get to Ulvik!" Harris clutched Lambert's arm. "I-I-I have people there. There's a fuel refinery with all the TEU we'll need. I have all the codes we'll need. It's a sequestered system, they won't even *know* the Hegemony is gone. It'll be business as usual for me to refuel the ship. Please. Please!"

Barnes tapped the metal-studded club on Harris' shoulder.

"Captain...he's likely correct," Lambert said. "With almost 700 TEUs, how far can we get?"

"Don't crush his skull yet, Mr. Barnes." Mehmet opened a star chart in the helmsman's station. "Ulvik is in range, but there's an interdiction order. Old one, all the current astrogation warnings have expired with the Hegemony. We come out of hyper without the right codes and the system pickets will either impound us or destroy us."

"These codes." Harris waggled another data cylinder in front of his face.

"Where else can we reach?" Lambert asked.

"Harruma, but that's a Hegemony naval post. Half the tracks we've seen leaving the system were going there," the helmsman said. "Aton VII, but that's in the Deseret sector—and didn't this guy say it was already in rebellion?"

"It most certainly is," Harris said.

"We can't even get to Alliance space," Mehmet spat. "He knew. He knew there wasn't enough fuel at this depot he just wanted to get his lying ass off this planet!"

Mr. Barnes growled.

"I didn't! But we've got enough fuel for Ulvik and there aren't any picket ships blockading that hyper point." He licked his thick lips. "We may have lucked out...in a fashion. And what're your other options, hmm? You go to Aton or Harruma or some dead star in range and then what? You think they'll just give you fuel to reach Bretton? No, whatever faction finds you first will either kill you or draft you and your men, Lambert. Mehmet, this ship's a bonus prize to them. I doubt your hazard insurance is even valid..."

Mehmet beat a fist against the station, startling the helmsman.

"Ding." Harris' head popped back and his eyes crossed. "Fuel transfer complete."

"I never should've taken this contract," the captain said. "Mr. Barnes, take Harris to his quarters and lock him in there. We're setting course for Ulvik. Lambert, load up your men. A deal is a deal."

Mehmet swiped a new panel open in the tank and entered a long digit code. A wire diagram of the ship appeared and the cargo ramp lowered. The captain's brows scrunched as he peered at a camera feed.

"I didn't deliver a tank..."

"Is its mass an issue?" Lambert asked.

"Not really. Suppose it's better to have one and not need it than need it and not have it." Mehmet shrugged.

"Fair enough, but I need your ship's auto-surgeon activated right now. There are wounded," Lambert said.

"Of course." Mehmet tapped in another code and watched as Flankers and Cataphracts ran up the ramp. The Wolverine idled at the base, turret scanning from side to side. "There were so many more when we arrived... I'm sorry, Lambert."

"I thank God for saving as many as we have. If you'll excuse me?"

Mehmet raised a hand and dismissed him.

Corre helped Mason off the back of the Wolverine. His breathing was labored and came in short huffs, likely from broken ribs. Noah was just behind his brother, arms akimbo in case Mason fell to either side.

Mason let out a pained yelp as his boots scuffed along the *Izmir*'s deck. Soldiers of Bretton sat along the bulkheads, helmets off. All had the long stare of fresh combat in their eyes.

"Sickbay's open," Boyle called to them as he trotted over. "Got Felix right in and he's in the recovery room, which is the mess hall, but whatever. Saw the major in there too. There's a line for everyone else that's not urgent or on a litter, but the auto-surgeon's going through people pretty quick."

"It giving out pain meds?" Mason asked. "The green pills are the best ones."

"I've got some now if you need some." Boyle tapped a chest pocket.

"Get him to the doc before you give him anything," Corre growled. "And how'd you get those so fast? Never mind. I don't want to know."

"Ah, hello there?" Colonel Lambert called out. He raised the tip of his cane as he limped over. "Who's the commander of this . . . thing?"

"Get him over," Corre said to Noah and Boyle, then turned around and approached Lambert. "I think I am, sir."

"Sergeant Corre, if I remember right." Lambert set his cane between his feet and leaned on the handle. "I don't believe . . . you are rated on this weapon system. These are rather complex machines; how did you even manage to drive it?"

"We didn't, sir. We recovered Ta'essa here and she came with a driver. We'll need to add her to our rolls. . . . We're going home, correct? Sir?"

"Yes, but actually no. The rumor mill is no doubt full of speculation, but I've secured our passage back to Bretton. Though our way back may be a bit zigzagged. Things are unwell between Dahrien and home, but we'll get there before too long. You've my word." Lambert tapped the Wolverine with his cane and a hunk of armor plating fell off.

"We'll need this secured properly," Lambert said. "The crew are rather strict about this sort of thing. Can't have a loose cannon bouncing about, can we?"

"Negative, sir. Let me ask our subject matter expert." Corre hooked a thumb towards the turret. "She's . . . a little different."

"Certainly, a main battle tank amidst infantry. We'll incorporate her one way or another, but the more the merrier on our way home. Well done securing the void port, sergeant. If you'll excuse me, there are no doubt many embers about the ship ready to burst into flames that only I can piss on." Lambert slipped his cane up in a pseudo-salute and walked towards the sick bay. He turned back and said, "'Ta'essa,' you said? I rather like it."

Corre raised a hand and was about to clarify his last statement but let it slide. He climbed back into the tank and dropped down next to the chamber. Felix's blood was smeared over much of the floor and the entire place reeked of body odor.

"Tessa?" Corre raised a hand to knock on the chamber but ran it through his high-and-tight haircut instead. Dried sweat and blood from a nick he didn't remember suffering came off.

The chamber rolled open. Tessa removed her air mask and headset, then sat up. She wasn't particularly tall, Corre realized, and her frame was slight enough that he wasn't sure she could carry a Flanker carbine into battle.

"Mission accomplished?" she asked. Her voice was a fair bit more pleasant when it wasn't through his earbud.

"Yeah, we're underway. This is a civvie ship. If some Navy vessel has issue with us, everything will be over pretty quick. But I guess we can relax now. You saved our asses back there. All of us. Whole battalion. I'll be sure the chain of command knows that. Soon as I figure out what it is." Corre sat against the hull and let out a sigh.

"Our performance was well below baseline standards." She raised her arms over her head and stretched from side to side. Her bodysuit framed her chest in such a way that Corre made a mental note to get her into a less flattering set of utilities as soon as possible.

"Ah shit!" He sat forward as a realization hit him. "You're the only female aboard."

"All Skien vehicle drivers are female. We tolerate the chamber better than males and our lesser stature makes for easier designs," she said. "Is that a problem?"

"No, Tessa, you did great as the driver . . . the problem is that you're the only female on a ship full of infantrymen and scumbag sailors," Corre said. "Something tells me that you Skiens didn't have *that* class during Hegemony Standard Schooling."

"I don't understand." She ran a hand through her short hair. "Sergeant, may I make a personal hygiene request?"

"You don't have to ask for permission for that sort of thing, Tessa. What do you need?"

"I need," she leaned closer to him and stared him straight in the eye, "a shower. A hose. A bucket of anything moist to—"

Corre got a whiff of compounded sweat and grunge emanating from her and the chamber.

"Saint's bones, you do need one, but we take care of our equipment before we take care of ourselves. You're my soldier, it's my job to take care of you even if you aren't from Bretton. Same with

Felix." Corre rubbed a hand under his nose and kept it there to mitigate the smell.

"Our drone magazines are empty. Further, the onboard ammunition supply is below standard. We will need a full inspection to assess damage to the hull and—"

"Tessa, you understand where we're going? We're going home. My home. Bretton. Where's home for you?" Corre asked. "We'll get Felix back to Syddan or his ship clan one way or another, but he doesn't seem to be in any real hurry."

"I do not understand the question." She scooted back to her chamber and let her knees dangle over the edge. "This is my station."

Corre rubbed his knees.

"What happens to Skiens once they finish their service? We were drafted for two years of active-duty time. The clock wasn't ticking while we were in transit," he said.

"Skiens entered service less than twenty years ago. None has ever been dismissed from their station. Those too injured to function are permanently retired," she said.

Corre's face darkened.

"I didn't know that . . . What do you want to do?" he asked.

"I do not understand the question. My station and my flesh are both viable for service. I estimate at least three more days of continued operation before compounding personal hygiene requirements will negatively impact performance," she said.

"You know what? Let's knock down the fifty-meter targets before we aim at the ones on the far end of the firing range," Corre said.

"Do I have permission to dismount my station?" she asked.

"Granted." Corre rubbed his face. "I need to secure us some barracks space. Then there's your privacy needs. This is going to be such a fucking headache."

"Hey in there," someone with a thick accent called from outside. "Can you give us a hand securing this to the deck?"

"Moving!" Tessa hopped up and set a foot against the top of the commo station's seat to boost herself up. Corre got a glimpse of how tight the rest of her bodysuit was.

"Wait, do you have some coveralls or something in here?" Corre asked.

"In a locker at the bottom of my chamber. Why?" She scratched her rear end.

"It's ... cold out there—no, just put some more clothes on before I have to beat someone to death today just to save myself the trouble later."

Felix hopped off the tank and landed hard on the *Izmir*'s deck. He touched his chest and let out a long sigh.

"Shipboard air ... finally," he said.

Boyle dropped down next to him.

"I am both disgusted and relieved to be back aboard this bucket," Boyle said. "We're going home, but the trip over was no fun. Nothing but combat drills drills drills and then we had to do ship drills and get in those nasty vac emergency suits." He shivered.

Felix looked the cargo bay over.

"The dorsal lights aren't rigged correctly, that's why the illumination keeps blinking in and out. Hey, do me a favor and don't tell the crew I'm a spacer. I volunteered for translation duty by accident, and I don't want to be doing anyone else's job for them," Felix said.

"Works for me." Boyle put his hands on his hips and leaned back for a moment. "I wonder if we'll actually get to walk under the Hero's Boughs. We weren't gone that long. Most come back after at least two years."

"What're these 'boughs' everyone keeps talking about?" Felix sat against the tank treads and Boyle joined him.

"The main avenue running up Armorica City has Salix oak trees on either side. Legend has it they were planted by Saint Robin himself. The branches arc over the cobblestones and vines native to Bretton will bloom into white flowers with each full moon. You should see it just after dawn, the golden light through the leaves, petals falling over everyone ... soldiers returning from war get to march under the boughs and then the Lord Bishop blesses our return. He uses Saint Robin's own Bible to do it, too." Boyle swiped a hand across an eye.

"You get back from war and they make you march in a parade?" Felix asked.

"It's worth it. Why, what do Syddan men do when they get off active duty?" Boyle asked.

"Most of them get drunk and fight." Felix shrugged. "But what you've got waiting for you sounds pretty good. Did you say there's a lot of bakeries where we're going?"

"Yeah . . . one on most every street," Boyle said.

"I was thinking about that bag-eat I had on shore leave once. Sat on a grassy field in the middle of a first diaspora city, just munching away on it. It was one of the first times I actually liked being dirtside. Later on I went back to the same bakery and watched them making these twisty things with salt. I wanted to see how they made the bag-eat but they weren't doing them then," Felix said.

"Okay, it's a baguette, and if you keep saying it wrong, a man of Bretton will take offense. And you bake baguettes first thing in the morning. *Baguette tradition*, but any bread that's not made as per *baguette tradition* is not a baguette," Boyle said. "Takes time to do it right."

"You guys take your bread seriously. Can you teach me to make it?" Felix asked. "Maybe there's more to life than void ships and war."

"His sister Marie can," Mason said from atop the tank. "She's got the best *pain de campagne* in the province."

"Hey hey hey!" Boyle raised a finger. "None of that talk."

"You have a sister? She . . . single?" Felix asked.

"We're not talking about her. Ever." Boyle stood up. "Now if you'll excuse me, I've got to take a dump and I want to get in and out of there before any of you stank-ass—ah shit."

Sergeant Corre turned around one of the cargo containers that held the battalion's 3D printer foundries. He had a determined look in his eyes.

"Felix," Mason said. When the other man was looking at him, he mimed a pair of impressively large breasts and canted his head at Boyle.

Felix's brows shot up.

"Where's Noah?" Corre asked. The last of the original squad stuck his head out of the turret. "Get down here. We all need to have a little talk."

"Should I get—"

Corre gave Noah the Look that only NCOs can, and Noah hurried down to the deck.

"Gentlemen . . . Felix, we have a situation with Tessa," Corre said.

"As you're aware, this entire ship is a sausage fest with the exception of her. Do I need to explain the problem any further?"

"Someone . . . might need a lesson." Boyle glared at Noah.

"Tessa is not hideous—and even if she was it wouldn't matter—it is our duty as her squadmates to keep her safe and her honor intact. The woman is . . . off. Apparently the Skiens don't learn normal human social interactions, so it is up to us to take care of her," Corre said.

"Yeah, she's a bit of a weirdo," Mason said.

"But she is *our* weirdo," Corre said. "No one outside of this squad is allowed to try and date her, make jokes about her or even imply she's a woman of poor character. Just like she's a nun back home."

Noah raised a hand.

"Don't you even fucking ask!"

Noah's hand shot down.

"At least we've got a dick shooter to back up the threat," Mason said. "Couple guys in Delta Company were asking about that."

"It wasn't intentional," Felix whined.

"Hell, the ship's crew were asking about who shot someone in the dick." Boyle nodded.

"You know what, we're going to lean into the dick shooting." Corre scrunched his lips and shook his head. "Sounded better in my head. I will have a talk with her and explain the standards to her. Anyone violates those standards and we are honor-bound to beat them within an inch of their life. Just like she's from a convent. As such, she will have a battle buddy with her at all times. We'll take shifts," Corre said.

No one objected.

"Boyle. Go find us some white paint and stencils," Corre said.

"Moving." Boyle hopped to his feet and sauntered off.

Felix waited until he was out of earshot.

"But we can ask about Boyle's sister, right? Not the same rules as Tessa."

"Oh, *her*." Corre's brows shot up. "Best *pain de campagne* for miles . . . if Boyle kicks your ass, it'll be because you deserve it. Now let's get our barracks secured before those assholes in Charlie Company take all the good spots near the only showers with hot water."

CHAPTER 24

Major Perrin awoke with a start. One arm was bent and bound to his chest; the other had more than one IV line plugged into it. He blinked until his eyes managed to focus on the ceiling and the tops of wall lockers.

"Ah, right on time." Lambert leaned forward from the one seat in the small cabin. "The medics said your sedatives would wear off about now."

Perrin bent his head forward and looked over his body. He wore a white smock with tight socks around his feet and lower legs. His left arm ended halfway below the elbow in a plastic cylinder.

"Well . . . that I am aboard the same cabin I occupied on the *Izmir* implies that we escaped Dahrien. How many made it aboard? Things were in doubt when I was hit." Perrin smacked dry lips.

Lambert gave him some water from a squirt bottle.

"Of the four-hundred-and-eighty-one men of Bretton we brought to Dahrien by the *Izmir*, three hundred and nine made it back aboard," Perrin said. "Saint receive them."

"Saint comfort them," Perrin said. He looked down at where his left hand should've been. "A whole career dreaming of leading men into combat and when I finally get there . . . my first battle lasts only a couple of minutes. I can still feel it. Can even open and close fingers that aren't there."

"The men have been most worried about you," Lambert said. "Bugging the medics for updates and such. I must say, Easton, I didn't know you had it in you. No complaints by me."

"Hmph." Perrin shimmied back onto a pillow and propped his chest up. "Nor I you. How did you manage to pull all this off?"

"I sold my soul to the devil." Lambert's hands gripped the handle of his cane. He gave Perrin a quick rundown of the deal with Harris and Mehmet. "Though like any deal with the devil, there are caveats and loopholes. We're not on course to Bretton just yet, but to some outpost named Ulvik where Harris believes he can bluff his way to enough fuel to get us home."

"Do you believe him?" Perrin asked.

"We don't have much of a choice, do we? Civil war has broken out across the Hegemony . . . though I don't think it's quite right to call it 'civil.' The Hegemony was a very weak glue holding a lot of different peoples together. Peoples that hated each other. We've just reverted back to the natural order of things. Tribe killing tribe. Clan against clan. Though the Skien warlord that threw the first stone into the whole castle of glass is a bit of a wild card. We'll have to beg, borrow and steal our way home . . . or fight for what we need. As such, I have high hopes that Harris can get us what we need and we're not shedding blood for our own ends. I'd rather hold my head high when we walk under the Hero's Boughs again."

"And what must we give this Harris to get us home?" Perrin asked.

"Like any intelligence officer, he's out to save his own hide. I'm sure Governor Engelier will grant him a stipend and an apartment at the very least for getting us home. Though, he's likely more valuable than that if his connections and knowledge of power brokers is to be believed," Lambert said.

"I don't know about you, but I'd call that a bargain," Perrin said.

"Indeed, but I still don't trust him. He's . . ." Lambert shivered for a moment.

"The men? Are they situated? Our equipment needs to be secured and—" Perrin tried to get out of bed and fell back, woozy.

"They're just fine." Lambert gave him a pat on the shoulder. "Rather easy, actually. We just put everything back where we had it. I gave the officers a general idea of what to do and let the NCOs do what they do best: organizing and controlling the soldiers. Though what to do with the Wolverine tank has been a project. Very nice find, I rather like it."

"You brought it with us?" Perrin gave him a confused look.

"Was I not supposed to? It's taken up a sizeable portion of the cargo bay, but we had room for it."

"I thought . . . I was going to leave it behind, but it's better to have it and not need it than need it and not have it. How long until we drop hyper at Ulvik?" Perrin asked.

"Two more days. I'll handle the battalion while you rest. You've earned a day off," Lambert said.

"Bugger that, the men need to see me up and about and in good spirits or they'll—" Perrin tried to sit up again and froze, his abdominals tight. "—why is the cabin spinning? I'm floating. Did we lose power to the gravity...things?"

He eased back down, one hand gripping the sheets.

"At least a day off. The men are assembling a prosthetic hand for you. It might end up being little more than a hook, but do try and appreciate their efforts. Captain Mehmet's preparing a meal for you from his personal stores once your eyeballs aren't floating in medications." Lambert stood and hobbled toward the door. "I'll let the medics know you're awake."

"Lambert...well done." Perrin raised his stump to him.

"Bah, you did better. Thank me when we're home." Lambert nodded at him and opened the door.

CHAPTER 25

Noah carried a stack of food trays covered in plastic into a berthing room. Double bunks were stacked against the walls with a long table down the middle of the room. Wall lockers nestled between the bunks had names written on strips of paper on them.

Felix lay on one side on a bottom bunk, a blanket up to the bandages covering his right shoulder. Boyle sat on the bunk over Felix's, a pair of headphones on. His eyes were closed and his head bobbed along to some song Noah couldn't hear.

"I've got chow." Noah set the trays down. "Crew made us some sort of churro-looking stuff— Ain't even listening." He glanced at a clock on the wall, then rushed to pull a small ticket from a pocket. "My shower chit's almost up! Damn it damn it son of a bitch!"

Noah flung a locker open and yanked out a white mesh sack with small bottles, fresh utilities from the battalion's foundry printer, and a towel inside. He went back to the passageway and turned a corner to a small recess with a shower bay and restrooms behind separate doors.

Noah double-checked his chit and narrowed his eyes on the timer over the shower door. It ran down to zero as he stripped off his shirt. A new timer began on the clock as the mag locks snapped off and the door went slightly ajar, releasing a waft of steam.

"Mason," Noah hissed. "Mason, you're cutting into my time and if you think I'm going to help you scrub your ass—"

He flung the door open.

Tessa stood in the shower, her legs slightly wider than her shoulders, a towel wrapped around her lowered head blocking the view of her more intimate areas. Noah froze as soap suds and water dripped down her legs and flanks.

Tessa flung her head back and locked eyes with Noah, who could now see everything.

"Ah!" Noah slapped a hand over his eyes and fell back. The shower door slammed shut.

Noah had his back to the bulkhead, his jaw open. Mason rushed out of the bathroom, one hand holding his pants up. Mason looked at the shower door, then at his shocked brother.

"Ahhhhh!" Mason raised his hands and shook them next to his head.

There was a bang against the shower door.

"Ahhhhh!" Noah shouted in panic and fear as he ran back to the berthing. He found Felix and Boyle both seated at the table, eating rice and kababs.

"Hey, you want your churro-looking thing?" Felix pointed at a tray laid out on the other side of the table.

"Ahhhh!" Noah slapped his hands to the side of his head.

"What's the prob—oh no." Boyle dropped his fork and swallowed a mouthful of rice. "*You* brought the food."

Mason ran to the doorway so fast he slipped trying to stop. He got one hand on the doorframe and pulled himself into the berthing, his breathing heavy and his face red.

"Corre's gonna kill us all." Mason put his hands on his hips.

"You were supposed to guard the door!" Boyle shouted.

"You were supposed to tell Noah not to go in there!" Mason shouted back.

"I was listening to music and didn't see him. You were supposed to guard the door!" Boyle slapped a hand on the table.

"You were supposed to be in the shower!" Noah thrust a finger at Mason. "It was your turn!"

"I had to take a shit—which I thought was okay because *Boyle* was going to tell Noah I gave my chit to her because *Boyle* said the hot water was running out—and it was my first shit in days and—"

"What is wrong with you guys?" Felix poked a fork into some rubbery carrots. "This some weird Bretton—oh no, Corre is going to kill us. He said we're honor-bound to kill anyone that messes with her because of Taessa or something . . . wait, maybe he didn't see anything."

"Well," Noah closed his eyes, "it was steamy—not like that!—and she's pale. Really pale all over and okay so maybe I got a good look at . . ." He opened his eyes.

The other three men were frozen in place.

"She's behind me, isn't she?" Noah asked.

Tessa cleared her throat. She strode into the room in baggy overalls, her hair still damp against her scalp. She stopped between the table and Noah, her back to him. She clasped her hands over the small of her back at parade rest.

"Boyle, if I'm to understand the rather unprofessional screaming I heard in the passageway, is it correct that you misled me as to my proper shower chit time? I did draw last from the hat before Noah went to pick up our rations," she said.

"Um, yes." Boyle swallowed hard. "I gave up my hot water allotment for you. So did Mason."

She looked at Mason, who nodded and looked away sheepishly.

"And why was I misled? This is suboptimal communication between stations," she said.

"You really wanted a hot shower," Boyle said. "And, if we're going to be all optimal and stuff . . . you needed one."

Everyone but Tessa nodded.

"And Mason was posted to 'guard my honor' that Sergeant Corre insists on protecting?" Tessa took a step towards Mason.

"I had to shit!" Mason extended an arm and wagged a finger at Boyle. "He was supposed to stop Noah."

Tessa whirled around and narrowed her gaze at Noah.

Noah went to the position of attention like he was about to be yelled at by an officer.

Tessa stood very close to Noah, her head coming up to his shoulder. She hooked a finger into his collar and pulled him down to be cheek to cheek with her.

"I believe there has been a series of honest mistakes," she whispered. "Do you agree with that assessment?"

Noah nodded.

"This will never be spoken of again. Is that clear?" she asked.

Noah nodded.

"The hot water supplies have indeed expired, and a cold shower is in order for you," she whispered into his ear.

"Yes, ma'am. I need a cold—I mean—"

Tessa let go of his collar and went to the table. She pulled the plastic off a tray and sniffed at the food.

"What is all of this? It doesn't look like any standard Hegemony ration pack. I am partial to the beef stew if that's ever available," she said.

"So I should just...go?" Noah backed toward the doorway.

Tessa snapped her fingers twice and thrust a finger towards the shower bay.

Noah stumbled over the doorframe and jogged down the passageway.

"You've never eaten *food* food before?" Felix asked.

"These small rubbery bits are curious." Tessa pushed rice around with the edge of her spoon.

"Everyone get the stank off?" Corre asked as he entered the bay.

Boyle, Felix and Mason acted like a grenade had just rolled into the room.

"What? Anything wrong?" Corre frowned.

"What? Nothing!" Mason shrugged.

"Shipshape." Boyle's head went north and south several times.

"Alright." Corre pondered for a moment then sniffed the air. "Hot chow, outstanding."

CHAPTER 26

Major Perrin stepped out of the lift and onto the *Izmir*'s bridge. The crew went about final checks in their native language as the ship approached the hyperspace exit. He'd pinned his left sleeve underneath his too-short arm and kept it bent behind his back as he approached Mehmet, Lambert, and the toadlike Harris at the captain's station: a comfortable-looking chair surrounded by holo displays projected up from a small dais.

"Major, glad to see you up and about," Mehmet said. He was sitting with his elbows on his knees, fingers steepled beneath his chin, as sensor readings poured into his screens.

"Your ship's auto-surgeon does good work," Perrin said. "I'm still a bit fuzzy around the edges."

"In my experience, good food, good pay," Mehmet glanced at Lambert, "and good living conditions attract the best crews. Also, a reputation for fair and stern discipline will get the bad apples to weed themselves out."

Mr. Barnes grunted from his post against the bulkhead.

There was a slight rock across the deck. Mehmet flipped a panel open and gestured to Harris.

"As we're exiting hyper, I will now upload my system access codes." Harris drew a data rod from his jacket and pressed it into a slot. A tiny needle popped out from the end. He pressed the flat of his thumb against it and held it there until the rod flashed blue. He sucked blood from the puncture.

"I'm aboard this ship, same as you, captain," Harris said. "I've the same vested interest in not being blown out of space."

"How long until you can get our tanks topped off?" Mehmet asked.

"The sky hook has a refueling platform." Harris curled the fingers of one hand in front of his face. "It should be fairly straightforward. Hegemony business and all. Just let me do the talking."

"*Kolay gelsin,*" Mehmet said. "*Inshallah.*"

"No need for superstition when one has the correct paperwork." Harris chuckled. "I suggest you broadcast the codes before we exit hyper. That's standard protocol for the Intelligence Corps."

Mehmet spoke to crewman to one side.

The *Izmir* left hyperspace with a shudder. Perrin put a hand to the back of Mehmet's chair and choked down something that tried to kick up his throat.

The system appeared on the screen in front of Mehmet.

A single pale blue primary star was several AU from the hyperspace junction. Ulvik was closer, a snow-and-ice-covered world with several Hegemony installations pinging around it. A massive asteroid was in a mining extraction frame orbiting a large moon.

"There." Harris traced a fingertip around a space elevator extending up from Ulvik's equator, topped by a massive space station at geostationary orbit. "There's the refueling station. Just like I said."

"We're being hailed." Mehmet gripped the armrests as a new field popped up in front of him. "Not from a Hegemony ship."

Harris' head bobbed back as if he'd just been hit in the forehead.

"That is . . . highly unlikely. The only system pickets would be Hegemony corvettes, not— One moment." Harris pulled a small data slate from his jacket and concentrated on the screen.

An alert screen appeared in Mehmet's tank. A ship appeared on an intercept course with the *Izmir*.

"I need you to give me access to a certain frequency," Harris said. "There's an override code I can issue that will—"

"Vessel *Izmir*," a rough voice came from speakers in Mehmet's chair. "This is system vessel UK-229. You will heave to and receive boarders. Per orders of system commander Goto."

The approaching vessel was a fast and sleek blur on the screen.

"That is . . . not what should be happening," Harris said. "That vessel should've acknowledged my overrides. Goto is read into the program and should've loaded my codes onto that ship!"

"Nothing seems to be playing out how you promised," Mehmet said. "And why is that picket ship using camo-shielding?"

"W-what do you mean?"

Mehmet grabbed Harris by the front of his jacket and pulled him down to see a screen.

"The ship is within visual range. My onboard scopes should be able to read the serial numbers on the damned rivets, but she's blurred!" Mehmet shoved Harris away.

"Similar to our camo screen," Perrin said. "Is there any legitimate reason the ship doesn't want us to see what it looks like?"

"System pickets are all Calatan Heavy Industry construction," Harris said. "The Hegemony obtained significant cost savings by using one manufacturer and one standard design. The most likely reason it's screened is because they *don't* want us to see they're not a Calatan hull."

"Pirates." Mehmet leaned back.

"Improbable," Harris squeaked. "Extralegal actors aren't projected to reach this far from naval bases for at least several more months."

"Oh, fine." Mehmet nodded slowly at him. "I'll just tell that ship it shouldn't exist yet! Our options are limited, gentlemen. I don't have the TEU fuel to get us anywhere else nor do I have any defensive systems rated for anything higher than minor space junk."

"Then we accept boarders," Perrin said. "We've plenty of weapons on board. I still have most of an infantry battalion under my command."

"This ship is not built to host a firefight." Mehmet held up his palms. "One solid hit from any missiles or rockets from that ship and the *Izmir* will not survive."

Perrin held up an earbud and turned his head aside for a few moments.

"*Izmir*! Signal compliance immediately or you will be treated as a hostile target," came from the picket ship.

Lambert tapped Mehmet on the shoulder.

"Do what they want," the colonel said.

"I don't seem to have much of a choice, do I?" Mehmet beat a fist against an armrest.

"Harris, you're certain that ship isn't complying with your codes?" Lambert asked.

"We should've heard from the real Goto aboard the tether station by now," Harris said. "Perhaps the variables were unweighted correctly. The destruction of the *Highest* did happen ahead of projections—"

"Yes or no!" Lambert whacked his cane against Harris' thigh.

"Yes, it's a pirate," Harris snapped.

"Heave to and batten down the hatches," Lambert said, "or whatever you sailors do. We can fight them back at the airlocks and storm their ship before they even know what's happening."

"Yes, hello," Mehmet spoke into a microphone, his accent much thicker than usual, "we are listening. Ready for inspect. So sorry for bad English." He made sure the line was closed and looked at Lambert. "I don't think that'll buy us much time."

"Here. Here!" Harris swapped out the data rods. "There's a Hegemony video decryption algorithm that's meant to counter this sort of obfuscation."

"Now? Now you tell me you have it?" Mehmet looked at him like he was some sort of an idiot.

"I forgot. I grabbed everything I could when I abandoned my post." Harris turned his nose up.

In the holos, the picket ship resolved into a vessel with a massively armored prow. Hegemony navy missile pods were bolted to the sides. It was barely half the length of the *Izmir*, but it carried an implicit menace to it. The words *Void Witch* were painted in tall red letters on the metal plates on the fore of the ship, angled like a sword tip.

"Definitely pirates," Harris said. "My analysis holds."

"So glad you're here," Mehmet said.

In the plot, the *Izmir* cut her forward velocity and slowed. The *Void Witch* changed course, approaching at an angle that kept the heavily armored prow straight on to the merchant ship.

Perrin slapped Mehmet on the shoulder several times and accidentally dropped the earpiece onto his lap. The major leaned over and whispered into Mehmet's ear.

"That's insane," Mehmet said.

"*L'audace l'audace, toujours l'audace*, as we say back home." Perrin smiled.

"I don't know what that means but if we're going to die anyway…" Mehmet pulled up a menu in the holo screen. "I'm not going before my maker and telling him I died for some 'loud ass' idea."

⊕ ⊕ ⊕

"Boarding vector locked in," the helmsman aboard the *Void Witch* said. The bridge was a mess of empty beer cans and food wrappers. Captain Jenks sat in his chair, his shirt open and greasy chest shining under the lights. He reached down and scratched the head of a canid chained to the deck. The genetically engineered animal struggled to breathe, its mouth full of irregular teeth that oozed spittle through the gaps.

"Tell the prize teams same drill." Jenks scratched his crotch. "We don't need the crew or passengers unless they're worth selling to the brothels. Any cargo gets divvied up equally, so don't break anything expensive."

"Second one this week," a man in Hegemony navy pants and a dress jacket with the patches and ribbons torn away said from the weapons station. "We're eating good. Even better once the bastard at the fuel depot surrenders."

"Boss Duarte likes a good ROI on any cruise," Jenks said, then belched. On the main screen, the *Izmir*'s outer air docks rolled open.

"About to pass through camo screen effective range," the former naval officer said. "Think they'll bolt?"

"Won't do them any good and they'll know it," Jenks said. "Ready a warning shot just in case. Target the bridge if they keep running. Just like last time."

"Aye aye," the gunner said.

On the screen, the *Izmir*'s main cargo ramp cracked open and a gust of air flooded out.

"Huh," Jenks leaned forward. "They dumping their hold?"

"Doesn't make any sense," the gunnery officer said. "Wait, what's that?"

Lashed down to the cargo ramp, the Ta'essa slewed its turret toward the *Void Witch*.

"Is that a . . . tank?" Jenks asked.

He got his answer when the main gun fired a sabot round at his bridge. With no atmosphere to pull the metal petals off the tungsten penetrator, the entire shell shot across the gap faster than the defensive screens aboard the *Void Witch*—rated only to destroy small bits of space junk while the ship orbited a planet—could intercept.

The shell punched through the bridge's hull and turned the compartment into a brief blender of metal fragments and flame. The

ship vomited the resulting flesh and metal slurry out from the bridge
and into the vacuum of space, leaving a gaping target for the Ta'essa.

DPAT rounds followed the first sabot shot. The interior of the *Void
Witch* was not nearly as well armored as the outer hull and the
subsequent main gun rounds stabbed deep through the vessel, each
shot ramming deeper. The boarding teams burned alive in the airlocks
as shells exploded inside the ship, leaving little to none of the payload's
destructive potential to go to waste.

A final shell punched through the engineering compartment,
igniting the TEU tanks. The residual thrust from the fuel burning
pushed the *Void Witch* past the *Izmir* and to the outer reaches of the
system where it would drift until someone came looking for it or it
encountered a deep space object ... which would likely be never.

With the threat eliminated, the *Izmir*'s ramp raised up and the
cargo hold sealed itself.

On the *Izmir*'s bridge, Harris beamed at the burning pirate ship on
a holo screen.

"See, nothing to worry about." Harris put his hands on his hips.

Mehmet reached behind his chair and threw a brass-colored
coffeepot at him. Harris ducked and Mr. Barnes caught the pot when
it hit him in the stomach. Lambert backed away as fast as his cane
could aid him.

"Exactly how much better off are we?" Mehmet waved an arm
overhead. "Do Hegemony pirates always operate alone, because in the
Union they travel in packs, and I don't think that trick will work again."

"We're being hailed," a crewman said. "This time from the planet."

"I accept apologies," Harris sneered as he brushed bits of coffee
from his jacket.

"On screen." Mehmet crossed one leg over his knee.

A man in dark blue coveralls and a sunburst on shoulder lapels
appeared. His features were Asian and he had a fair amount of gray in
his goatee.

"Ah, Director Goto." Harris leaned into the camera view.
"Pythagoras. Braised. Puce. Keratin."

One of Goto's eyes rolled back.

"Onion. Fealty. Trojan. Book," Goto replied and his eyes returned
to normal.

"Everything's fine." Harris slapped Mehmet on the shoulder.

Mehmet took a deep breath to compose himself.

"Harris, you rat bastard, nothing is on schedule," Goto said. "I've been stuck in my tether fortress for weeks while goddamn pirates plunder everything on the ground and any ship dumb enough to show up in system. What's the situation with the plan?"

"Ah, best not to discuss that on an open line," Harris said quickly. "As part of my contingency efforts I had to procure transport. We need a TEU transfer right away. Which docking bay?"

"Slight problem there," Goto said. "All the TEU reserves are down tether on the ground. The base platform is held by the pirates who've been looting everything. The only reason they haven't tossed me out of an airlock is because I locked all the lifts here with me. Negotiating with them has been useless and every time I open a channel to them, they execute one of my workers to send a message."

"Ah . . . another variable I didn't account for." Harris plucked at his bottom lip.

"So, unless you've got some way to take back the ground station so I can run the TEUs up tether to you, you're stuck here with me," Goto said.

"Actually," Harris raised an eyebrow at Lambert, "I just so happen to have a workable solution."

Corre slapped his thigh. The glove of his emergency vac suit squeaked like rubber against his leg. He leaned over from the main gun cradle and waved at the squad below, all in the same vac suits.

"Hey, anyone hear that?" he spoke into his microphone.

"I think I did," Felix said. He picked up a wrench and banged it against the deck. "Was that sound going through atmo or just the echo through the hull?"

"Not so close to my chamber," Tessa said.

"According to this screen everything is blue." Noah tapped on his sleeve. "But nothing's in Standard. Can we breathe yet?"

"All Father, I hope so," Felix said. "These vac suits haven't been washed in years. Years, I tell you! They're an embarrassment to voidsmen everywhere."

"You're the lowest-ranked one in the tank," Boyle said to Noah. "Pop your helmet seal and see if your eyeballs pop out."

"Felix is the new guy!" Noah pointed at the drone operator.

"There is .93 bar and rising atmospheric pressure," Tessa said. "There are atmospheric sensors as part of the targeting systems. It's safe to remove your helmets."

"Noah, you first," Corre said. "That's how things work, private first class."

"This-this-this is—this sucks!" Noah pushed a button on the underside of his helmet and air hissed out. He raised the visor up and took a breath.

"It's cold," he said. "But it's okay."

The rest of the crew removed their helmets.

"So, are we Marines now?" Boyle asked. "That's what they do, right? Ship-to-ship combat."

"We didn't actually go to the other ship," Mason said. "Maybe we're navy instead? Besides, I don't like eating cray-sticks."

"Stop jaw-jacking." Corre touched his earpiece. "Major wants us to dismount now."

"You think I can get another hot water shower chit?" Noah said as he unzipped his vac suit. "We did save everyone's ass and this thing's a damn fart sack."

Corre pushed the top hatch open. He stuck his head and shoulders out.

A cheer rose up from the men of Bretton in the cargo bay. Most were in varying states of combat readiness, but all were gathered around the tank shaking their fists and hollering at Corre and the rest of the team as they climbed out and sat on the turret.

The pilot was the last to emerge.

"Ta'essa!" someone shouted.

"Ta'essa! Ta'essa! Ta'essa!" The chant continued until she was helped all the way out of the hatch. She sat on the gun mantlet, a confused look on her face.

"Sergeant Corre?" She leaned over to yell in his ear over the cheers. "Why are they repeating your designation for me?"

"It's not you, exactly." Corre pointed to the fume extractor hump halfway down the main gun barrel. "Ta'essa" was stenciled on it in fresh white paint. "We had to name the tank. Bad luck to fight in a tank with no name."

"What does it even mean?" Tessa asked.

Corre cracked a smile.

"Little sister."

Major Perrin emerged from the main entrance and walked with obvious pain in his stride, his truncated arm bent behind his back.

Senior NCOs called for a formation and the soldiers arranged themselves into loose rows and columns.

Perrin stopped next to the tank and gave the crew a quick nod.

"Men of Bretton," he said loudly, "...and Tessa. Much has been asked of you to get us this far. But we are not home yet. We have another fight. We have another mission. I don't know if this will be the last one. But together we will return home. Together, we will walk beneath the Hero's Boughs with honor, and as greater men of Bretton than our home sent to war.

"Our next mission is as follows..."